Here's what critics ar
Kerri Nelson's

"Nelson's novel (*Courting Demons*) is full of fun. Readers will love the hilarity and underlying danger that pushes the story forward."
- *RT Book Review.*

D1527237

"Kerri N   *urting Demons*!"
- Linda Wisdom, Bestselling author   *e a Girl's Best Friend*

"I was so into the book (*Falsify*), I even gasped out loud once... It will definitely keep readers turning the pages to see what will happen next."
- *More Than A Review*

"(*Miss Taken*) Is an electrifying romantic adventure that crackles with danger and sizzles with sensuality! Don't miss this debut!"
- Roxanne St. Claire, National Bestselling Author of *The Bullet Catchers Series* and RITA Award Winner

"I was pulled in (to *Double Take*) from page one...the story will restore your faith in love. An entertaining read that will leave the reader wanting more."
- *Book Wenches Reviews*

BOOKS BY AUTHOR NAME

Working Stiff Mysteries:
Remote Consequences

Other works:
Cross Check My Heart
Vegan Moon
Making the Ghost of It
Double Take
Kissing the Bull
Falsify

REMOTE CONSEQUENCES

a Working Stiff Mystery

Kerri Nelson

Folks in the
River Region are
the very best !

Dedication & Acknowledgements:

To all the hard working women out there who routinely put their families first and their careers last. You have something to teach a girl like Mandy.

To Gemma, for believing in me and my cast of crazies. You remained patient and calm in the midst of my editorial insanity and for that I'm forever grateful.

And to my husband for coming up with the idea of a cable girl who solves a mystery. Thanks, baby.

I'd also like to apologize to the real Mayor of the real Millbrook, Alabama (whose last name is Kelley not Mills). And who is neither a country club snob nor involved in the cover-up of any crimes whatsoever. And from what I hear, is an all around amazing guy and one heck of a dancer!

For those of you who live in or have visited Millbrook—you'll find that I took some literary license with the business names and locations. Please forgive me or thank me, whatever the case may be. For those of you who have never visited our fair city—you don't know what you're missing. Please come by and see us sometime. I can't promise that you won't fall in love with it, but I can promise that the city's motto is more than true...comfort...convenience...community. Oh, and lots of great food. If Mandy left any there by the end of this book.

CHAPTER ONE

———

It is better to exist unknown to the law. –Irish Proverb

"Your buns will be firm in no time or your money back."

The shrill television voice squawked, and I reached for the remote on the end table but found a large, furry head instead.

Jerking my hand back, I turned to peer into the square face of my sister's dog—Pickles. A mix between a retriever and bullmastiff, also called a Bullmasador, his head was bigger than the entire cramped sofa that held my exhausted body.

The truth was, I didn't sleep much anymore and I'd just sort of zoned out here after my latest night shift. Who knew being a cable installer would be such physical work? All the crawling around and juggling dust bunnies behind sofas was taking a toll.

"Hi, boy." I patted his head as he clutched the missing remote between drool-laden jowls. Pickles climbed onto the sofa with a graceful nonchalance uncommon for a dog his size.

He yawned in response, releasing the device.

"Gee, thanks."

I punched the channel up button up to The Forecast Network and was not surprised to learn today's temperature was a high of ninety-eight. The end of summer might be rapidly approaching, but the weather couldn't care less. I was, however, surprised to see the current time flashing in the right-hand corner of the screen.

I'd missed Paget's breakfast time and hadn't heard so much as a peep out of little sister. A niggle of concern pinched at my neck. It was unlike Paget to get off schedule. Paget's diagnosis of Kenner syndrome, a form of autism, was something I'd lived with for years and something I'd studied in greater detail more recently. The bottom line was that there was no cure in sight, but keeping her on a tight schedule was the best way of reducing her "episodes."

A rather insistent knock sounded from the kitchen area. Someone at the back door. Probably another neighbor or someone from the church bringing the umpteenth covered dish. They meant well, but if I never saw another plate of pear salad, it would be too soon.

I dragged myself up from my aunt's crummy sofa, cringing at meeting the sympathetic face of another neighbor in my ratty novelty T-shirt sporting *You're my Favorite Dish*, which I suspected had traces of my new best friend, Pickles "the drooler," on it.

Pickles followed me to the door to check out our visitor. The bright morning sun reminded me how little sleep I'd gotten, hurting my brain and blinding me as the door swung open. I cupped my hand over my brow for much-needed shade as I made out the silhouettes of two people.

"We found her in Village Park on the swing set."

Blinking them into focus, I saw a young police officer beside my sixteen-year-old sister, who was grinning like a child on Christmas morning.

"He let me turn on the lights," Paget exclaimed.

"Oh, Paget. You know you're not supposed to go out alone."

My words came out a tad too harsh, and the grin fell from my sister's face.

The sandy-haired officer looked apologetic. "She's fine, but I don't have to remind you that with the interstate running nearby, we get drifters through here from time to time."

I nodded. The warning was clear enough. I was already falling down on the job. Only a month back home, and big sister had put sweet, innocent, autistic Paget into harm's way.

I sighed.

"Uh, thank you, officer. It won't happen again."

I pulled Paget inside by the hand, and she fell to her knees, embracing Pickles with dramatic flair.

"Have a nice day, then." He tipped his hat and allowed his eyes to linger a moment too long on my bare legs before shuffling back off the porch and into his cruiser.

Paget looked up at me. The grin had returned. "Did I tell you about those blue lights on the *real* police car?"

* * *

As soon as I'd settled Paget and Pickles in front of her favorite reality show rerun with breakfast, the house phone rang. It was the dispatcher from Flicks Vision Cable Company, my new employer. She'd alerted me, with a generous thirty-minute notice, that my shift would begin early today because Mayor Mills had requested an emergency service call. So much for sleep.

That was one thing that hadn't changed in the ten years since I'd escaped Millbrook. The powerful families in town were still the Mills and the Brooks. And I'd not been lucky enough to be born into either.

However, I had been lucky to catch the day sitter at home, and Kendra lived only two streets over. In a matter of minutes, Paget was in good hands, and I was free to rake in some much-needed cash. Not that I was looking forward to my next shift in those medieval torture devices they referred to as blue coveralls, but with student loans and other assorted debt piling up, I'd take all the hours I could get.

Half a banana and a travel coffee mug in hand, I headed for the work van parked in our postage-stamp-sized yard.

"Woo-hoo, Mandy Murrin, is that you, dear?"

My mouth stuffed full of over-ripened banana, I nodded and waved at my neighbor. Ms. Lanier was all of about four foot, eight inches tall and ninety pounds soaking wet, but her voice did not belie her size. She may have been considered frumpy by most, but I knew that there was a sharp wit contained in that small but nosey package.

"I saw that Prentiss boy over there this morning. Is everything all right?"

I forced the mush down my throat and chased it with a scalding slurp of bitter coffee while I tried to recall who the Prentiss boy could possibly be.

The cop?

"Oh, yes, Ms. Lanier. No problem at all."

I kept moving toward the van, tossing my tool belt into the passenger scat as I fumbled with the key in the ignition. This was the last thing I had time for this morning.

"Well, I'm glad I caught you before you left for work, dear. Can you pop by later this evening?"

"Sure thing. Gotta run now, though. Duty calls."

I plastered on my customer friendly smile as I started to swing shut the van's creaky door. But before it clunked into place, I heard Ms. Lanier's follow-up words.

"Oh, that would be wonderful. I have this boil I need you to look at *on my left buttock*."

The last few words were spoken in an exaggerated stage whisper, but I caught them nonetheless.

Gag.

The engine roared to life, and I dialed the air to full blast as I waved once more at the now overjoyed Ms. Lanier. I may not have completed my medical degree, but apparently a four-year undergraduate degree in biology and one semester short of completing med school was good enough for my neighbor. And if this was what I had to look forward to after work, a full day of remote-control programming didn't seem like such a chore after all.

CHAPTER TWO

It is better to be a coward for a minute than dead for the rest of your life. –Irish Proverb

Mayor Douglas "Dougie" Mills lived in a two-story, Georgian-style home overlooking the eighteenth hole of Sugar Pines Golf Course. I pulled the van up the circular drive and parked it behind a shiny new BMW.

My long legs came in handy when exiting the mile-high van seat, and I was soon at the front door, tool belt affixed to my waistline and clipboard in hand. A real blue-collar soldier, ready for battle.

As I reached up to knock, the door swung open, revealing a tanned, twenty-something male in starched tennis whites. He gave me a dismissive once-over and then yelled back over his shoulder, "There's someone at the door, Amika. I'm gone to the club."

I stepped aside as he trotted toward the BMW Z series roadster. I gave a small finger-twirl wave as the hot car roared to life.

Goodbye, my fair stallion.

I meant the car, of course. Not the apparently spoiled rotten mayor's son.

My mourning was interrupted by a voice with a moderately strong German accent.

"Are you from the cable place?"

I turned my focus to a rail-thin woman with crystal-blue eyes and pearlescent skin. She was probably in her early sixties, but she'd aged well and was still very attractive. I could tell she'd been a true knockout in her day.

"Yes, ma'am. We received an emergency call from Mayor Mills. What seems to be the problem?"

I stepped into the crisp, cool air and admired the marble floors, the cherry wood stair banister, and a vase full of fresh roses perched on an antique secretary near the entryway.

Nice digs.

"This way."

I couldn't remember if I'd ever seen her before, but I could tell from the tidy yet inexpensive dress she wore that she was not related to the Mills. No Mills would be caught dead in anything but the most designer of outfits. I assumed she was the housekeeper and followed as she led me toward a large open den with a theater-sized television mounted on a corner unit. She pointed toward the blank screen that flickered with muted static.

"Can you fix?"

"No problem. I'll have this up in a jiffy." I spoke with a confidence that I did not possess. Consulting my checklist, I made my way to the television and began troubleshooting a digital diagnosis.

* * *

Two hours, three sneezes, and a half a box of Tic Tacs later, I was crouched in the oppressive heat of the attic. After two phone calls back to the office to ask my boss questions, I'd finally deduced that there must be a faulty coaxial cable somewhere in the house's wiring. Finding it was going to take time and patience. And I was low on both.

My stomach grumbled with hunger, and the dispatcher had radioed twice to ask when I might be able to take the next service call. But I was stuck here in the mayor's dreadful attic until I could find the source of the problem.

I inched along the perimeter in the near dark. When it came to blood and anatomy, I could stomach almost anything. But when it came to bugs and creepy crawlies, I was as girly as they came.

Holding my Maglite XL at arm's length to warn me of potential eight-legged predators, I scooted my knee forward another notch and winced as a splinter made its way through my pants leg and speared my tender flesh.

"Dammit."

I eased back onto my bottom and surveyed the damage. A shard of laminated wood about three inches in length protruded from my pants leg. I yanked it free and tossed it behind me. I'd have to tend to my wound later. A brief daydream image of sitting on a sunny beach—margarita in one hand, and a hefty worker's compensation check in the other—made me grin. Not a likely outcome for a splinter-induced injury, though.

Boxes of holiday decorations, an old baby crib, stacks of books, and a deep freezer cluttered the area. Standard stuff. Nothing special about His Honor's attic.

Deep freezer?

Who had a deep freezer in their attic? My head snapped back to the opposite corner where a standard eight-cubic-foot, chest-style freezer sat in the shadows. I stood up, brushing off the back of my pants. Deep freezers were heavy suckers. I knew this because I'd once had the corner of one dropped on my toe in my aunt's cellar basement.

As if in response to the memory, my toe ached deep inside my boot.

I'd never seen anyone lug a heavy deep-freeze up to an attic. It didn't make much sense, but at the same time—wouldn't it feel great to open that lid and feel the mist of ice-cold frost caress my face? Memories of homemade ice cream and preparing containers of summer vegetables for the fall trickled through my memory. Summers had been good once. A long time ago.

Back and knees stiff from the attic crawl, I limped toward the freezer. I doubted it was even running. Who would be stupid enough to run it up here? What if it defrosted and leaked down through the floorboards? Imagining worst-case scenarios was kind of like a superpower to me.

But as I reached out to touch the dusty lid, I heard the humming thrum of the motor inside.

Probably shouldn't mess with it.

I looked around the attic as if someone were going to pop out and shake their finger at me for snooping. But when no one appeared, I lifted the lid.

The blessed frost hit my face, and I inhaled the frigid glory. But when the mist cleared—my breath caught in my throat. Lungs frozen in an ice block of silent shock.

There, among the Tupperware containers, curled into a fetal position was...one dead body.

CHAPTER THREE

Don't tell your complaint to one who has no pity.
—Irish Proverb

The body was on its side and appeared to be male, but that was about all I could tell from this observation point. Well, except for the fact that it had major freezer burn.

I dropped the lid of the freezer and backed away, conking my head on a shallow roof beam in the process.

"Ouch. Crap."

I rubbed my head. Tried to think. What should I do? *Diagnose the patient? Wait. What the heck am I thinking? Get the heck out of this attic. Call the cops.*

My mind flooded with ideas, but my body remained motionless. The sound of shoes squeaking on the attic's dropdown ladder brought me back to reality. I spun around and shone the flashlight directly into glowing eyes.

"Do you mind?"

It was the housekeeper. The accented voice came at me with short-clipped words that seemed to leave off the end of each syllable. I lowered the strong beam of light and saw a glass containing some sort of refreshing beverage extended toward me.

"You thirsty, no?"

The kindness of those simple words almost made me feel better. Almost. A chill was still sweeping up my spine at the memory of the frozen man-sicle just two feet behind me.

Should I tell her? Show her? Call the cops? But something told me to get out of the house. A sudden sense of being trapped nearly overwhelmed me, and spots swirled before my eyes, causing me to sway slightly.

"You okay? Too hot up here for working." The housekeeper observed me warily.

"Uh, you know. I'm going to need to go."

I forced my legs to propel me forward.

"You want Amika should call someone for you?"

Who's Amika?

Her big eyes blinked slowly. Once. Twice.

Oh, *she's* Amika. My brain stumbled over the third-person reference.

"Uh, no. No. I just need to get *out*."

My last word came out a little more stressed than I'd intended.

Amika shrugged and backed down the stairs. I followed suit. One step at a time. Get out of here and call the police. Who was that dead guy, and what was he doing in the mayor's attic? My mind raced. My heart raced.

"Cable all fix?" Amika waited at the bottom of the ladder. Moisture on the glass, of what appeared to be lemonade, frosted the sides. It made me think of the freezer, and I shivered.

"I need some help."

Amika watched me carefully. Did she seem suspicious? Did she know about the body? Maybe *she* was the one who'd hid it there. Maybe I would be the next one preserved like the summer squash if I didn't get the heck out of here.

I sidestepped down the hallway, keeping my eye on the wary housekeeper and making my way to the stairs leading down to the foyer.

"You come back today? Mr. Mills not happy if cable broken." Amika sing-songed the last few words of warning.

No, he won't be happy.

This was not something that any politician wanted to face. And now, I was right smack dab in the middle of a small-town scandal.

* * *

Drumming my fingers on the steering wheel, I considered my options. I could phone the cops from right here. I could drive to the police station. I could drive to the cable office and tell my boss. Or I could drive home and forget any of this ever happened.

I liked the last choice best.

But it wasn't really an option. I was quite familiar with what a cadaver looked like, and I was certain I'd found one in the Mills' attic just minutes earlier.

I cranked up the air conditioner another notch and the not-yet-cooled air sent my hair back in waves, making a flapping sound against the vinyl headrest. I closed my eyes a moment.

What to do? What to do?

If I went to the office with my story, my boss could fire me on the spot. I hadn't completed the job I was sent to do, and, better yet, I'd snooped inside their personal belongings. Both were on the big "no-no" list that Barry, my passive-aggressive boss, had given me the first day on the job.

I'll probably be fired anyway.

Why did I have to look inside the freezer? If I'd never seen the body, I wouldn't have to worry about telling anyone. Any attempt at rationalizing my fears and actions now wouldn't help me or anyone, and there was still the matter of the dead body. He was someone.

Maybe someone's father. Someone's brother. Definitely someone's son. Whoever he was, he didn't deserve to spend an eternity curled up in a perpetual frozen ab crunch.

Aunt Patty had once told me that death was never pretty, but it was a necessary part of life. After all, I'd learned about death at a very early age—back when my parents were killed in a car accident. This was so *not* the time to go there. I flushed the memory back down and refocused.

My aunt would have known exactly what to do in a situation like this. But, once again, I was alone in the decision-making adult world, and I felt less than equipped to star in this role.

It was so much easier to read and study books. Write term papers and dissect a willingly donated cadaver. There was a certain art and beauty to be able to look at the human body from an objective, scientific point of view. I'd learned this in medical school—maybe one day I could finish that. It had been so close I could still almost taste it.

Now all I tasted were bitter regrets, fear, and the lingering tingle of my very last Tic Tac.

A check of my phone revealed the time to be almost one in the afternoon. I'd put this off long enough. It was time to be a responsible adult. Take action.

I cranked the engine and pulled out of the mayor's drive. *Millbrook Police Department, here I come.*

CHAPTER FOUR

————

The apple falls on the head that's under it. –Irish Proverb

I parked the van between two squad cars and jolted out of my seat. I did not look forward to my second police interaction of the day.

Reaching the station's double doors, I caught a quick glimpse of my haphazard reflection, but my terrifying image was interrupted by the outward swing of the door.

There, before me, stood the voluptuous body of Allyson Harlow.

One look at the short, stacked vixen sent my stomach into a tight clench of dread. All those old school memories came flooding back with a vengeance.

Mandy...Mandy...rotten candy...

From the first day of kindergarten until the last day of high school, we'd had two things in common. We'd both loved Ty Dempsey, and we'd both hated each other.

"Well, lookie who's back in town."

Allyson's molasses-thick voice drawled out between perfect teeth, which were clamped in a forced Crest-white grin. She stood there in five-inch stilettos and a short polka-dot sundress, its seams strained to the max with her well-endowed chest that taunted the laws of physics. Ready to attend the weekly Millbrook Service League meeting and throw daggers at anyone who got in her way, no doubt. Or maybe she'd just claw their eyes out with her newly manicured fake acrylic nails.

"And look who's still wearing hooker heels." The comment sprang forth from my mouth in a rapid-fire response.

My words surprised Allyson for a split second. They surprised me, too.

The smile fell from Allyson's face as she lifted her neck a little higher and turned her attention to the empty gingham-style cloth-lined basket swinging from her left arm.

"Oh, I just had to bring by some fresh-baked brownies for Ty and the boys. You know how he *loves* the sweet stuff I have to offer."

Ugh.

"Yes…still stalking Ty, I see," I mumbled beneath my breath.

"I'm sorry. What was that?" Allyson's eyes pinged ice picks my way. But the thought of ice picks brought me back to the matter at hand.

Ice picks equals ice equals freezer equals…dead body.

"Wish I could stay and chat, but I have something important I need to talk to Ty and the boys about." I reached around Allyson for the door handle, catching a lungful of her over-the-top perfume.

"I'm sure he'll be glad to see you." Allyson gave me the once-over, and her look was easy to interpret. I looked like crap, and Allyson looked perfect.

Some things never changed.

I pushed my way past and entered the lobby, but before the door closed the last words out of Allyson's mouth reached my ears…

"Ty and I will be at O'Hannigan's tonight. You should join us if you're not busy."

The invitation was fake. Just like her nails. Just like everything else about her. But I got the message. Allyson was still chasing Ty, and I was still watching from the sidelines.

Oh well, I have bigger and colder things to deal with than Hussy Harlow.

* * *

I shouldn't have been surprised to see Ty Dempsey as a cop. After all, every Dempsey man was a cop. The Dempseys only made cops it seemed. Three generations of cops from what I remembered. But I'd never actually *seen* him in cop mode.

And I had kind of hoped he'd do something different. Once upon a time, he'd had such big dreams. All those years ago he'd talked of nothing but getting out of Elmore County. He was a rebel. A troublemaker. A football star. And a heartbreaker. My heart, specifically.

And now, he was here…at the police station. Right where I needed to be and exactly the person I needed *not* to see.

I shuttered the memories out of my mind and focused on his glare from across the station house. I couldn't help it if he still blamed me for losing his college scholarship. It really wasn't my fault. Well, mostly not…

A rotund man in a black uniform studied me from behind the front desk. I focused on his curly hair and the police radio clipped to his shoulder lapel. His icy blue eyes, quite similar to the Mills' housekeeper's eyes, caught my attention and made me think of my own Irish-green eyes passed down from my father.

He cleared his throat and a few crumbs trickled down the wrinkled front of his uniform, where it bulged out just over his belly. The look in his eyes was one that said he didn't expect to see much action outside of a jelly donut today, and, unfortunately, as I told him my tale of the thwarted cable mission, the look didn't change much. Except to crinkle his eyes at the corners into a hint of a mocking expression as he ogled my B-cup boobs.

"So, you say you were in Mayor Mills' attic, and there was something dead in the freezer?"

His voice was half amused and half bored. But his beady eyes never left my breasts as he spoke.

I swore I could feel Ty staring at me from what must've been twenty feet away, but I refused to look up. I had to stay on target. It wasn't time for another high school reunion. I'd already survived one this morning before entering the building.

"Yes, I was there to handle a cable problem." I took the opportunity to point my index finger at the Flicks Vision patch that hovered over my left breast. If he was going to stare at my chest, at least I could verify my legitimacy for being at the house in question. "And there wasn't something dead in the freezer, there was *someone* dead in the freezer."

He let out a cough and turned to look over his shoulder. I followed his eyes and saw Ty watching the exchange from the desk of the young Officer Prentiss, whom I'd met this morning at my kitchen door.

"Is this some kind of joke?" Officer Chubby asked as he glared at his fellow patrolmen.

I slapped my hand down on the countertop, and he spun his glare around to me.

"This is no joke. You need to get over there now. Call the coroner and a forensics team. Didn't you hear me? There…is…a…dead…body…in…the…freezer. Do you need me to write down the address for you?"

His face colored beet red, and he emitted another cough. This one a little wheezy.

In the distance, I could see Ty rise from his chair and head our way.

Officer Chubby continued to stare at me as he tried to calm his sudden bout of asthma.

"Well? What are you gonna do about it?" I prompted.

Ty eyed me under heavy lids as he approached. I swallowed back nerves and turned my attention to him.

"Uh…" Cough. "…Detective Dempsey…" Cough. "…Ms. Murrin here…" Cough. "…claims she found a dead body…" Cough. "…in Mayor Mills' attic." Cough. Officer Chubby finally got the words out in between hacks.

Ty's eyes studied my face. "A mere few weeks back in town, and you're already stirring up trouble?"

I had the sudden urge to storm out of the office and never look back. But I reached in my pocket instead. Unfortunately, my supply of Tic Tacs was long gone.

"I was at work. Doing my job. Now, you need to do yours."

The words came out clearly, and I stood a little taller as I said them. Despite my attire and the way he studied my disheveled state, I refused to appear anything other than confident and knowledgeable. If there was one thing I was sure of, it was what a dead body looked like.

"Okay, Mandy. We'll check it out. But maybe you need to spend a little more time focusing on *your* job."

His words made no sense to me.

"What are you talking about?"

"It's your responsibility to take care of your sister, isn't it? I know for a fact you weren't doing that this morning."

My spine tingled. "If you're referring to her disappearing act. Aunt Patty told me that it has happened in the past. I'm working on it. Don't give me a hard time about it, Ty."

What was with him? Still holding grudges.

"No. I'm not talking about that. I'm talking about the scene she caused at Ingram's right before she darted out in front of traffic on Main Street."

His words struck me with a shocking blow. My face numbed, and the confidence I'd tried so hard to exude faded.

"Paget? What happened? Is she hurt?" The panic in my voice was clear even to my own ears, as all thoughts of freezers, dead bodies, lost scholarships, and pervy cops faded in comparison to my sister's wellbeing. I watched his face and saw a twitch of discomfort. "Ty? What happened?" My pulse was racing. My throat began to squeeze.

Ty hooked his thumbs in the belt loops on his khaki pants and did a little backward sway on his dress shoes.

I reached out to balance myself on the edge of the counter, waiting for him to continue and yet almost not wanting to hear what he had to say.

"Let's not forget the running off after the accident before the ambulance could arrive."

My voice came rushing back with a certain volume that shocked even my own ears. "Where is she? She's missing?"

"You might want to check the hospital," Chubby Face interrupted.

We both looked down at the cop sitting between us.

"You hear from Adam Owens, sergeant?"

"Yes, sir. I was just on my way to tell you when she walked in."

"Adam Owens?" I tried to place the name, but my mind was blank with fear.

"Did he find her?" Ty asked.

I reached out to balance myself on the edge of the counter. Paget was missing? What was going on in this town? What was going on with my life?

The rotund cop nodded vigorously—as if eager to please his superior with his newfound information. He patted his own chest to ward off more coughing.

"He took her to Millbrook Memorial. She was admitted for head trauma."

Ty and I made brief eye contact. I thought I caught a hint of remorse in his expression as he opened his mouth to speak. But before I could hear another word from him, I turned and ran. All I could hear were the words that reverberated between my ears.

Paget.
Head trauma.

CHAPTER FIVE

———

See not what you see and hear not what you hear.
–Irish Proverb

Millbrook Memorial was a five-mile trip from the police station, but it seemed as if every other driver on the road was out for a leisurely drive. I swerved in and out of traffic, a sense of dread squeezing my ribcage into a knotted mass of cartilage.

Ignoring the red and white warning signs, I whipped the van into the ambulance bay and cut the engine. I swung my legs out of the van and slammed the door behind me.

"Hey! You can't park that here," the hospital security guard yelled at me from his kiosk perch at the entry.

I ignored him and ran inside in search of the information desk. I found it a few feet in front of me. A gray-haired volunteer sat behind it reading an issue of *Redbook*. Surrounded by a semi-circle desk with a half-dozen floral arrangements on it, the woman looked up at me with kindness. "Hello, dear."

I wasn't in the mood for a meet-and-greet. I had to find Paget. Make sure she was okay.

"I need the emergency room. I thought this was the entrance."

Why wouldn't the ambulance bay not enter directly into the emergency department? I wished I had my hospital credentials from UAB Hospital with me. Being able to flash that med student identification was something I would pay money for right about now.

"I'm sorry, dear. We don't have an emergency room here. We do have the Acute Care Clinic. It is right around…" She pointed down a wood-paneled hallway, and I took off in that direction, the woman's words fading behind me. I'd find it myself. I couldn't play polite and wait for a long, drawn-out explanation from the elderly volunteer today. My patience was beyond gone at this point. I needed to know if Paget was safe.

I heard Paget before I saw her. Her voice, edged with concern but slightly slurred, vibrated against my eardrums before I reached the end of the hall.

"But why did he have to go? So cute."

I turned the corner and found my sister on a hospital bed. Head bandaged. Intravenous fluids dripped into one pale arm while a blood-pressure cuff was secured on the other. My heart knocked against the back of my breast like the *thwop*, *thwop*, *thwop* of helicopter blades.

Paget looked so innocent, so fragile, so little in that huge bed. An image of her as a tiny girl came to mind. A red snow cone spilled down the front of her white Sunday dress. Daddy laughing. Momma fussing. Me embarrassed. Always embarrassed by my sister.

I swished the dry-erase board of my mind as Paget looked up and grinned widely at me.

I should be the one embarrassed. I had not been a good big sister, but I needed to find a way to be better. Needed to make up for all the times I wasn't here for her.

"How're you feeling? What happened?"

Paget stopped smiling and looked down at her hands. "I was hungry." That was her response.

I took a deep breath. Reaching for her chart in the clear bin on the wall, I flipped it open and read the physician's notes.

Minor head laceration to the medial scalp. No stitches required. Monitor overnight for possible concussion. Treat with anti-anxiety meds as needed.

She must have been very agitated when they'd brought her in. They'd given her a fairly large dose of meds to calm her down, but it didn't sound like a serious injury. Ty Dempsey and his cop cronies had nearly scared the life out of me. Would he ever stop trying to make me take the blame for everything? Even after all these years.

"You should wait for the doctor. You're not supposed to touch that."

A bleached-blonde nurse stepped into view. Her face was pinched with an I'm-over-worked-and-underpaid sneer as she snatched the chart from my hand and replaced it in the drop box.

"Sorry. I'm a third-year medical student from…"

The nurse pierced me with a look that stopped my explanation. It was obvious that the woman couldn't care less that I had *almost* been a full-fledged doctor. All that really mattered was that I *wasn't* a doctor here and I *was* a patient's family who shouldn't be acting like an almost-doctor at any rate.

"Sorry," I repeated.

"Oh, Darlene. Don't give her such a hard time. She's always been a nosy little thing."

I swirled around to see the freckled face of Dr. David Cavello. I stepped forward and right into the bear hug of his embrace.

"We missed you at the funeral," I told him.

He squeezed me tightly and then stepped back to examine me with his knowing eyes. Eyebrows crinkled. A mix of love, loss, and intelligence poured out of him and into my still-smarting heart. "I couldn't." His chin quivered slightly as he spoke.

And as strange as it seemed, I understood. I'd loved Aunt Patty, too, and had almost opted not to hold a funeral at all. It was expensive and sad. I hated funerals. But it was a big deal in a small town. Everyone out in their Sunday best. It was a rite of passage that all locals expected, and I didn't want to let Aunt Patty down. In the end, I'd honored her wishes.

Dr. C. had been a part-time father figure to us growing up. I knew it wasn't a coincidence I'd chosen medicine after having him in my life all these years.

He'd loved Patty, but they'd never married. I'd never asked why, and it had never mattered to us. But I had noticed his absence at the funeral. Deciding that now wasn't the best time to push the issue, I motioned to Paget.

My sister had become distracted by the reflection of the nurse's watch on the wall. It had caught a beam of sunlight coming through the window as she checked Paget's blood pressure. Paget was following the light around on the ceiling as if it were the North Star.

"Our girl is going to be just fine," Dr. C. reassured me, and then he motioned for me to walk with him down the hall.

With Paget occupied for the moment, I chose to follow him.

"What happened, exactly?" I asked once we'd cleared the room.

He made his way to a door marked *Doctor's Lounge* and opened it, motioning for me to enter.

"Am I even allowed in here?" I scrunched my nose at him.

He winked at me in return—those same bushy salt-and-pepper eyebrows dipping down at the top of his nose in a caterpillar maneuver. I giggled. It felt good to laugh, if only for a moment.

"I don't know all the details, Mandy. But I do know that she somehow ended up on Main Street and walked in front of a car."

My hand went to my mouth. "She was hit? But her chart says—"

He shook his head. Leaning over to pour a cup of steaming coffee in a Styrofoam cup, he continued, "No. She was shoved out of the way in the nick of time. The head lac is from when she hit the pavement."

I caught my breath between gritted teeth. "The driver?" I ground out.

He turned and handed me the coffee, along with two sugar packets and a red plastic stirrer. "He's okay. A little shaken up. But no damage."

My heart rate tried to return to normal. I hadn't realized how accelerated it had been for the last twenty minutes or so since I'd run from the police station.

"I don't know what she was doing there. I had her with a sitter. I had to work."

I sat down on the art deco velvet-covered sofa and sipped the coffee. Despite the heat outside and the flush in my cheeks from the adrenaline overdose, I was chilled inside.

"It's not your fault, Mandy. You don't know how many times she's done things like this in the last year. It was getting harder and harder for Patty to deal with."

I looked up at him as his voice caught on the name *Patty*.

"She didn't tell me. Why didn't she tell me?"

Dr. C. joined me on the sofa with his own cup of coffee. He stirred it absently. "You know she was one tough cookie. She liked to handle things her own way. Even when she got sick—she refused any help with Paget until...well, until she finally called you."

I knew my aunt had been one of the strongest women I'd ever known, but I didn't know how much she'd struggled to keep up with Paget in the end.

He shook his head, set his coffee down on the table, and reached over to pat my knee.

"Not to worry about that now. You can go check on Paget and then get back to your work. I'm going to keep her here overnight. Just to watch for signs of a concussion. I'll keep her under close watch. You can get a good night's sleep."

I was disappointed with myself yet again when I felt a twinge of relief at the idea of sleeping through the night and not being worried about the police showing up at the door with my sister—little girl lost—again.

"Everyone in this town will think I'm totally incompetent—if they didn't already."

Dr. C. reached over and touched my chin with his index finger.

"Chin up, Panda. No one thinks that. You're doing the best you can."

"Am I?"

I had all but forgotten the pet name he'd given me all those years ago. Panda. I sighed. I was convinced the answer to my own question was "no," but knew that he wouldn't tell me that in a million years.

"I think I need help."

He looked at me, eyebrows raised. "I may know some nurses who are looking for a little extra work. Can you afford nursing care?"

I shook my head. "No, I mean, what about a place for her to stay…where she can be safe?" The words came out of my mouth, but it was as if I'd spoken them involuntarily. As if my very subconscious had snuck them into the conversation when I wasn't looking.

Immediately, I wanted to withdraw them. But the look on his face was non-judgmental. I loved him for that. He never judged.

"I'll do a little research for you, but I think you can do this, Mandy. I know you can do this. Won't you give it more time?"

I nodded. Set my coffee down and stood, wiping my hands along the front of my grimy coveralls.

"I need to check on her and go. I need to get back to work and…other stuff…"

I remembered the dead body in the freezer and opened my mouth to tell him all about it, but decided to refrain for now.

"Okay. I'll see you in the morning, then."

I nodded and then paused at the door. "Thanks, Dr. C."

He gave a nod of acknowledgement. "You betcha."

I walked out and back down the hall to Paget. She'd fallen asleep, and I decided not to wake her.

Today was quickly becoming more than just a bad hair day. At this rate, I'd need a total makeover before sundown.

* * *

I'd reported my frigid find to the authorities and I'd been all but laughed at by Ty and Officer Chubby. He'd said he would check it out, but I hadn't gotten the immediate sense of urgency that I'd expected. It was just like being right back in high school all over again. He'd always considered me his little sister's friend and he'd never taken me seriously, even when it really counted.

There was a small, curious part of me that wanted to revisit the mayor's house. If for no other reason than to dig a little deeper into my discovery. But there was also the matter of reporting to my boss that I hadn't been able to complete the job. Maybe he'd send another crew. Maybe he'd fire me on the spot.

Sitting in the cable van once again, I pondered my next move. The security guard continued to eye me from behind his kiosk. He'd probably already put in a call for a tow, but I hadn't been inside long enough for the truck to get there.

Before I did anything else, I had to get something to eat. There was only so long a girl could live on a cup of coffee, half a banana, and a box of orange Tic Tacs. Speaking of which, I needed to make a stop at Thrifty Mart before I headed to the office. A girl without Tic Tacs was not a happy girl.

Of course, I hadn't been exactly what you'd call giddy in a while now. Thoughts of the letter that had come in the mail zinged through my brain. I arched my back and dug deep into my pants pocket. I'd shoved it there yesterday.

I hadn't wanted to dwell on it too long. I knew it was a drop letter from school, but somehow opening it made it too real, so I'd opted to remain in denial about the contents. Pulling out the wrinkled paper now, the window-style envelope crinkled in my hand. I shoved it back inside my pocket. Now wasn't the time for pondering my future. Now was the time for eating, getting rejuvenated with caffeine and carbs, and then facing my boss. Ugh. Well, at least the caffeine and carbs sounded good.

With the decision made, I rolled through the faux ambulance bay and was on my way to my favorite eatery in town, The Back Porch Café.

CHAPTER SIX

_____

Never give cherries to pigs or advice to fools. –Irish Proverb

Entering the café was always like coming home. Kind of like it felt at Aunt Patty's house, but with a lot more clatter. I'd grown up in this café, and for a brief moment, my father had owned it. I paused to inhale the scent of fresh-brewed coffee. To listen to the grinding blades of the blender whipping up yet another peach pie shake. Add to that the tinny sound of forks and spoons scooping heaping helpings of goodness from over-filled plates, and you had a normal day at The Back Porch.

I walked toward the bar and then decided it might be a good idea to detour to the restroom and wash up. I'd been crawling around a dusty attic all morning, and there was that freezer situation as well.

I moved to the left side of the main dining room and down the paneled hallway. The ladies' room had a sign on the door that read *Belles*, and the men's room door sported the *Beaus* sign. I was definitely back in Millbrook. Pushing through the door, I studied myself in the mirror.

My appearance made me want to gag. My dark auburn hair was a disaster of epic proportions. Matted with dust and cobwebs alike, it hung from my head like a curtain of filth. My face held several smudges of unidentifiable markings as well.

Dr. C. hadn't bothered to mention my appearance. Of course, guys rarely took the risk of telling a woman they looked like crud on a stick. But still… Help a girl out.

Ty's face danced in my mind's eye. No wonder he and the other cop had looked at me as if I'd just escaped the local loony bin. Take my baggy coveralls and state of disarray—then add in my surprise tale of finding a frozen corpse in the attic of

Mayor Mills. It was no wonder they'd looked at me as if I were a wrench short of a toolbox.

I made quick work of scrubbing my hands like a well-trained surgeon, followed by a quick splash of cold water on my face and a make-do finger-combing of my hair. That was the best I could do for now. It would have to be enough. My stomach rumbled like a monster truck show.

Okay. Okay. I'm going.

I exited the bathroom looking down at my dusty boots. Great, now I was talking to my stomach. I was truly losing it.

I didn't see the woman in the doorway until I had ungracefully crashed into her. We did an awkward dance while trying to keep our balance. It ultimately spun me around into the hallway and left my dance partner standing just inside the open doorway, glaring at me with no shortage of annoyance.

"Oh, excuse me."

I had always been a royal klutz, and today it seemed more pronounced than ever. My knee gave a sharp sting as I recalled the splinter incident from earlier that was still lacking in first-aid attention.

"Mandy Murrin." The voice both comforted me and made me feel ill at ease.

I took a closer look at my dance partner. Short stature, dark, curly hair, and thick but stylish glasses topped off her look.

"Henny Penny? Oh, my gosh. You look amazing!"

The woman's half-smile faded into a full-on smirk. "Wish I could say the same of you, and no one calls me that anymore."

I beamed at her despite the obvious putdown. "Sorry, Penny. It's just…I haven't seen you in ages. How have you been?"

"I've been fine." The woman across from me had once been my best friend. We'd grown up together, played precocious pranks on the boys, and taken many a swim in the Alabama River. We'd shared first days of school together, first crushes, and even first periods. Then it had all gone away. One night, one decision had destroyed our friendship. It had been my fault, and I'd apologized more times that I could count. Surely all that was behind us now. It was all ages ago and long since forgotten.

I reached out to touch my former friend's arm. But Penny pulled it back and out of reach. Her lips pressed together.

Perhaps it wasn't so long ago or so far behind us after all. Seemed like Penny and her brother Ty could sure hold on to old grudges despite a decade-long respite.

"Are you still working for the paper?" I tried a different approach. It would be so nice if I could patch things up with Penny now. I could really use a friend right about…this minute.

"Not really," Penny said, standing as tall as her five feet of stature would allow.

"I know how much you've always loved to write. What are you doing now, then?"

"Oh, I still like to write from time to time. You know, I wrote a piece about Patty's funeral."

My face flushed. I hadn't even bought a copy of my aunt's obituary, much less checked the paper for any articles about her death or services. I'd been so wrapped up in finding a job and trying to find care for Paget.

"I must have missed it. Been real busy, you know?"

Penny gave me the once-over…or maybe it was a twice-over, and she took in the grungy coveralls and flyaway hair. "Yes. It does seem you're quite busy doing…things."

The condescension in her voice sent a burst of discomfort through me.

She knew I had left town to become a doctor, and now she'd seen me in the Flicks Vision uniform. There was no way to hide my fall to menial labor. I was a working stiff, and news of Mandy Murrin's mediocre Millbrook existence would be all over town by morning.

A little of that schoolgirl envy began to boil beneath the surface. I wanted so badly to throw it back in Penny's face. An idea whisked through my mind, and before I could stop myself the words were churning out.

"I found a dead body in the mayor's attic."

Penny's mouth opened and then closed. This happened several times in a row, making me recall one particular summer when we'd learned how to bait our own hooks and fished off the pier. Penny never had wanted to touch the wriggling worms, but she'd been aces at casting that line.

"Let me buy you lunch," Penny offered, and stepped back into the hallway to join me.

I smiled vaguely, but I knew I'd just made a terrible mistake.

* * *

I finished my late and awkward lunch with Penny and headed back to the cable office. I parked in the company lot but delayed the confrontation with Barry by taking a detour next door to the Thrifty Mart. Browsing the aisles in the well-air-conditioned building, I loaded my arms with chips, cookies, coffee filters, a two-liter Coke, and my beloved Tic Tacs.

"Why you don't get a basket?"

I spun around, nearly dropping my loot. There, standing too close behind me for comfort, stood Amika—the mayor's housekeeper. What was she doing here?

"Uh…oh, I was just grabbing a few things." My voice stuttered out the words. I took a step back to try to put a little space between us. My back bumped into a rack of beef jerky, and it began to topple over. Amika stopped its fall with one pale hand and quick reflexes.

"Hmm…you have time to eat and shop but no time to fix cable television?"

My nerves twinged a little beneath my skin at her words. How did she know where I'd been since I left the mayor's house? Was she following me?

Oh, don't be ridiculous, Mandy.

I shook my head and forced a smile on my face. "Well, I'm headed in to work now, and I'm sure they'll get it taken care of as soon as possible."

She lifted the corners of her mouth, but it still looked menacing. "You should eat better. That stuff will *kill* you." Her eyes indicated the junk food I was holding in my arms. Then she turned and marched out of the store.

I let out a breath I hadn't known I was holding on to. Kicking myself into gear, I unloaded my stash onto the counter. As I waited for the cashier to ring it up, I wondered—had her warning about the food really been about something else? Did I actually hear her stress the word "kill," or was my imagination getting the best of me?

What if Amika knew what I'd found in the attic? What if she was watching me to see what I'd do about it? What if she knew that I'd already told both the cops and Penny?

I gathered up my bags and left the store. My eyes darted around the parking lot, but I saw no sign of the mayor's hired help.

Mandy, stop creeping yourself out.

I chastised myself and tried to get myself together. I still had to face Barry the boss, and technically my shift wasn't over yet. My day was just beginning.

Hip hip hurr—blah.

* * *

After a full recounting to my boss about what happened in the attic, including the Siberian-solid stiff and a quick rundown of how the rest of my morning and afternoon had been spent, he was not impressed. He was a man who lived for money and television. People had to have their television—apparently the world revolved around it. At least Barry's world, anyway.

"Look, just as soon as we get the all-clear from the Millbrook police, I want you to go straight back there and finish the job. This is the mayor we're talking about here. It's our top priority. Are we understood?" Barry said, staring down at me and scratching his head simultaneously. Little flakes of dandruff coated the collar of his matching, company-issued blue coveralls.

"But—" I started.

"I can't spare anyone else," he cut in. "As it is, the mayor is going to be royally teed off that he can't watch his game tonight. What were you thinking leaving the assignment before completing your work order?"

Was this guy serious? Who could finish a job with a dead body hanging around? It seemed like the mayor would have bigger worries if and when Ty and company showed up to check out my report. I was trying to focus on his rant but found myself scratching at the neckline of my own uniform, wondering who else had worn this before me and what cooties I was catching at the current moment.

But he didn't wait for a response before saying, "Just go on home, Mandy. Take the rest of the evening off. You said your sister is in the hospital? Go check on her or something. I'll call the station and make sure it was all just a false alarm." Barry's face had reddened. His head scratching had grown more vigorous.

Barry hadn't been exactly nice to me since I'd been on his payroll. Then again, being on his payroll was all the kindness I really needed to have from this bundle of joy at the moment. I had to take care of Paget while I figured out what to do about med school, and up until today, this job had been tolerable.

"I'm sure it will turn out to be nothing. There's no way Mayor Mills would be involved in something like that." Barry mumbled the words as he turned to look at his computer screen, thereby dismissing me.

Hearing Barry's confidence in the mayor and his good reputation made me want to believe maybe he was right. Only... I knew what I'd seen, and that couldn't be erased. But I let it drop for now and headed for my locker in the break room to drop off my gear and change clothes. I had a lot to think about tonight. I needed to do a bit of brainstorming. And nothing went better with brainstorming than food.

CHAPTER SEVEN

———

The well-filled belly has little understanding of the empty.
–Irish Proverb

Ten minutes later, I exited the back door of the building and headed toward my car. My red 1963 Buick Skylark convertible, the only thing I had left to remember my parents by. More important, it was affectionately named…Stella.

I'd left the car here last night since I'd gotten off duty so late. I'd wanted to get home and crash after my last work order. Now, at the end of another very long day, I was finally sliding inside once again.

I blew out a breath of relief and then inhaled the scent of old leather.

"Nice car."

The unexpected voice from the back seat made my throat emit a high-pitched squeak as my eyes darted up to the rearview mirror.

A thirty-something male sat in my back seat. His eyes were piercing, hair cut military short, and his mouth—dangerous. I reached for my bag. It contained an industrial-sized pepper spray, and I intended to use it.

"Don't bother. I'm not here to hurt you. I'm here to help you."

My hand froze in mid-motion.

"Who are you? How did you get in here?"

"That's not important. I heard you found something today, and I think I can help you."

My mind raced through possible scenarios. Find cell phone, call cops. Jump out of car, run for help. But he didn't seem aggressive. He seemed calm, almost unnaturally calm. Fear did not overwhelm me, but caution remained.

"I'd be more comfortable chatting if we'd met under, say, any circumstances other than you breaking into my car."

His expression softened and the tension in my shoulders lessened a notch.

"My apologies. Old habit."

I turned to look at him directly. One hand on the door handle. Ready to bolt if not for the fact that I'd be abandoning Stella. "Old habit? What are you, a friendly retired robber?"

This entire conversation seemed like something out of a wicked dream. In fact, this day continued on its course of the sublimely strange.

"Let's just say, our government trained me how to enter places quietly, and besides…I didn't break in. Your car was unlocked."

I thought about his words. Government training? Military haircut?

"Well, what is it you want from me?" Getting to the point was another one of my personal superpowers.

Another disarming grin from the secret agent man in the back seat. "It's not what I want from you. It's what you need from me."

"Great. Riddles."

He chuckled softly, and the sound caused a few stray bumps to emerge and salute him from my forearms. Whether the chills were from fear or attraction, I couldn't quite tell yet. But one thing was certain: I needed sleep in a serious way. A man breaks into my car, and I'm getting chills from his laughter.

He interrupted my thoughts. "Sorry. I overheard you chatting in the café today. You found a body at Mayor Mills' house."

I turned my upper torso around to face him. He wasn't asking a question—he was making more of a statement of fact. "You heard that?"

He nodded. "What can you tell me about the body?"

I swallowed. Someone actually wanted to hear my story and not make me the punch line. This was the fourth person today I'd discussed the body with, but the first person who'd made me feel at ease about it. "Why should I tell you? Who are you?"

He seemed to ponder my question carefully and then made a move to reach behind his back. I darted for my bag and tried to locate the canister of spray. I wrapped my hand around the first oblong object I found and pulled it out—thrusting it toward him.

"Nice bone."

My eyes cut over to the object I was holding. One of Pickles' chewed bones. Mangled and dirty. So much for my self-defense training. If he'd been reaching for a weapon, I'd be dead by now.

Luckily, what he'd retrieved from his back pocket was a newspaper clipping.

I dropped the chew toy on the car seat and reached for the paper.

He spoke in a calm, deep voice. "I think I know who the body belongs to."

* * *

I pulled up to 973 Edgewood Road just after five. I'd never been so glad to see Aunt Patty's house.

It seemed a bit like a mirage after the day I'd had. I stepped out of the car. Blue jeans and a white tank top adorned my tired body. I could almost hear Patty telling me to eat more— fatten up, men like a little something to hold on to. The memory made my heart ache for her wit.

My mystery man had left the article with me and told me he'd meet me for breakfast at the café. I'd told him that I had to be on duty by seven thirty, and he'd asked if six a.m. was fine. I'd agreed, but early mornings weren't my thing. Of course, there'd been a time just a few weeks ago that I'd been at the hospital doing rounds with the residents at five every morning. Only then, it had seemed important and exciting.

My booted feet clomped up the porch steps to the kitchen door, and I pulled open the screen. Before I could get inside, I heard the door screech open next door.

"Mandy, honey, is that you?"

Crap on a stick.

I'd forgotten about Ms. Lanier and her boiled buttock.

I turned and waved. "Yes, Ms. Lanier. I'll be right over. Let me just wash up."

"All right, then. I made camp stew. Are you hungry?"

My ears perked up at the offering of a home-cooked meal. Unfortunately, I'd never paid much attention when it came to cooking. It wasn't the first time I'd wished I had paid more mind to the things Aunt Patty had tried to teach me. Camp stew. A mixture of barbecued pork, chicken, potatoes, lima beans, corn, and tomatoes. It was a heavenly creation that would save me from a night of yet another leftover casserole from the funeral stash in the fridge.

"Be right there," I called again, and entered the kitchen just long enough to drop my purse, pat Pickles on the head and refill his food and water dishes, and give my hands a thorough washing at the kitchen sink. I placed the newspaper article next to my bag and decided to deal with that later.

Right now, I had a date with a huge bowl of stew and a woman with a sore bottom. I was living the dream life.

"At least I've got you, huh, Pickles?"

He snorted but didn't lift his head from the bowl of food.

* * *

Two bowls of stew, two dozen Saltine crackers, and a glass of sweet tea later, I was still eyeing the dish of peach cobbler steaming on the nearby counter. Obviously, my appetite was still lingering after the less-than-stellar lunch I'd endured with my old *friend* Penny. There'd been nothing wrong with the food, but it had been difficult to eat when Penny was tossing nosey questions at me left and right.

There were no secrets in Millbrook. At least, that was what I'd always thought until today. Someone had a secret. Someone in the Mills family. And I intended to find out what it was if for no other reason than pure medical curiosity. I wanted to know more about this ice man. Maybe without the help of the police. Maybe *with* the help from my breaking and entering mystery man. I really needed a name for him. Maybe he'd reveal it tomorrow at breakfast.

"I'll wrap up some peach cobbler for you to take home. Will Paget be able to come home tomorrow?"

At the mention of my hospitalized sister, I popped back to reality out of my fantasy world of secret agent men and mysterious dead bodies. My life was usually much less intriguing and much more plain old frightening.

"Yes, ma'am. Dr. C. is keeping her over night just for observation."

Ms. Lanier nodded as she cleared the table and placed the empty bowl and spoon in the suds-filled sink to soak.

"I expect it'll be a good night's rest for you, too."

I nodded, but the nod didn't even convince me. "Ms. Lanier. I came across something today when I was working at Mayor Mills' house, and I was wondering if I could talk to you about it."

Ms. Lanier propped herself against the clean counter and waited.

"So, I found a dead body in the freezer." No sense recounting the entire story again. Frankly, I was tired of telling it. Better to just jump to the punch line.

She didn't even blink at the news. No shocked expression. No eye rolling. No tone of disbelief when she said, "I'll bet it was that Myrna Mills. I never did trust that bitty."

Now it was my turn to gawk and express shock. "Now, Ms. Lanier…you don't know that. This all could have been just an accident. Maybe the police will go by and get this sorted out. Maybe there is a perfectly reasonable explanation."

She puckered her lips at my words. Then emitted a tsk-tsk sound. "You can't be serious, Mandy. What possible reasonable explanation could there be for a dead body in a freezer? What did it look like, anyway?"

I thought about it. "You know, I didn't hang around long enough to come up with a real description. It was kind of shocking. But it was a grown man, and he was curled up."

"Mmm hmm. Huh." She began to pace around the kitchen with a bit of a limp. "Well, I was gonna say if it was a woman that it was Myrna's doin' for sure. That Dougie never could keep his pants on."

I let out a little laugh. "Wow. A politician who cheats. What a novel idea."

"Yeah, the word is he's been sleeping with that housekeeper for years. So what did you do after you found it?" She stopped behind one of the table's chairs and balanced herself with one of the seatbacks.

Amika.

"Wait...Amika? The German-sounding housekeeper with those vivid blue eyes?"

"Yep. Oh yeah. Everyone knows about it, but no one says anything. You know how most of this town treats them like the royal family."

Oh, I knew, all right. But I decided to get back to our conversation at hand.

"Anyway, I went to the police station and told them, but they kind of gave me a hassle."

She shook her head slowly. "Those boys down there don't know how to handle this stuff. What you need is a real man like that Gil Grissom."

I ticked off names in my mind and couldn't seem to place the name. "Gil who?"

"I know he's out there in Vegas, but he'd know what to do with this body situation."

"Vegas? What are you talking about?"

"He comes on television every Thursday night—well, he used to, anyway."

The pieces finally snapped together in my mind. "Do you mean from the show *CSI*?"

She gave me a short grunt. "Of course I do. Who do you think I'm talking about? This kind of body discovery would be perfect for that show."

I opened my mouth to explain that it was a fiction-based show. That those weren't real forensic experts. But I just let it go. So much for Ms. Lanier being a true genius underneath all that body powder and hairspray.

"I was kind of thinking about doing a little investigating of my own, but I don't know where to start."

She grinned at me. "I'll think on it and let you know."

I might have officially lost it, but I was about to take the advice of one little old lady and agree to the help of a man who claimed to be a government spy.

"Well, I guess I'd better head home for now. I need some rest if I'm going to embark on this new adventure. Plus, I have to figure out who is going to care for Paget while I'm off working and snooping. I called Kendra and had to let her know that I wouldn't be needing her services any longer."

"What did she say happened?" Ms. Lanier inquired.

"Oh, she seemed really nonplussed about the whole thing. She claimed she was in the bathroom when Paget slipped out and she didn't even know she was gone until she couldn't find her at lunchtime. I mean, Paget has slipped out on me before, but it was really Kendra's lack of concern that worried me. Of course, now I'm back with zero care lined up."

Ms. Lanier opened a cabinet over the sink and extracted an old whipped-topping container and the matching lid. "I may have an idea on that."

She pulled a long-handled spoon from the drawer and began scooping heaping mounds of cobbler into the plastic container. My eyes were nearly watering with anticipation.

"Oh, yeah? Like what?"

Ms. Lanier finished filling the container and then turned toward me, eyes sparkling. "I know someone who is looking for a little extra work. But you have to be open-minded."

I wasn't sure how much more open-minded I could be. I'd take anyone responsible enough to keep Paget safe at this point.

"I think I can do that."

Ms. Lanier was beaming. "Oh, good…good. I'll set everything up, then. You go on home and get some rest now."

I wanted to ask more questions about the new caregiver idea, but Ms. Lanier was ushering me out the door with the covered bowl of sugary goodness.

My bed was calling to me, and I figured tomorrow would be another long day.

"Oh, but before you go…can you take a look at this?"

I was almost to the door with my container of bliss when I stopped and turned around. Ms. Lanier was untying her apron and lifting up her dress. Her belly bulged over a tight pair of pantyhose. The hosiery had started to roll downward over her generous midsection.

"I hope you don't mind taking a look at my little problem. I can't imagine showing this to that handsome Dr. Cavello."

Oh, geez. Appetitus interruptus.

CHAPTER EIGHT

———

You never miss the water till the well has run dry.
–Irish Proverb

Towel wrapped around me, I waited in the after-shower mugginess for my reflection to become visible in the fogged mirror. Chewing on my lower lip, I shed the towel and donned hot-pink panties and an oversized T-shirt before swiping my damp towel across the mirror to create one clear corner.

Tired eyes stared back at me. I'd stayed in the shower until the hot water heater had finally given up. Despite my best effort to wash away the stress of the day, worry still lingered in plain sight. Were those wrinkles forming on my forehead? Wasn't I too young for wrinkles?

I shrugged at myself and then pulled a red-tipped vent brush through the long, wet strands of my hair. Opening the bathroom door, I was greeted by the lonely face of Pickles.

"Hey, boy, ready for bed?"

He stood and trotted down the hallway toward the back of the house. I watched as he stopped just outside Patty's closed bedroom door.

"No, boy. I'm sleeping in the den. Remember?"

He sat down in front of Patty's door and emitted a small whine.

It would be nice to sleep in a real bed. I hadn't had a good night's sleep since I'd arrived here, and that ancient sofa was likely the culprit. I walked down the hall and stood above him. We both stared at the closed door.

Another whimper from Pickles.

I reached down and patted his firm but smooth head. "I know, boy. I miss her too."

I turned the doorknob and pushed the door open. Pickles trotted into the darkness. I flipped on the switch, and the bedside lamp responded with a soft glow. Pickles placed his front paws on the foot of the bed and then, with some effort, managed to vault the lower half of his heavy frame onto it.

As if all his remaining energy for the day had been spent, he stretched out along the foot of the bed on a multicolored afghan and yawned a big, drool-producing yawn.

No one had been in this room since the funeral. I'd closed it off after I'd chosen the dress for Aunt Patty. I could have slept in here at any time, but it seemed like an invasion. This was Patty's room.

Stepping farther into the room, I caught a whiff of gardenias. It was Patty's signature scent. I missed her so much. Over the years, she'd been more like a mother than an aunt to me, and the only mother figure that Paget had ever known. Our parents had died when Paget was just a baby, but I was nearly twelve when it happened. Their deaths had spiraled my world out of control. Aunt Patty, my father's sister, had moved home to Millbrook from her life in Las Vegas and we'd moved in with her. I'd become reclusive, a bookworm, and hadn't spoken for over a year.

I didn't like to think about that year. Parts of it were clear in my mind while others drifted in and out of my memory like unwelcomed spirits. I'd been at school when it happened, but Paget had been in the truck with them. It was my father's work truck, and they had taken it to Paget's doctor's appointment because it was snowing and he didn't think Stella would be a good choice for the bad weather. The only day that year that it had snowed, in fact. On their way home, they'd been hit by a semi-truck that'd lost control on an icy bridge. Icy weather was a rarity in the Deep South, but there it was…just the wrong moment on the wrong day. Paget had survived the crash, but I'd struggled to survive the aftermath.

I shuddered at the recollection and then shook it from my memory like shaking the wrinkles out of a sheet. Now, I sat at Patty's three-mirrored dresser and studied her silver hairbrush and comb set. It had been passed down from Patty's mother—my grandmother, whom I'd never met. It was the only other link I had to my dad's side of the family—besides his car.

Turning away from the mirror and the past for the moment, I looked back at Pickles. He was already snoozing. The deep, rumbling snore sounded like an invitation to join him in slumber land.

I tiptoed to the bed and peeled back the covers. I slid my legs underneath and scooted down into the floral-scented cocoon. It was almost like hugging Aunty Patty. I closed my eyes. If Patty were here right now, what would she tell me to do about Paget?

I knew the answer, but I was too tired to admit it tonight. As I drifted off to sleep, I recalled the headline of the article that my mystery man had left for me. How it connected to the body I'd found today, I wasn't sure. But I was sure that I was dead tired and sleep was beckoning.

* * *

A knock on the door awoke me from a sound sleep. The digital clock confirmed that it was six thirty in the morning. I peered over the covers at Pickles, and he raised his head to peer back but made no effort to leave his comfy spot. I couldn't blame him.

Another knock on the door.

What was it about early-morning visitors around here? Did no one sleep past sunrise anymore?

I shuffled out of my warm cocoon and back into the now too-cold morning air of the house. I snagged Patty's rose-patterned housecoat from the back of the door and pulled it on as I headed to the kitchen.

I opened the door, and there stood my mystery man holding two to-go coffee cups and a bag that was emitting sensuous smells, like bacon and sausage.

"Oops."

I'd forgotten to set an alarm, and I'd left my cell phone in the bathroom. Obviously, I'd missed our early a.m. breakfast meeting, and obviously he'd tracked me down at home anyway.

He smiled. "Nice robe."

I returned the smile with some trepidation and motioned for him to enter. The idea did cross my mind that I was admitting a complete stranger into my home. As he entered, I stealthily made my way to the counter and removed a rolling pin from the ceramic utensil holder. I moved it behind my back as I turned around with a look of utter innocence and nonchalance.

It was an unsettling feeling, having him show up like this, but I kind of wanted to trust him. I wasn't sure why, but I did.

His compliment had made me aware of the old-lady-style floral housecoat I was wearing. It came complete with a zippered front. My hair was probably very interesting about right now, as I'd had fallen asleep with it semi-wet. Probably looked a bit like Einstein's hair on a good day.

I shrugged. "Thanks. Is that bacon I smell?"

Pickles let out a resounding bark at my question. I saw he'd made his way to the kitchen to inspect our visitor and offer me protection. Oh, who was I fooling? He had smelled the food and had come running. He was no dummy.

"Your dog?" the international man of mystery inquired.

"No, he belongs to my sister. His name is Pickles, or as I like to call him, Señor Drool. I would introduce you, but I'm not privy to your name."

He ignored my question and began to set the Styrofoam boxes of food out on the kitchen table in a precise manner, folding napkins and arranging the plastic utensils as if preparing for a formal dinner party. I watched and caught myself admiring his muscled arms, which bulged from the sleeves of a pressed white golf shirt. As he reached across the table to set down my coffee cup, I thought I caught a hint of a tattoo on his left bicep, but the sleeve covered it before I could make out the design.

My eyes moved down his back to note his crisp khaki trousers fit snugly in all the right places. He turned, and I redirected my eyes upward to a more appropriate vantage point. But he'd caught me checking him out. Thank goodness he had the manners not to point it out.

Nonetheless, I clenched the robe a little tighter as a blush crept up my cheeks. Dang Irish heritage—it was impossible to hide a blush on this fair skin. It wasn't like me to be embarrassed, but this whole scene playing out before me was beyond odd. Of course, what in my life wasn't odd these days?

"Shall we?"

He pulled out a chair for me, and I took a seat. Pickles moved to me and placed his heavy head on my thigh. His eyes twitched up at me with immense longing. I pushed the rolling pin between my legs. At least I had some sort of weapon handy in case he was bribing me with food just so that he could distract me before he murdered me. What if he *was* the murderer?

I swallowed back my nerves as I opened the box of food and gasped with surprise.

It was loaded with scrambled eggs, home fries covered with cheese, crisp bacon, long links of sausage, and a huge buttered biscuit. It was…perfect.

I hand-fed Pickles a piece of bacon and then sliced up a link of sausage and placed it on a napkin. I slid it to the floor, and he made quick work of it.

I looked up at my guest and found he was watching me under hooded eyes.

"Aren't you going to eat?" I asked as I scooped mounds of peppered eggs into my mouth. I'd never been one to act shy around guys when it came to eating. Hated it when girls acted all silly about not wanting to eat when they went on dates. I'd never ordered "just a salad"—ever. No one would ever call me a cheap date.

"Have you had a chance to read the article I gave you?"

I nodded in sync with my munching mandible. "I did read through it, but I'm sorry to say that I don't understand how this explains anything."

He nodded and reached across the table to where I'd left the article next to my bag and scooted it toward me.

I took this to mean he wanted me to read it again here and now. Well, he had brought me a breakfast to die for. I guessed I could take a moment to scan the article.

It was a faded newspaper clipping. The paper was the local *Main Street Mile*—named this because the most happening part of town was located in a one-mile stretch that ran between Smoke Pit Barbeque Grill and City Hall. The date in the top right corner was a decade ago. In fact, it was the summer after I'd left for college—when I'd spent a summer working as a waitress to save money for the books and food that my scholarship wouldn't cover. Of course, that was only the beginning of how hard I'd had to work to put myself through medical school—something I was still paying for even though I wasn't currently attending. And the fact that I was right back to the blue-collar world, even with all those expensive student loans looming, didn't escape me.

The article's title was "Search for Local Man Called Off." I scanned over the text. It was about one of the men in the Brooks family. The Brooks were the other founding family of Millbrook. Douglas Mills IV and Cyrus Brooks had been best friends once upon a time. They'd grown up in nearby Prattville, but had aspirations to create their own town—which they did successfully in 1977 when Millbrook was established. But even long before that time, the two families had been close allies since multiple generations earlier when they'd fought side by side in the War of Northern Aggression—better known to most as the Civil War. They'd been members of the local encampment known as the Prattville Dragoons. In the end, the South may not have come out on top, but both families had survived and subsequently built their families into a "local empire" when Douglas and Cy put Millbrook on the map.

As ambitious young men, they'd created the small but charming Millbrook. But while the original duo may have fought side by side, somewhere along the line, the families became bitter enemies. For as long as I had known of them, they were rivals in just about everything. From who had the biggest house, to who had the best lawn, to who had the best athlete in their family, to who had the most beautiful debutante daughter. Most of the Brooks had gone on to serve in high political offices for the state and had spread out and away from Millbrook, but a few remained. Mostly the Mills family had remained to run the town.

I finished the article and looked up to find my mystery man still watching me. I took another bite of eggs and munched on the end of a slice of bacon.

"Okay. I read it." I mouthed the words around the cholesterol-coated sticks of delight I was polishing off at record speed.

He studied me closely for another minute. Then he finally spoke. "That man in the article, Caden Brooks."

I nodded. I hadn't known the man and wasn't sure what this had to do with anything.

"I believe he's the man you found in the freezer yesterday."

I nearly choked on a sausage link and covered my mouth with a napkin as my eyes watered. The ever-helpful mystery man reached over and smacked me on the back a few times, and I shook my head.

Geez.

He was stronger than crap, and he was beating me to death with his helpfulness. I waved him off and took a sip of coffee from the cup he'd provided. With all the choking and back smacking, I lost my grip on the rolling pin, and it clattered to the floor then rolled across the kitchen. Our eyes followed its journey until it came to a stop after bumping into Pickles' water bowl.

His knowing grin took me off guard, and I was slightly embarrassed, but shrugged. "Look, I don't know you. A girl has to protect herself by whatever means necessary."

His grin turned up a notch. "What were you going to do? Bake me to death?"

I bit my lip to keep from smiling, and tried to get back to the business at hand. "Okay. Why do you think that the body I found was this Caden Brooks? The article says he was a known skirt chaser and probably ran off with one of his conquests."

Mystery man sat back in his chair and crossed his arms. "He didn't run off. He was murdered. He and Dougie Mills hated each other, and Caden Brooks had submitted his paperwork of intent to run for mayor just one month before he disappeared."

I certainly hadn't heard anything about that. And usually if it was news in Millbrook, everyone heard. A big campaign between the Mills and Brooks for control of the city would have been big stuff. Of course, I'd had my own stuff going on then. Ty's face sprang to mind, but I erased it immediately.

"How do you know about all this? No one has ever had the guts to run against Dougie Mills in my lifetime."

Mystery Man watched me closely as he said, "Because Brooks told me the night before he disappeared."

"He told you?"

He nodded, opened the box of food in front of him, and scooped up a portion of eggs on his fork.

I stared at him, waiting for him to continue. When he didn't, I reached out and stopped his hand. It was midway between the plate and his mouth, and bits of egg spilled back into the container as I held his wrist.

His eyes met mine.

"Why did he tell *you*?"

"'Cause I'm his son."

CHAPTER NINE

___

It is no secret that is known to three. –Irish Proverb

I finished my questionably healthy breakfast and my questionably safe visit with Mystery Man, who'd now identified himself as Colin Brooks—a member of one of Millbrook's founding families. I'd wanted to continue our conversation, but he'd disappeared while I'd been busy filling Pickles' bowl with Colin's leftover breakfast. Unfortunately for Señor Drool, no food remained in my box.

I'd been surprised at his hasty retreat, and how he'd seemed to vanish into thin air was anybody's guess. But I didn't have time to ponder his skills further, 'cause after a rapid teeth-brushing effort and a change into clean jeans and a fresh tank top, I had to zip off in Stella once again as the daily grind awaited.

I barely had time to stop in for a quick check on Paget before I was due back at work for yet another glee-inducing shift with Flicks Vision.

Despite the early-morning hour, there was no chill to be had as I guided my red missile through town with the top down. Hair blowing in the breeze, I tried to clear my mind from the clutter of thoughts by tuning in to the local radio station, but apparently music had been replaced by the yakking of "Married in The Morning with Mick and Matty." Since when did Millbrook have a morning talk show? And who really cared about what those two mumble-heads had done last night?

Snapping off the radio, I took a few cleansing breaths and tried to prepare myself for the day. I'd left my morning meeting with secret agent man half an hour earlier.

Of course, now that he'd identified himself as Colin Brooks, that made referring to him as the international man of mystery a little less fun. I found Colin's theory about his father interesting, but I wasn't sure I could trust him. He'd failed to satisfactorily explain where he'd been all these years and why I'd never heard of him—despite the fact that we were only a few years apart in age. Maybe he'd reveal more when we met again.

But I was willing to suspend disbelief for the moment—at least until I knew more about the identity of the dead body. A body that I hoped had been found by the police by now.

I made a mental note to do a little research on Colin when I had time. Surely there was some record of him somewhere. No one could hide out these days with the power of the internet.

Could the body really be Caden Brooks? Son of one of Millbrook's founding fathers?

Colin seemed interested in helping me discover the truth. After a good night's sleep, my curiosity was more than nagging me. So, like it or not, I was headed back to the station after checking on Paget and clocking in at the cable company. I needed to know if Ty was taking my report seriously, and that, regardless of his apparent memory of my one "big lie" back in high school, I shouldn't be considered a liar upon sight. I wasn't that immature girl anymore.

And, frankly, when all was said and done, I'd never been a fan of the Mills. If I could play a part in taking them down a notch and maybe solving a mystery in the process—well, it was all about honesty, and that was part of the Hippocratic Oath, wasn't it?

Maybe that was stretching the oath a little too far.

Plan in mind and car ride complete, I swung the wide car into a parking space—or two—and then pulled my hairbrush from my bag. Looking in my rearview mirror, I saw two things that concerned me.

One, my hair was going to need more than a quick brush-through after the wind damage I'd just caused it. And two, I had a bigger problem. Ty Dempsey was in the row of cars behind me, leaning against the hood of his police-issued sedan with his arms crossed.

He didn't look happy.

* * *

I exited my car and watched Ty's eyes carefully as he studied me with a cop's glare. "We need to chat."

I slung my bag over my shoulder and turned toward the entrance. "Well, I have to check on my sister first, if you don't mind."

It wasn't a question. I was going to check on my sister, and I didn't feel like talking to Ty Dempsey right now. Something about him still made me act out. Even after all this time, he could get under my skin without speaking a word. He'd been my whole life, back in the day, and then he'd been the reason I'd started a new life when I left town. I'd all but cut off communication with this town, with the exception of limited contact with Aunt Patty and Paget. But I didn't have time to reminisce right now.

"Actually, I do mind. I need to get to the mayor's office pronto, and your little stunt yesterday could cost me my job."

At his words, I stopped and spun around.

"My little stunt? I came to your office, reported a possible crime, and your guy laughed it off as if I were a nutcase. Then you sprang the news on me that my sister was injured and sent me off in a panic. Nice job, officer."

A twitch at his jaw line revealed that I'd zinged him with my words, but no other emotion was visible behind his green eyes.

"That's *detective*. And I'm referring to your little stunt of going to the newspaper and spreading rumors about Mayor Mills before we'd had a chance to secure the crime scene."

My breath caught in my throat, and the smugness I'd felt a moment ago slid down to my stomach, which lurched into a spin cycle.

"I did no such thing. I wouldn't go to the newspaper about something like…"

My mind raced back to my lunch with Henny Penny, who'd said she didn't work for the paper any longer. But that didn't mean she hadn't spread the news herself. Or maybe it was

Colin. He'd overheard our entire conversation and come after me the same evening. Who else had heard the story? My boss, Barry?

I went with the most likely culprit. "Penny said she didn't work for the paper anymore."

Wasn't that what she'd said? I had to focus in order to swallow.

He lifted one eye and crinkled his forehead at me, and I had the sudden memory of him doing the same thing when I'd confronted him behind the stadium on one rainy night eons ago. I tamped down the memory.

Not now, Mandy. Not now.

"No. She doesn't work for the paper. She *owns* the paper, Mandy."

Gulp. "Well, I asked her if she worked there, and she said she didn't. I needed someone to talk to. I'd had a bad day."

The explanation sounded lame even to my own ears, but he was watching me carefully. The muscles in his face were taut—locked into place. His jawbone shifted slightly as he ground his teeth, but his eyes were soft, and the heat emanating from them, combined with the heat off the asphalt parking lot beneath us, was unbearable. It was as if he wanted to console me in some way but was torn between compassion and anger. I'd seen that look before as well.

"Look, I didn't exactly handle your visit to the station well, either."

I looked down at my worn work boots. "Is that an apology?"

He let out a soft bark of laughter. "Let's not get carried away."

I avoided eye contact with him as I lifted my head. "I need to check on Paget and get to work. I need this job, and after yesterday…"

He nodded. "Can I join you?"

This brought my eyes back to his face. "Join me? At work?"

Now he smiled full force at me, and I felt fifteen again. Saying the wrong thing in front of the cute guy. I was a virtual pro at this maneuver.

"No, when you check on Paget. I haven't seen her since the accident."

"Since the…"

I was finding it difficult to form rational thoughts and sentences this morning. Maybe I didn't get enough sleep. Or maybe it was being around Ty that caused it.

"Oh, didn't they tell you?"

"Tell me what?" My heart did a little boogie against my chest plate again.

"I'm the one who pulled her out from in front of the car. I'm the one who saved her."

CHAPTER TEN

―――――

Fences have ears. –Irish Proverb

"Do you think Dr. C. will let me get an x-ray so I can see inside myself?"

I squeezed her hand. "I doubt it. Why would you want to do that?"

Paget jabbed at the wiggling block of gelatin on her plate and scrunched her nose. "I wanted to see if it still jiggles on the inside?"

"I see you're feeling better."

Paget frowned deeply. "I'm sorry I messed up again, Mand. Are you mad at me?"

"I'm never mad at you. I'm mad at myself. Sorry I can't be with you all the time. Sorry I have to work."

Paget gave a wide grin. "Want some Jell-O? It's orange, that's your favorite."

I laughed, and Paget reached up to press her small finger to the corner of my mouth. Our mother had had the same dimple at the corner of her mouth. I remembered it. Mom, hanging clothes on the clothesline. Smiling in the sunlight. Back when she was young and happy and alive. I wondered if Paget had seen a photo of our mother like that.

"No, I think I'll pass for now. Pickles and I had a huge breakfast, but thank you."

"Pickles…is he okay?"

I patted her hand calmly, pulling her attention back into focus. "Pickles is fine. He and I slept in Aunt Patty's bed last night."

"But…but…that's Aunt Patty's bed."

"I know, and I'm sorry I didn't talk to you about it first. I was so very tired, and Pickles demanded to sleep on that afghan—you know the one."

Paget beamed at me with pride. The green and purple afghan was the crooked one that Paget had helped Aunt Patty knit. It was uneven and oddly colored, and it was Aunt Patty's favorite thing in the world.

Now Pickles never wanted to get off it. Now it was *his* favorite thing in the world. Well, besides Paget.

"Paget, I'm going to work for a little while, but I'll be back after lunch to pick you up. Will that be okay?"

A small coughing sound from the doorway caught our attention. Paget peered around me as Ty walked in. Paget gripped my hand tighter at first, but then she relaxed as she seemed to recognize him.

"Oh, you…you're my hero." She looked at him sheepishly.

Ty smiled back and winked at her.

"Do you know the Tall Winking Stranger, Mand?"

Tall Winking Stranger? Ugh. I nearly gave myself a headache with the large mental eye roll that ensued. "Uh, yes. I know him. Is it okay if he says hello?"

Paget's face turned red. She looked down at her hand, still clasped inside mine. "Yes. He's nice."

I murmured, "That's debatable," under my breath, but neither of them paid me any attention. Paget seemed infatuated with Ty as he walked over and touched her shoulder.

There was silence for a moment, and then Paget's shrill voice set both me and Ty on high alert.

"A gun…he's got a gun!" Paget screamed, and I tried to calm her.

Ty, seeming to understand, backed out of the room slowly, and I tried to hold Paget in a reassuring embrace until the nurse came and slipped something into the IV.

After Paget returned to bliss-filled sleep, I eased out of the room and returned to the parking lot. Ty had slipped a note on Stella's windshield. Apparently, there was no need to stop by the station this morning—Ty wanted me to come by during my lunch break to fill out an official report. Lunch with Penny yesterday and lunch with her brother today.

Huh. So now he wanted to hear what I had to say. What a difference a day makes.

* * *

"Have you seen this?"

I stood in the Flicks Vision office. Barry's eyes bored into me as he held a newspaper in one hand. I scratched the back of my neck while thinking of diagnosing myself with coverall-itis. *Wonder if I can add it to the* Physician's Desk Reference*?*

I shrugged. This couldn't be good. "No, I just got in."

Barry's face was a red color, kind of like the shade of a bad summer sunburn. A thick vein in his neck throbbed under the fluorescent lighting. He tossed the paper in my general direction

The headline read, "Local Girl Returns Home, Accuses Mayor of Murder." I looked back up at Barry, who was now wiping his forehead with the back of his hand, a nervous gesture.

"Do you know anything about this?" he asked.

I shrugged again and then scanned the article quickly. I needed a plan and needed one quickly, or I wouldn't have a job by the end of the day.

I looked up at Barry. "You know how this town is, Barry. This is nothing new. The gossipmongers know about everything. You can hardly kiss someone goodnight without it making the headlines around here."

His bulging vein seemed to expand another quarter-inch. I began to worry that it might explode from his neck at any moment like an alien invader who'd inhabited his body.

"You told someone besides the police and myself? Is that what I'm hearing?"

Despite my calm outward demeanor, my pulse raced at Barry's accusation. I knew I'd spilled the beans directly to Henny Penny at the café. I was totally to blame here.

Well, partially to blame. The police hadn't exactly jumped on this at record speed. And I hadn't really accused anyone of anything. The headline was a bit premature.

"Uh, well…what should I do? Do you not want me to finish the job at the mayor's house now?" I asked. Weirdly enough, I wanted to go back to that attic now. After all, you had to see all the clues to solve the mystery, didn't you?

"You bet your bottom dollar I don't want you back over there. You are to stay as far away from Mayor Mills and his family as possible. I wouldn't be surprised if he pulls our business license by the end of the day as it is."

I bit my lip. "Maybe I could go and apologize?" I had no idea where this idea had come from, but it seemed the right thing to say at the moment. I wondered if I could get in to see the mayor—or maybe his wife. Ms. Lanier had seemed to think that she was the key to everything.

Barry released a pent-up breath and shook his head. "I'm certain this whole thing is a big misunderstanding, but girly, you've got to keep out of it now. I've assigned you to The Country Club for this morning."

And there certainly won't be any Mills there.

My boss could be a nice enough guy, but I wasn't sure what he was thinking. The country club, which was aptly named The Country Club, was where the wealthiest, most hungry gossip hounds lived and breathed.

I thought about reminding him of this, but instead I gave a nod and reached for the clipboard he was extending toward me. Better not push my luck with old Barry. The redness in his face was screaming "potential coronary" already.

I headed out of the building but stopped to read the article before I pushed through the door. There was a quote from me at the bottom, it read:

"I know what I saw, and it was indeed the frozen body of a male subject. I've attended medical school for three years now, and if there's one thing I can recognize—it's a dead body."

Oh, shumbunnies.

* * *

As I drove toward The Country Club in the dreaded work van, I thought of Paget and could still hear her scream. It was always like that. You'd have a few good moments with her, and then everything would go to hell. Her brain worked that way, and there was little you could do about it. I'd been away too long. I'd left her care up to Patty for too many years.

Now, I had to learn how to cope with it all over again.

The welcome sign for The Country Club came into view as I crested the hill, and I wondered what was worse...coping with Paget's illness or withstanding the snobbery of Millbrook's elite?

CHAPTER ELEVEN

———

Great mansions have slippery doors. –Irish Proverb

I'd worked at The Country Club one summer during high school as a lifeguard. Honestly, it had been the only way to spend the summer near a pool for me, but I'd not been fond of a job where I was forced to sit around all day and watch the wealthy lounge about and spend their family money.

I didn't know what it was like to have luxuries such as country club memberships and private tennis lessons. But I did know what it was like to work for an honest day's living, and that's what I was doing here today.

No sense dwelling on the past. I was here to focus on my job.

Exiting the vehicle, I heard the screech of tires and looked up to find the same sleek BMW I'd seen at the mayor's house yesterday. The license plate read *Matson*—it was the mayor's son again. I watched as the driver haphazardly parked across two parking spaces one of them a handicapped spot.

What a jerk.

He exited the car, wearing the same type of tennis whites I'd observed him in yesterday, but today he had a certain weariness about him. Dark circles under his eyes and less-than-perfect hair sprang out from beneath his cap.

Bad night at the mayor's house? The thought occurred to me as I affixed the tool belt to my waist and watched him bounce a tennis ball on his racket as he made his way through the gated entrance and toward the courts.

Ty had mentioned that my lunch chat with Penny may have comprised his crime scene, so I assumed that even though the cops hadn't given me a proper welcome at the station that they'd checked out my gruesome discovery nonetheless. But I wondered how the family had responded to the exposure this and the news article was sure to rain down upon them.

My mind worked through the possible scenarios of how the mayor would have found out about this. Did Ty get a warrant and search the premises after I'd left? Did he give the mayor a heads-up and the opportunity to explain before he headed to court for that warrant? Or did he drag his feet until the paper came out and then was forced to follow up? I imagined the cocky Ty Dempsey standing in front of the mayor's desk this morning, hands clasped behind his back, and chin down like a petulant school boy caught ditching class.

The thought more than appealed to me.

He hadn't really been clear on it this morning, and I kicked myself for not asking for more details. There were too many distractions in my life. But it would have been cool to have something to report to Colin this evening. The thought of playing sleuth suddenly held a growing appeal to me. In some ways it was like being a doctor. You looked at the symptoms as if they were clues and then solved the mystery of the illness when you issued a diagnosis. This was kind of like that—of course, as a doctor you tried to avoid turning your patients into corpses.

Clipboard in hand, I headed toward the clubhouse, my mind sorting through the possibilities of how best to kick-start my own little investigation. After all, what if the Mills family managed to sweep this entire thing under the proverbial rug? I suddenly felt that it was my responsibility to ensure that didn't happen.

"Excuse me. You can't park that work vehicle there." A gravelly voice broke through my mental wanderings. I stopped and turned to find a dark-complexioned man wearing gardener's attire, complete with gloves and a rake in hand.

"What?"

"I said, you can't park that van there. Those parking spaces are for club members only. All work staff and contractors have to park around back."

What he meant to say was that the menial labor had to stay out of sight. I frowned. It was difficult to get back into the swing of being on the low end of the totem pole. I didn't know why it should come as any surprise after a lifetime of being treated this way in this town. But somehow, after the last ten years away, I'd begun to think of myself as worthy of respect. In college and med school, we were all at the same level, and our backgrounds hadn't mattered all that much. Here, who your family was or *wasn't* made all the difference in the world.

"Well, they can tow it if they want to. Wouldn't be the first time I've parked where I'm not supposed to."

He frowned at me as if my bad attitude was bringing him down. Then he shrugged. "If you want to lose your job over a parking space, who am I to judge, chica?"

"Doubt I'll lose my job over this in particular. I'm already on thin ice over something much bigger."

He stifled a smile, and I smiled back at him. I liked this guy.

"I'm Mandy. Mandy Murrin." I held out my hand, and he hastily removed his right glove and shook it.

"I'm Rigo."

"Nice to meet you, Rigo. Have you worked here long?"

He squinted slightly as if recalling. "Been about eight years now. My family moved here after the hurricane."

I bit my lower lip. He must mean Katrina. It had brought quite a few new families into town. I remembered Patty telling me that she'd helped fix up a temporary shelter in the school's gymnasium for displaced families. I wondered if Rigo's family was one of them.

"Well, I'm glad you found our town and hope everyone is treating you well here."

He tilted his head from side to side. "It's okay. I like the area. Most of the people are nice."

I gave a nod. I understood completely. There were two distinct classes in this town. Those who were the Mills or the Brooks, and those who worked for them. I'd always been in the latter category, and my new friend Rigo was as well.

"Yep. Well, looks like I'll be back in town for a little while. Maybe I'll see you around."

He seemed a little puzzled, and I got the sense that he thought I was flirting with him.

I laughed. It was funny, but I hadn't been flirting with him or any other man in what seemed like ages. My personal life had consisted of weekend study sessions in the library and weeknights at the lab. In other words, I was an absolute bore when it came to romance these days.

He tipped his hat then continued his raking of straw into the bricked-in circumference of a flowerbed.

"Hey, Rigo. Thanks for the parking tip."

He shrugged. But I could see him smiling as he turned back to his work.

Some folks were still nice in this world. That was another reason I wanted to get back to school. I wanted to complete my studies and become a part of something important—make a difference.

I headed for the clubhouse door but paused to look back at the tennis courts. There was Matson Mills stretching for his expensive tennis lesson with the club pro.

I wondered: had he ever done anything to make a difference?

* * *

I duck-walked along the baseboards of the pool house. The room had more than its share of humidity, and my hair inched up the back of my neck in response. The floor of this particular building did not sport the club's standard hardwood flooring. Instead, it was covered with green artificial turf. There were slightly sunken drains located at key junctures in the floor, and I couldn't help but think of the floor drains in the autopsy suites back at school.

I would never forget the first time I'd had to see and touch a cadaver. I'd been surprised at how hard and cold a body could feel, even through gloves. I'd learned to detach myself from the body. I tried to never think of it as a person. Someone's brother or father or boyfriend—nope, it was just a body. That was the only way I could cut into it, dissect it, and learn from it. Of course, that didn't mean that you lost respect for the body.

You always had to respect this person for making a sacrifice so that others could learn. Giving your body to science takes guts— no pun intended.

A small shiver racked my body as my mind wavered back to the sight of the body in the freezer. I hadn't had the same detached reaction to this body. Why? I hadn't known the person. Why had I been so flustered by it? Why hadn't I taken the time to examine it a little further before I'd high-tailed it out of there?

I should have been glad that I didn't have to go back to the scene of the crime. But instead, I wished for a second chance. My reaction had been so out of character for me.

"Well, isn't this just the most awkward thing ever?"

The tightly wound voice of Allyson Harlow somehow managed to shrivel my hair another half-inch shorter. I looked up from the outlet I was wiring to find the busty brunette decked out in a yellow polka-dot bikini and a straw hat with matching yellow bow.

What is it with her and polka dots?

She twirled her sunglasses around and around by the ear stem in one hand and sloshed a cocktail around in the other. The pink umbrella in the drink was being sucked down into the whirlpool of what smelled like Malibu rum.

I faux-smiled at her and returned to my work with concentrated effort.

"Do you think you could hand me a towel from down there?"

I turned to look behind me and saw that there was, indeed, a wicker cabinet door that concealed shelves of large, fluffy white beach towels.

"Uh…let me think…no."

Allyson gasped in mock horror. "I mean, since you're down there already and all. You can't do me this one itty-bitty little favor, Mandy Candy?"

A tightening at the base of my spine threatened to rocket boost me up from my crouched position and knock the daylights out of this pest. But I took a deep breath and continued to work. I refused to stoop to the level of petty catfighting. It just wasn't worth it. We weren't in high school, after all.

That was when the sticky, ice-cold drink hit the top of my hair.

"Oopsie…"

I shot up and smacked the glass out of Allyson's manicured hand. It hit the turf-covered floor with a *thunk* but managed not to break.

"Are you out of your mind?" I snatched a towel out of the now-open door to the cabinet.

"Well, you see, that's why I asked you to get it for me. When I bent over to open the cabinet, I must have accidentally fumbled my drink. Oopsie…"

"I'll oopsie you." My eyes were on fire as I fought back the sudden urge to cry. I towel dried my now-sticky strands as I tried to control my emotions. I would not—absolutely would *not*—let this jerk get to me.

"I said I was sorry."

"No, you didn't."

"Oh, well, I'm sure you know it was an accident. I know it is early in the day, but I've been having brunch with Mrs. Mills, and she does enjoy a morning cocktail by the pool."

My hand slowed its motion as I immediately began to wonder if Allyson and Mrs. Mills had chatted about the matter of a little dead body situation in the attic. I wondered how to broach the subject.

"I wanted to tell you that I loved the little article you starred in this morning. Too bad they didn't include a picture of you. I know how much the town will welcome you back with open arms now that you've become enemy number one of the Mills family."

Yep. If Allyson and Mrs. Mills were in cahoots then it had definitely been spoken about already. That was probably why the mayor's wife was at the club drinking such strong refreshments long before noon. But I had to wonder what Allyson had in common with Myrna Mills.

"Look, I know what I saw, and the police will follow up on it, I'm sure. It is best you stay out of it." I was surprised at my own words. They were smart advice. A real reasonable warning for Allyson.

"I think you should be the one to stay out of it. No one wants you here. No one wants to hear a word out of your smart mouth."

Oh well, so much for Allyson taking sound advice. That little snarky remark plus the "accidental" spill on my head was the reason I couldn't hold back my next retort.

"Well, there's at least one person who wants to hear what I have to say. I have a lunch date with Ty."

No sooner had the words come out of my mouth did Allyson turn and grab a pitcher of water off the counter. She began to swirl it in the same motion as the cocktail, only this was a gallon-sized pitcher of ice-cold water with lemon slices in the mix. Trapped between the demon and the door, I braced myself for another cold shower.

Only Allyson turned and splashed the pitcher's contents into the open outlet in one swift motion. She dropped the pitcher on the floor; shards of glass rained down over my boots and a hissing sound from the outlet filled the air.

Then she turned and sauntered out of the pool house without another word. Slipping on her sunglasses as she exited the mirrored doors. A gray-haired man awaited her exit, and she giggled when he took her arm and led her away.

I stared down at the mess before me. This was a battle I hadn't wanted, but somehow—all these years later—I found myself right back in the same drama I'd endured once before in my life. Yep, high school *was* back again.

CHAPTER TWELVE

———

One man's meat is another man's poison. –Irish Proverb

I swung by the Flicks Vision office and gave Barry the thumbs-up on the country club job. He seemed happy about me completing my assignment despite the fact that, due to Allyson's little cocktail party with the cable outlet, the assignment had taken all morning shift long.

He'd seemed more than a little perturbed about my needing the rest of the afternoon off to meet with Ty and pick up Paget, but I managed to escape before he went into full face-reddening mode. I swapped out the rusty work van for my gorgeous beast of a car, stopped by the house for a quick shower and shampoo, and then I was en route to the police station. I was doing pretty good, only running half an hour late as I drove toward the station, my mind swirling over the events of the last two days—not to mention the dreaded conversation I was about to have with Ty Dempsey. I'd held a lot of resentment toward him for many years, and now he was back in my life and, apparently, Paget's new "hero" with a scary gun.

The thought of him as anyone's hero was hard for me to grasp. After taking advantage of my tender, school girl crush and stealing my virginity—things had gone downhill from there. Well, he didn't exactly *steal* it. I'd pretty much offered it up on a silver platter. Or the hood of his silver Camero as fate would have it. And then when he got offered that huge football scholarship to Auburn University, I may have told one little lie—well maybe not exactly *little*…

But the fact that I'd once looked up to him and cared for him deeply was enough of a disappointment after the way things had ended between us. He'd humiliated me and then he'd blamed me for everything in his life that had gone wrong. And…well…I didn't know if I could ever fully trust him again.

Pulling up to the station a mere twenty-four hours after my first visit still brought up the same feelings of anxiety and dread. But this time, Ty was outside the building, speaking with an older, white-haired man in uniform. They both gave me a glance and then wrapped up their conversation.

Ty headed my way and took no shame in studying both me and the car as I cut the engine and stepped onto the asphalt, shoving sunglasses atop my head.

"You've kept it in great shape." His words seemed to reference the condition of my classic muscle car, but his eyes roamed my bare arms and low-cut tank top as he spoke.

I pursed my lips. I wasn't in the mood to chat about cars with him. Although I did wonder what he was driving these days. A passion for hot cars had always been something we'd had in common. But I didn't have time, nor was I in the mood for idle chitchat today.

"I've got to get to the hospital before they are ready to discharge Paget. What exactly do you need from me, Ty?"

"Uh, that's Detective Dempsey." His quick retort took me a bit off guard. It shouldn't have surprised me. He was the master at turning off personal feelings at the drop of a hat. Of course, I wasn't here for personal reasons. And he didn't know that I'd just been remembering his hot rod and his hot…*rod*.

I felt a rise in my blood pressure, accompanied by a whooshing sound gathering behind my eardrums. "Fine. Detective Dempsey. Ask your questions, and let me be on my way. I have things to do."

He pulled out a small spiral notebook and a pencil from his back pocket. His forearms flexed as he turned his arm over to check the time on his watch. I waited. Impatiently.

"Is everything such a big production with you? Am I supposed to be impressed that you're a detective with the police department now?"

The condescension in my voice must have stung, as he looked up, green eyes penetrating mine. His face deadly serious. He knew how we'd left things that night after the graduation party. It had been the last time we'd spoken, and it had been the night I'd lost my battle to keep him. My life had changed into a big dream on the horizon as I'd left for pre-med at the University of Alabama. And his dream had died just a few months later when he'd blown his knee out at spring training—a career-ending ACL tear. It had been surgically repaired, but his scholarship had been lost.

"I have a job to do, Mandy. Do you want to cooperate inside my air-conditioned office or do you want to keep smart talking me, and we'll just stand out here in the parking lot while I question you?"

Neither. I wanted to get back in my car and go home. Forget everything I'd seen and done the last two days. I wanted to pack my bags and drive back to Birmingham, where I'd been forced to sublet my adorable apartment to a geeky lab tech. I sighed. None of those things were going to happen. Not today. Not any time in the near future. It looked like we both had something new in common these days. Both of our dreams had been lost and we were both back home once again.

"Okay. In your office."

Ty led the way to the front door and then opened it for me, adding a sweeping arm-motion gesture for me to enter.

* * *

"Tell me exactly what you found and when you found it."

It wasn't a question, it was a statement. Obviously he was done playing Mr. Nice Guy or "Tall Winking Stranger."

"I was on an emergency service call at the residence of Mayor Mills yesterday morning. I was supposed to have the morning off. I've been working the one-to-ten shift and had been out late the night before. Somehow, I've been switched to the day shift now—go figure."

He tapped the end of the pencil on the pad as if boredom should be accompanied by an annoying drumbeat. "Let's get to the part where you *allegedly* found a dead body."

I swallowed. The word *allegedly* had come out with the same terse undertones he'd used yesterday. He still didn't believe me? Could one lie in high school follow you this far into the future? Why hadn't he just gone to the house and checked it out? Why was that so difficult?

"I was in the attic looking for a bad patch of coaxial cable line, and I hurt my knee."

The pencil stopped tapping and his eyes stabbed me with a steely glare. "You hurt your knee? Is this going to get to the dead-body part of the story sometime today, or should I call for backup while you dictate your autobiography?"

I crossed my arms over my chest and balled my hands into fists. I wanted to punch him. Right here. Right now. In his windowed office that overlooked the parking lot. I wanted to give him a one-two punch sequence he wouldn't soon forget.

"As I said...I'd hurt my knee and sat down to tend to it. That was when I took notice of my surroundings and became intrigued by the sight of a deep freezer. I thought this was suspicious."

He cleared his throat and interrupted me for the third time. "So, you decided to unlawfully snoop through the mayor's frozen green beans and preserves in search of what...an icepack for your knee?"

"Do you want to hear my account of the event or not?" I'd had enough of his attitude. One minute he was charming my sister into a schoolgirl blushfest, and four hours later he was about to get assaulted by a woman half his size. He really knew how to push my buttons, and I didn't doubt that he took joy in it. He scratched his chin with two fingers and then resumed the pencil's drumbeat.

I reached forward and snatched the pencil out of his hand, flinging it across the room. We both watched as it pinged a filing cabinet, poked the bulletin board, and landed in an empty vase atop the corner credenza.

He straightened what seemed like a foot taller. "Are you out of your mind? What'd you do that for?"

I took a deep breath and then leaned back in my chair, propping my boot-clad feet on the edge of his desk. "You obviously take great joy in annoying potential witnesses. So I'll make your job easier. I'll wait here while you fetch the captain. With such a high-profile case at stake, I'm sure he'll make the time to hear my boring story about a dead body that may belong to the Brooks family. Will that work better for you?"

He opened his mouth to speak, but no words came out.

Ha! I'd sure put him in his place. Take that, Tall Winking Stranger.

But then his words found their mark, and my heart began to race once again. The brief bravado faded in an instant.

"Did you say Brooks family? How would you know that?"

Uh-oh.

CHAPTER THIRTEEN

Sense doesn't come before age. –Irish Proverb

"Mandy?"

"Look, I met someone who has a theory, and that's all. I don't know anything other than the fact that I opened the freezer and saw a man, curled on his left side in the fetal position. He was dead and frozen solid. I know what I saw, and that's the extent of my report, *sir*."

He raised his eyebrows at my sarcastic "sir" but remained silent for a few moments. We both had our hackles raised from this interaction.

"Who is this person who thinks the body is related to the Brooks family?"

Studying my fingernails, I offered no response.

"Mandy?"

"I'd rather not say."

"You'd rather not—"

I continued to study my nails. I dared not make eye contact with him at the moment, as I knew the look on his face without actually seeing it. I knew that his eyebrows were drawn together. I knew his forehead was doing that scrunchy thing. I knew his ears were slightly reddened and I knew that his tongue…his tongue…his tongue was pressing against his teeth.

His tongue. What am I doing focusing on that?

"I have a meeting with the mayor, the chief, and the captain in less than an hour, and you want to play games?"

"Not games, per se…"

He slammed the palm of his hand down on his desk.

My head shot up, and we had a stare-down.

"Ty, don't get huffy with me. I came here yesterday. I tried to report this. Your desk sergeant ogled me and all but laughed me off. Then you sent me on my way with scary news about Paget in the most indelicate way ever. Don't try to bully me now."

I wasn't sure where the words came from, but they felt darned good. I was surprised at myself and at the look I received from Ty. He seemed to settle down considerably at my response. He took a deep breath and leaned back in his seat. He crossed his arms over his chest, and I could tell he was considering his next words carefully.

"Listen, I'm sorry about that. I wish I'd handled it differently. But you have to understand that I don't have time for this now, Mandy. I need your help. So, one more time, I'm asking you…who told you this might have something to do with the Brooks family?"

I shrugged. "That has nothing to do with my report. It's probably nothing. I shouldn't even have mentioned it. That's all I know. I've got to go get Paget now."

I pressed my hands down on the wooden chair handles and stood before him.

"Mandy, come on. This is a police investigation. You can't make a statement like that and then leave me hanging. These are serious accusations. "

I turned to leave and then looked over my shoulder, piercing him with a look. "No, driving off and leaving a person hanging is what *you're* good at. Remember?"

With that, I took two steps closer to the door before his voice stopped me.

"This isn't personal. This is my job, Mandy."

I stepped into the hallway and pulled the door closed behind me.

Damn.

* * *

I wasn't sure why I was protecting Colin. It didn't exactly seem smart, but I'd held it back for now. Ty hadn't exactly confirmed whether or not he'd searched the mayor's house yet.

Though, I'd gotten the idea that he was still trying to figure out how to handle this mess and this was a huge deal from anyone's perspective.

There was nothing more I could do for now. So, I did what I do best. I stepped inside The Back Porch Café and closed my eyes as I inhaled the scent of country cooking at its finest.

I made my way to the bar and took a red-topped stool, hooking my boot heels on the footrest below.

"What'll it be, Panda?"

I lit up at the familiar voice. A gray-haired woman with her hair in a bun and soft tendrils framing the side of her face grinned at me from across the countertop.

"Ms. Maimie, only you and Dr. C. still call me that."

The woman let out a smoker's crackly laugh as she patted my hand and leaned in on her forearms for a kiss. I kissed her cheek. It was smooth, but heavily coated with foundation.

"How come you are just now coming in to see me? I haven't seen you since the funeral."

I blinked at the statement. "I'm sorry."

"I miss her, Mandy. Your Aunt Patty and me worked here together for nearly twenty years. And that was after our Vegas days. She was my best friend in the whole world..." Her voice caught on the last word, and I watched as she shook her head to fight off the emotion.

"I know. I'm sorry. I've stopped by a time or two, but I must have missed you. I should have swung by the house to see you. Brought Paget by."

Ms. Maimie made a kissy-kissy face and gave my cheek a pinch. "What do you have to be sorry for? I know things have been tough on you and little sister. How is she doing, by the way? I've never been so scared in all my life as to when I saw her run out in front of that car."

My spine straightened a notch. "You saw her accident yesterday?"

"Of course I did. I was on the night shift and was heading out to my car as soon as the breakfast shift took over. She was crossing the street from Ingram's over there, and she just walked right out in front of that car. I saw it happening, but there was nothing I could do."

"Oh my God. I didn't know that. No one told me the details…" My voice trailed off as I remembered Ty telling me this morning that he'd been the one to pull her out of the way. I hadn't thanked him for that. I'd been too busy giving him a hard time over this matter with the body.

"Thank goodness Ty was there. It was like something out of an action movie, I tell you. He just came running and grabbed her, and they both flew through the air. Everyone was watching out the window."

My mind raced with the images that Maimie's words created. *Thank goodness for Ty.* It seemed that he was back in my life every time I turned around this week.

"Well, I was here yesterday afternoon, and no one mentioned it. How come *that* didn't make it into the paper?"

"'Cause Ty asked me not to." Penny's voice reached my ears, and I turned to see my old friend take the stool next to mine.

Maimie gave Penny a purposeful glare and then dropped the topic of conversation.

"What can I get you?" she asked me, returning to the business at hand.

"I'll take the burger, well done…almost burnt…and some fries."

"And a peach pie shake…" Maimie completed my order and wrote nothing down. She knew the order by heart. She gave me a nod and left to holler out the order to the kitchen crew.

"What do you want, Penny? Haven't I given you enough?" I pulled a straw from the dispenser in front of me and began to twist the white paper wrapping around my left index finger.

"Oh, I'm just getting started." The tone of Penny's voice screamed *hurt*. I hadn't picked up on this yesterday. Had it been there all along? Had I been too preoccupied with my own day's events and troubles to hear it?

"So, Ty didn't want you to print the story about his heroic efforts with my sister, but he did want you to print a story about me finding a dead body in the mayor's house?"

Penny's nostrils flared a little at the comeback. "You don't worry about what goes on between me and my *family*. You worry about your own problems. And you're fixing to have a lot more problems rain down on you. Trust me on that."

I hadn't missed her stress of the word *family*. She'd once been like family to me, but then after all the mess with me and Ty—things had changed between us. I'd retaliated by revealing her biggest family secret and, well...I wasn't proud of it. I'd hoped she moved on, but I guess there was no chance of that happening anytime soon. "Tell me, Penny, buying the newspaper—is that your way of trying to control what news is released and what news is kept a secret?"

Penny seemed to study me for a moment, and then said, "What was your medical specialty going to be up there at big-shot UAB?"

The question took me off guard. I cleared my throat before responding, "Well, you don't actually have to choose your specialty until you're well into your residency."

She did a slow nod. "Was it going to be psychiatry?"

I gave a nose scrunch at the thought of me sitting in a dark room with a mood fountain trickling nearby and listening to my patients' mother issues all day. "Uh, no. Most definitely not psychiatry. I was leaning toward pediatric neurosurgery."

She took a sip of the water that had been placed before her. "That because of Paget's condition?"

"Yeah." I looked down at my hands. Hands meant for a career in surgery, not for a career in cable splicing. I wasn't sure where this conversation was going.

"Well, until you get your degree in psychology, how about you don't go around trying to analyze everyone and their reasons for doing things. Oh, and while you're at it—how about you do your current job. I think I might like to add a cable box to my guest bedroom, think you can handle that?"

The jibe should have hurt me, but I knew that I'd hit close to home with my analysis of her decision to own the *Main Street Mile*. My public revelation, though accidental, of her adoption in retaliation for Ty's leaving me in the lurch had embarrassed her family and broken our relationship off completely.

"Look, you're pissed at me. I get that. I guess you'll never be able to forgive me no matter how many times I've apologized. But you're the one who took everything from our conversation yesterday and turned it into front-page news. You let me sit here under the impression that you didn't work for the paper anymore when, in fact, you *own* it? How's that for dishonesty?" My voice carried a certain mocking singsong quality, but I couldn't help it. I'd had enough of all this old high school news in my dealings with both Allyson and Ty. I thought I had escaped all that and moved away and moved on. But it seemed everyone was bent on rehashing their grievances—Penny most of all, it seemed.

"Just don't think you can leave town and go off for ten years and then expect everyone to welcome you with open arms. We did just fine without you. "

I turned to face Penny. I thought I caught a brief flicker of something behind her eyes. Pain? Sorrow? It was gone in a flash. I softened my tone. "Look. I'm just home because I have to be. I'm here for Paget. That's it. Until we can figure something else out, I'm here for the time being. I'm not here to make enemies."

Penny laughed, but there was no mirth behind it. "Oh, Mandy. You don't need to make enemies. You already have them all over town."

I stared at her with incredulity. I'd said I was sorry over and over again. I'd attempted to reach out to her several times over the first few years of college. But when she'd rebuked my efforts, I'd finally given up. I'd moved on, and I'd hoped she had as well.

Without another word, Penny pushed off the stool and headed toward the door. I watched her leave and caught the eyes of several folks in the diner watching the two of us and our heated exchange.

How could I have forgotten? Everyone knows everything in Millbrook. There were no such things as secrets here. Of course, it had been a secret that the Mills had a body in their attic. A body that Colin Brooks believed belonged to his father—the missing Caden Brooks.

But there was no such thing as discretion unless you could buy it with money or power. I had neither. And not for the first time since driving past that Millbrook city limits sign, I longed to get in my car and drive north. Away from here. I eyed my shiny car outside the café's window, and for the briefest of moments I seriously considered turning, walking out the door, and driving away without ever looking back.

Then Maimie set my food down and gave me a wink.

Well…maybe after I ate.

CHAPTER FOURTEEN

―――――

A good beginning is half the work. –Irish Proverb

"Eeew! I can't believe you like green Jell-O. Who likes green Jell-O?"

Paget's voice squeaked down the hallway as I approached her room. The voice, filled with laughter, made me quicken my step. If Paget was in a good mood, I wanted to catch it. But as I turned the corner into the room, I stopped short.

There, sitting on the edge of her bed, was a hulking teenage boy wearing a football letter jacket. His head was covered with blond curls, and he was holding Paget's hand. She *never* let anyone hold her hand. It was one of her triggers.

"What—" my mouth spat out the word but then stopped for lack of anything better to say.

The giggling duo turned to look at me. The boy abruptly stood up, releasing Paget's hand. Paget blushed, and then she stared down at her hand as if wondering why it was suddenly alone.

"Hi, Ms. Murrin." His voice was deeper than I'd expected, and his smile was frat-boy charming. I was immediately on guard.

"And who are you, exactly?" I stepped closer, still eyeing Paget, who seemed to be both embarrassed and excited at the same time.

"Oh, yeah, sorry. Umm…I'm Adam Owens. I'm a friend of Paget's." He reached out in an effort to shake hands with me.

I took his hand and again was surprised by how large it was and by the firmness of his grasp. This was a boy in a man's body. What was he doing with my sister?

"Is that right? I didn't know that the doctor had allowed Paget to have visitors. In fact, I believe I requested that visitors be limited to family only." The instinct to protect my sister never wavered. I might not have done the best job of it lately, but that didn't mean I was any less fierce when it came to someone else's potential to take advantage of her.

"I'm sorry. My mom works here, and she probably pulled some strings. I guess she thought you wouldn't mind since I found Paget yesterday—you know, after the accident, and I brought her here. She knew how worried I was about her, and I came by today right after football summer camp to check on her."

I felt a little bit like a jerk. The name had sounded familiar, and now I knew why. Ty or Officer Chubby had mentioned the name Adam Owens yesterday at the station. "How did you come about being the one to bring her here, Adam?"

"Oh, well…she sort of ran off after the incident, and I offered to go and find her. She knows me, and I thought I could convince her to come get checked out. She seemed a little overwhelmed by all the cops and the crowd of folks around her."

"Okay, Adam. I guess it's all right. Thank you for bringing her here. I do appreciate it."

He shrugged then looked down at Paget, who was now watching him with shy eyes.

"I've got to go now. Coach is making me run extra laps since I was late getting to practice yesterday on account of the accident situation." He looked back down at Paget. "I'll see you tomorrow, though, okay?"

Paget nodded and bit her lip, but she didn't verbally respond.

"Nice to meet you, Ms. Murrin, and thanks for the job."

He sauntered out of the room before his words registered with me. Job? What job?

"Paget? Paget." Getting my sister's attention was sometimes difficult. I sat down on the edge of the bed right where Adam had been moments before. I took Paget's hand and felt the familiar recoil as Paget jerked it away and turned her eyes away from the doorway in response.

I sighed.

"Paget? How well do you know this Adam Owens?"

"He likes math."

"That's nice, Paget. But how do you know him? Did you just meet him yesterday?"

"Yesterday." Paget's attention seemed to drift off into fantasyland again.

"Paget?"

"What?" She came back around.

"How do you know Adam?"

"Oh, he helps out sometimes with Ms. Barnette's class at summer school. He loves math. Just like me. He's sooooo good at it. And he likes me. He really likes me." Paget's face, full of pure adoration, tugged at something inside me. Something that felt a little like…hope.

"What did he mean by 'thanks for the job'? Do you know?"

"What job?"

"I don't know, Paget. I'm asking you."

"Mandy, could you stop yelling at me, please? It hurts my head when you yell at me."

I shook my head. That was Paget's normal response whenever she didn't want to talk about a particular subject. Or when she didn't know the answer to a particular question. Sometimes it was hard to know which was which.

"Okay, Paget."

Paget returned to smiling.

"Hello, girls," Dr. C's voice boomed. "Are you ready to go home, Paget?"

Dr. C. approached the bed, focusing on Paget. The happiness had fallen from her face. She didn't have to respond. I knew what she was thinking. She didn't want to go home with me. She felt safer here at the hospital than with her own sister. I wasn't sure I blamed her.

"Mandy, I've signed off her release. Everything looks good and she had a quiet night."

"Thanks so much, Dr. C." I smiled at him. He gave me a pinch on the arm.

"Give me a call tomorrow, would you?" he said.

"Sure. Is everything okay?"

"Oh yes…I just did the research that you asked for and have some information for you."

Research?

Oh, right. About alternate care options for Paget.

"I'll talk to you then." He left the room and a wave of guilt toppled through my heart. Would handing her off to strangers be the best thing for her? I watched as she stared out the window, a dreamy look in her eyes.

My life was definitely taking an unexpected direction. I only wished they made a GPS for this type of journey.

* * *

When we left the hospital, I decided to take a quick detour on the way home. I was already on this side of town. Why not take a little drive by the old Sugar Pines neighborhood?

Paget sat in the passenger seat with her iPod earbuds in. She was zoned out on whatever they'd given her before she'd been discharged. She was calm, and I was curious.

Stella cruised into the subdivision and rounded the circle. I slammed on brakes and backed up when I spotted three cop cars around the bend. My heart leapt in my chest.

They were there. I wondered if they'd removed the body and if the identity had been confirmed. I tapped my bottom lip with my finger and turned to look at Paget, who appeared to be dozing. Did I dare leave her here for a minute while I went to check out the situation?

No. No, I couldn't risk it. If she woke up and I was gone, we might have another disappearing situation to contend with. And I probably shouldn't be here anyway. I'd come by and seen that the police were on the case, and that should be enough. I should head home and mind my own business. But just seeing them here wasn't enough…I wanted to know more.

A knock on my window sent me lurching over toward Paget, and a gasp escaped my lips.

I glanced over to see Ty staring at me. He was bent over at the waist staring in through the driver's-side window. This was one of the few times I had my car's top up.

He made a motion for me to roll down the window. I took a deep breath and then did as he instructed.

"What are you doing here?" He looked around me at the sleeping Paget, and his lips pressed together in a thin line of aggravation.

What *was* I doing here?

"Well, I just… I wanted to see what was happening. I have a right to know what happened here." It didn't sound exactly concrete, but it was the best I could do at the moment.

"Mandy, you have no rights here whatsoever. You made a report, and we're checking it out. You are not a part of this investigation, and you'd do yourself a big favor by staying as far away from it as you possibly can." His voice slapped me.

"Is that a threat, Ty? Are you threatening me to stay out of it, or else?" I didn't like to be told what to do. Particularly by a Dempsey.

He stood up and stretched his back. Placing his hands on his hips, he looked up and down the street before responding. "I'll let you know as much as I can, Mandy. I know how concerned you are about this, and I'll keep you posted. But this is a police matter now. You can't be turning up at the mayor's house any time you want to."

"Well, what if he still needs a cable technician to check into his problem?"

He looked down at me in such a way that I thought he might pat me on the head like a good dog.

"Barry sent Shane out here earlier, and that has been taken care of. You won't need to go back in the house for work-related purposes. But nice try."

I ran my tongue over my upper teeth. I was at a loss for words. How could I investigate this case if I couldn't even get near the scene of the crime?

"Go home, Mandy. Take care of Paget. Is she okay?" He motioned to her with his head.

"She's okay. She's resting." I stated the obvious.

"I see that. Why don't *you* get some rest?"

A nap did sound good. Food sounded even better. It had been at least three hours since I'd eaten last.

"All right, but you promise to let me know what happens?" I hated being on the outside, but it probably was for the best.

"Yeah. Yeah." He gave me a grin and stepped back. I rolled up the window, and he waited there on the curb. I guess it was to make sure I exited the premises. I wasn't so sure he was going to keep his promise. It wouldn't be the first time he'd told me one thing and meant another.

I put Stella back in drive and putted down the street, making a choice to pull forward toward the mayor's house and pull into his neighbor's driveway in order to turn around. I could have backed up instead, but that would have been too easy. I caught sight of Ty in my mirror as I did my big, clumsy driving maneuver. He was holding his hands out in a "what are you doing?" gesture. I gave him my most brilliant smile. I could still frustrate him—good to know the feeling was mutual.

As I backed out of the neighbor's drive and began to turn the wheel back to the right, I did a little more than a cursory glance back toward the mayor's house. There, sitting on the front porch, was Myrna Mills—the mayor's wife. She swung back and forth on the porch swing and she didn't look happy. In fact, if I could use one word to describe her expression it was: murderous.

* * *

Twenty minutes later, we were home, and Paget was awake and alert in her room, singing along with the music on her iPod. Dr. C. had given it to her for Christmas last year, and she kept the earbuds in almost all the time now. Of course, she didn't always have them hooked up to the unit itself, but she liked the way the ear buds blocked out the yelling. Or so she said.

I couldn't stop thinking about the police search ongoing over at Sugar Pines. I wondered what had happened when Ty found the body.

I wondered if it was a murder? *Murder?* This was the first time the word had really sunk into my mind. Sure, it didn't look good that a body was in the mayor's house. But what if it had truly been some kind of accident? What if there was a perfectly reasonable explanation for a body…in a freezer…in the attic? Ms. Lanier had been right. This was a job for a real man. If we couldn't get one of the guys from *CSI*, maybe Colin Brooks would be the answer.

Where to begin? I searched my brain for possible suspects as I started a load of laundry. Getting myself into a domesticated state of mind wasn't easy for me. I'd spent so many hours at work back at school that I rarely did laundry anymore. How odd was that? Living in scrubs day in and day out, there'd been little need for a civilian wardrobe. I needed to go shopping.

But the thought of shopping pained me. I hated shopping. I hated the hustle and the bustle and the whole shopping atmosphere. Maybe I could just do some shopping online. The thought appealed to me immensely.

So after I had the laundry sorted and chugging away in the laundry room off the kitchen, I peeked in on Paget for the tenth time in less than an hour. Still in her room. Still singing.

I padded down the hallway to the living room. Pickles eyed me from the sofa.

"Fine. You can have the sofa. I'll sit at the desk."

That dog ran the house. If only he paid the bills. I gave him a quick ear rub as I slid my laptop off the coffee table and settled in the desk chair nearby. I used my toes to push the rolling chair to the window and looked out on the yard. Small tufts of grass protruded from the cracks in the sidewalk. A sea of dandelions covered the lion's share of the lawn. I'd always liked them. They were cute and soft and delicate. But they were weeds. And they spread like wildfire.

Yep, the grass needed cutting. Something else to add to my growing list of things to be done.

One, do the laundry. Two, find some clothes to buy online so that I didn't have to wear jeans and tank tops every single day. Three, hire someone to cut the grass. Four, try to keep sister in the house for the rest of the night. Five, get ready for Colin to drop by at eight. A small flicker of some emotion I couldn't define hit my belly at the thought of the new mystery man in my life. Was it fear? Was it excitement? Maybe just the thought of embarking on some sort of wayward adventure with him had me feeling giddy. God knows I needed some sort of distraction in my life. I didn't know if becoming a sleuth was what I needed, but somewhere between wearing a cocktail on my head and facing off with my first love today, I'd decided to give it a go.

At least Colin didn't have a past with me. He didn't insist on bringing up old grudges and ridiculously petty arguments that had absolutely no place in the current moment. He was someone new with a past all his own. The only question was, what was his past? Was he really a spy?

He hadn't said the word, but he'd alluded to it.

Could my life be any stranger right now?

I fired up the laptop and waited for it to boot up.

* * *

Two hours later and I'd not purchased any new clothes. Instead, I'd been researching the Brooks family. I'd found no mention of Colin. In fact, the only possible mention of him was in his grandfather's obit. Part of it read that he was survived by "two grandsons," but then no other mention of the elusive Colin. I knew of one grandson, of course, who just so happened to be the current Lieutenant Governor of Alabama. But having a second grandson who was completely a secret? In a town this small, with mouths this big, this was absolutely unheard of.

Was it possible to have your entire history erased? On purpose?

A tap on the door made me jump, and I hurried to close the computer and shuffle to the door. The darkness outside was almost complete now, coming later these days, thanks to the genius who invented the Daylight Savings Time idiocy.

Don't get me started.

With my earlier thoughts about the business of murder back on my mind, I snatched a golf umbrella from the bin by the door. I answered with caution pounding in my gut, hoping to see Colin; my stomach growled in expectation of the food he'd promised to bring.

"Well, aren't you in a better mood?" The voice wasn't the raspy tone belonging to Colin, and it certainly wasn't accompanied by heavenly scents of my future stomach contents. Instead it was the infuriating voice of Ty Dempsey.

I bit down on my lip to quell a smarty-pants reply of my own. "Can I come in?" He nodded toward the kitchen behind me.

I stepped back and allowed him to enter. How many times had he been in this very same kitchen over the years? After he cleared the doorway, my eyes did a sweep of the front porch. No mystery man. No food. Sigh.

I closed the door behind me, crossing my arms over my chest, umbrella still in hand.

He turned to face me. He looked tired. Eyes dark. Stress evident on slightly scruffy cheeks. "What's with the umbrella?"

I uncrossed my arms and let it slide down to the floor. Wrapping my hand around the curved handle. "A girl can't be too careful with a possible murderer on the loose."

At the pointed words, he squinted. "We didn't find a body, Mandy."

I attempted to swallow, but my mouth was dry, and the mechanics of the simple throat-clearing maneuver eluded me.

"But it was there, Ty. I don't know what else I can do to convince you."

"I believe you." His words were simple and yet surprising.

"Well, it's about time." His eyes caught mine, and I knew he was biting back his temper. I pressed on. "Did you find the freezer, at least? There might be some DNA in there."

He shook his head. "We went through the official motions. Got the judge to sign off on a warrant and everything. But, when we arrived, the mayor consented to the search, and we found mostly nothing."

"Well, when your sister bends and molds the news to fit her liking…it sort of tips off the suspects, don't you think?"

"Leave Penny out of this…" He swept his hand out toward me in an I'm-drawing-the-line motion. The Dempseys stuck together, and when one turned on you, they all turned on you. It was the story of my life, but I let it drop for now.

"So, what now?" I asked.

"The floor had been recently swept. Who sweeps out their attic on a regular basis?"

I nodded, looking down at the umbrella in my hand and then returning it to the bin by the door. I knew the implications of what he was suggesting. "Did you find anything else suspicious? What did they say when you questioned them?"

Ty rapped his knuckles on the kitchen chair's seatback and seemed to study the chair for a moment. "Same chairs you've always had. Floral Naugahyde. We did our homework here over Aunt Patty's brownies more than once."

The nostalgia in his voice surprised me. It almost sounded longing.

"I miss her." My own words surprised me. I hadn't taken the time to express my grief to anyone. I'd had to remain strong for Paget. I'd had to handle Aunt Patty's affairs, find a job, and get organized. Well, I still wasn't organized, but I'd been a little busy in the last few weeks. I hadn't taken any time for myself.

Ty's study of the chair had refocused into a study of me. I watched his Adam's apple move up and down as he managed that swallow that had failed me earlier.

"I'm sorry about everything, Mandy."

Now *that* was a loaded apology. What exactly was he referring to? About Patty? His accusations about how I'd been negligent in my care of Paget? Or sorry for all those things that happened so many years ago? My mind whirred with the possibilities.

"Listen, I wanted to bring the mayor and his family in for questioning. But the captain says that we just don't have enough. There is definitely something suspicious going on here, but without the body…"

His words brought me out of my deep analysis. "I understand. I guess we just wait, then." My voice was suddenly thick with held-back tears.

"You okay?" He took a step toward me, and I took a step back.

My response seemed to surprise him, but he didn't pursue it. He took one more look around the open kitchen and nodded.

"Guess I should go. Tomorrow will be an interesting day. We're reopening the missing persons case of Caden Brooks."

His words reached my ears, but my brain took a few beats to catch up. I'd been momentarily lost in my own world.

"Wait. I thought you didn't find much there. How can you have enough to open that case?"

Ty walked to the door and pulled it open. The white lace curtain swayed, and he looked back over his shoulder as his booted feet crossed the threshold.

"Based on your statement, Mandy. You're now our star witness."

Oh, great.

CHAPTER FIFTEEN

———

It is a lonely washing that has no man's shirt in it.
–Irish Proverb

Ty closed the door behind him, and I stood there with my arms crossed over my chest, feeling it swell and deflate under my shirt. I was the star witness. The only thing between the mayor's family walking away scot-free and the possibility that they could be harboring a murderer amongst them.

A light tap on the back door interrupted my thoughts. What was it now? Ty had forgotten to tell me something? I took the two short steps and yanked open the door.

"Chinese?"

I blinked at my mystery man. He held a huge paper bag from which heavenly scents were escaping. He also held a box with the word *Chopstix* on it.

I stepped back and motioned for him to enter. This man spoke my language.

"You just missed the police."

He gave a single head nod. "A particular talent of mine. Kind of like a superpower."

"Oh, I have superpowers as well."

"Really?" He seemed very interested in hearing more. He placed his presents on the table and began to remove the boxes of food from the bag.

"Mandy, who is *he*?"

How could I have forgotten that Paget was in the house? For all I knew this man could be dangerous. It was one thing for me to put myself in danger, but Paget was a different story altogether. It was almost like I kept forgetting that she was in my life. It was a terrible realization that seemed to slap me in the face. The muscles between my shoulder blades tightened in response. My eyes darted around for something I might use as a weapon if needed. But, sadly, there were no rolling pins or umbrellas within my immediate reach.

"Uh, Paget…this is a friend of mine. He brought us some dinner. You like Chinese food, don't you?"

"Friend" might have been a strong word, but I didn't want to frighten her. I took a few cautious steps forward and put myself between him and her.

She started to sway from foot to foot. A nervous gesture. I began to regret having Colin show up like this. I should have thought to have him come by later, when Paget was asleep.

He'd been watching the exchange between us and stopped his food distribution to open the Chopstix box. I'd wondered what was in the box, and as he extended it toward my sister, I became even more suspicious.

Paget lifted her chin, and we both took a curious look. Inside, it was lined with thin rows of paper-covered wooden chopsticks. Just stack after stack of disposable sticks. It was a bulk quantity box of chopsticks.

"These are for you." Colin presented them to her as if he were presenting a queen with a jewel on a pillow.

I watched the exchange between the spy and the sister.

Paget studied Colin and then studied the box. She seemed hesitant for a moment. Almost as if it was a trick that she was scared of falling for. Then she took the box and hightailed it back in the direction of her room. Pickles stood in her place eyeing Colin in apparent hopes that he'd be next to receive a gift.

"How did you know?" My heart did a little flutter step that surprised me.

He shrugged. "I've done a little research on her condition. You hungry?"

"Always."

We sat and ate. The room was silent—save for the smacking of Pickles' jowls as he wolfed down some beef lo mein. This man was a mystery with an agenda of his own. But he had taken the time to learn about my sister. He knew that with her type of illness she loved numbers. She loved to count and she loved large, neat quantities of the same item. That box of chopsticks would thrill her more than any diamond ever could.

I knew that I'd have to force her out of her room and make her take time to eat—but in the meantime, she'd be happy. And that was a big score for the mystery man. I found myself liking him almost a little too much. This could be dangerous—in more ways than one.

* * *

After dinner, he dropped the bombshell.

"I guess you heard from your cop friend that they moved him."

Him. For the first time in the last two days, my brain focused on the fact that this body I'd found was someone important. He was important to Colin. He believed this was his missing father.

"I did. But what now?"

He shrugged then leaned back in the chair. It tipped onto the rear legs. I'd always wanted to master that seemingly cool move, but I knew that I'd definitely tip over and kill myself in the process. I noticed a small scar at the bottom of his chin. It was short, about half an inch in length. But I could tell that it was from a deep gash that may not have been sutured properly. I wanted to ask about it but held back.

What did I really know about this man? He claimed to be a Brooks, but I'd found no reference of him online. I'd never heard of him even though he was only a few years older than I was. In a town this small, and with as big of a deal as the Brooks family was…I found it more than a little odd that he'd been kept completely secret. There had to be some record of him. I made a plan to do a little research—as soon as my schedule allowed.

"Any idea who moved him or where?" I asked.

He shook his head. "I was watching the house, but somehow I still missed it. I don't know how I could have missed it. That's not like me."

He seemed both pissed off and sad at the same time. He was too close to this case. Even someone with specialized training, and the obvious ability to come and go like a ghost, could get emotional when the case involved a loved one. I knew this from my medical training. The worst patients in the world were doctors themselves. I figured that the same rules applied here.

"Look, you know as well as I do that the Mills have a lot of friends in this town. Who knows how they get away with half the crap they do? Let's just play by the rules and let the police take care of this. Ty said that he believes me and that the attic floor was recently swept and cleaned up. He's suspicious now, and on the case. Let's give it a few days and see what happens. I'll do some snooping around with some of the town gossips and see if I can dig up anything meaningful. I'm already beginning to suspect Amika—the housekeeper. I think she was following me yesterday. And Mrs. Mills, she looked ready to kill someone tonight when the cops were searching the house."

My best effort at a pep talk met steely blue-turned-gray eyes. He seemed to be studying me, and I seemed to be failing to make the grade.

He lowered his chair legs and stood, all in one swift motion. "I'm tired of waiting. I'm ready to bring down that family once and for all."

Uh-oh.

"Colin…wait." I stood and took a step in his direction. "Ty said that they are going to reopen your father's missing persons case."

He was already moving toward the door. I'd said the wrong thing. I didn't know exactly what that wrong thing had been, but I'd screwed up somehow. I was suddenly overwhelmed with grief for him. I had, after all, lost my father too.

He stopped and turned to face me. "Why would they do that?"

"Uh…oh…well, I might have mentioned something about the possible identity of the body."

He raised his eyebrows. "Did you tell them how you made the connection?"

I scratched my left arm and felt goosebumps under my nails. "Not exactly. I didn't tell them about you. I'm not sure why—but I didn't."

He studied me with a blank expression. It made me nervous, to say the least.

A loud series of knocks erupted from the other side of the door.

"Yoo hoo! Mandy! I've brought an apple pie and good news." Ms. Lanier's unmistakable voice graced our ears.

"Just wait in the den. I'll get rid of her."

He didn't respond, just headed toward the back of the house without another word.

I opened the door. This house was busier than a supermarket this evening. Who else should I expect?

"Hi, Ms. Lanier, I was meaning to come by and chat with you."

She pushed past me and set the tin-plated pie on the table. My nostrils flared at the scent of fresh-baked apple pie, and Pickles lifted his head off the tile in response.

"Looks like you girls just finished dinner. Perfect timing."

I closed the door and cast a furtive glance toward the living room. No sign of Colin, and nothing from Paget since she'd disappeared down the hallway with her chopsticks delivery.

"Yes. Thank you for the pie. I can't visit right now, though. I need to get Paget ready for bed."

"Oh, yes, well, that's what I wanted to talk to you about. About taking care of Paget."

A brief image of the tall football player from Paget's hospital room came into focus.

"Is this about Adam…?" His last name escaped me.

"Yes. Yes. Adam Owens. Did Paget tell you about him?"

I ran my fingers up the back of my neck and squeezed. A pinch-like pain had started to visit more often in this region of late.

"Not really. No. He was in her hospital room this afternoon when I went to pick her up. He indicated that he had some kind of job…" I had the sudden clarity of what was transpiring here. My conversation with Ms. Lanier from last night followed by Adam's news.

"Oh, good. Isn't he the nicest young man?"

I busied myself by clearing the table and surveying the leftovers. Paget needed to eat something before she went to bed.

"Uh, yeah, he seemed nice. Paget seems to like him, but if you were considering him for—"

"Listen." Ms. Lanier grabbed my lower arm and squeezed, pulling my attention away from my task at hand. "I know this is unusual, but you have an unusual situation here. You may feel uncomfortable with Adam looking after Paget, but she's crazy about him, and I just know that he'll take good care of her."

I pulled my arm loose and began to toss empty boxes into the trash bin in the cabinet under the sink. "I appreciate your thoughtfulness in setting this up, but I can't have a teenage boy watching Paget—unsupervised."

Ms. Lanier made a "tsk tsk" sound with her tongue. "I knew you'd say that. That's why they'll stay at my house, and I'll keep an eye on them."

I wiped my hands on the yellow-striped kitchen towel as I considered her offer.

"I can't ask you to do that."

"You didn't, dear. I offered."

I looked back at her. She stood there in her pajamas and pink house shoes that were worn through at the toe on one foot. Her hands were on her hips, and her wrinkled neck swayed slightly as she inhaled.

"But why Adam? What made you think of this? Because Paget has a crush on him?"

"No. Not entirely. But don't you think that she'd be much more likely to hang around if he's there? Maybe we'll put a stopper in some of these running-off episodes she's been having."

The plan had its merits. But still…

"What if he takes advantage of her?"

Ms. Lanier nodded. "I thought of that, and I don't believe he would ever hurt her."

"How do you know?"

"Because he loves her, dear. He loves her."

I pursed my lips and then squished them together. "Love? What are we talking about here?"

"Adam had a little sister that was…well…she died at a young age. She and Adam were watching a movie together while their mother was taking a shower. She managed to get outside and fell in the pool. She drowned."

I'd seen many cases like this come through the ER when I was on emergency rotation. It was heartbreaking.

"I'm sorry that happened, but what does this have to do with Paget?"

Ms. Lanier opened a nearby drawer, removed a pie cutter, and started to slice into the steaming pan of ecstasy. "He's always felt responsible for it. He took it really hard. And he's just developed a sort of protective nature. When he met Paget a couple years ago at Vacation Bible School, he just took her under his wing. And things have just sort of progressed from there."

"But you said he loves her. Does he have romantic feelings for her?" I wasn't prepared to deal with teen love right now. I didn't even know how to have a love life of my own these days.

She served up a piece of pie on a plate and then moved to the fridge. I hoped she was in search of milk to go with the pie.

"I'm not exactly sure about that. But I know he loves her and she thinks he hung the moon. What can be wrong with someone who cares about our girl that much? Why wouldn't we give him a chance to help her?"

She had a point, but I wasn't totally convinced that this was the way to go.

"I guess we can give it a try on a temporary basis. But I'll have to pay you to supervise them. I can't ask you to do this for free."

She filled a glass with milk. Moving about the kitchen and serving me dessert as if this was her own kitchen.

"Oh, hogwash. I don't need any of your money, Mandy. I just want you and Paget to be happy. I'm not sure just yet what I can do for you, but I can do this for Paget. Patty would have wanted me to. Just let me do this. It will make her happy."

I wasn't sure which she was talking about. Paget or Patty. Or…both? But I didn't exactly have a game plan in motion with such short notice, and it seemed that she'd already offered this to Adam and he'd agreed.

"Okay. Okay." I acquiesced and she left as quickly as she'd arrived. But the pie stayed with me.

* * *

It had been another long day and I needed to wrap things up with Colin and get Paget fed and to bed. I had to be at work early. Another day of paradise at the delightful Flicks Vision.

"Colin?" I spoke his name softly as I entered the living room.

No reply.

"Colin?" A little louder now as I tiptoed down the hallway to see if he had made a pit stop in the bathroom. The door was open, the room dark.

"Where did you go?" I stood there waiting for his response.

"Who are you looking for?" Paget's voice sounded from the end of the hallway, and I jumped. She waited just outside her bedroom door. Her right index finger twiddled a lock of hair near her face.

"That friend of mine from earlier. The one who gave you the chopsticks. Where did he go?"

Paget shrugged.

"Are you hungry?"

Another shrug.

"Let's go to the kitchen and see if we can find you something. Then we need to get you to bed." I spoke with a soft tone to my voice, not wanting to upset her further. Maybe Colin had left through the front door while I was in the kitchen with Ms. Lanier.

"I tried to make it, but I couldn't. I'm sorry, Mand."

It took me a minute to follow her train of thought. My eyes followed her frown down to her legs. A wet circular pattern stained the upper thigh area of her jeans. She'd wet her pants…again.

"Don't worry, Page. Just go get into some dry clothes and bring me the wet ones. I'm about to start a new load of laundry anyway."

She stood there, shuffling from foot to foot. The fingers entangled in her hair moved quicker now. She tugged them out of her hair, pulling out a strand or two as she went.

"Don't do that, Paget. You'll hurt yourself."

"I don't mean to," she said. Her eyes brimming with tears.

"I know that." I walked to her and reached out. I tickled her belly with my fingertips. Just like old times. But this time she turned away, and I withdrew my hand. *I don't know her anymore. I don't know how to take care of her anymore.* I started to bite my lower lip.

"That man—with the chopsticks…"

"Yes?"

"He said to tell you something…"

"Okay. What was it?"

"He said to tell you…"

I waited. She stopped twirling her hair and seemed to be drifting away from the conversation.

"Paget? What did he say?"

"There are exactly fifty-eight sets of chopsticks in that box. One hundred sixteen if you pull them apart."

"Paget…what did the man say?"

She turned to look at me. Her eyes were blank. Absolutely expressionless.

"What man?"

CHAPTER SIXTEEN

————

If you meet a red-haired woman, you'll meet a crowd.
–Irish Proverb

Main Street in Millbrook is the ebb and flow of the community. Like most small towns, it hosts City Hall, a small structure sitting on the corner with a neatly trimmed lawn and wooden picket signs along the edge of the road. This week's sign was for the upcoming Back to School Bar-B-Q Festival. If I wanted to enter my homemade camp stew recipe, I might win cash or prizes.

Unfortunately, I didn't have a homemade recipe, but the smell of Aunt Patty's cooking whizzed through my sensory memory as I drove past the sign. Also, the image of Mayor Mills sitting behind his big ornate desk inside City Hall did a dance through my mind's eye.

What was he hiding? What had he done with that body, and was he responsible for murder? If not him, then was someone else in his family to blame?

As I drove the requested thirty-five-mile-an-hour speed limit, an unexpected horn blared at me, and a white blur flashed by me on the left.

What the heck?

I had turned and caught sight of the profile of Matson Mills as he sped by and then cut in front of me, leaving barely enough space between his shiny new car and my old classic.

Jerk-o-rama.

Did he drive like this all the time, or did he know who I was? I had a suspicion that Matson had no clue who I was and didn't give a flip. I had an idea that he was on his way to his next adventure and that I was simply an obstacle that was in his way. I was not in his world and therefore was as insignificant as the average mosquito.

Nonetheless, I wondered where he was going this early in the morning, and in such a hurry. My curiosity gave me a fluttering sensation in my stomach. In response, I slipped my cell phone out of my pocket and eyed the time. It was six fifteen. I had forty-five minutes until my shift started at Flicks. I'd planned on grabbing a breakfast burrito at the Back Porch—they made one with hash browns inside—but now I had the sudden inexplicable urge to tail him.

Tail him?

Who did I think I was all of a sudden? Cops at my door. A mystery man claiming to be a spy who arrives and vanishes from my house in the blink of an eye. A dead body. A star witness. What had my life become these days?

Thoughts raced through my head, and my car raced through the streets of town. Soon we had crossed over the county line and into neighboring Prattville. We sped down busy Cobbs Ford Road and then back out and away from the shopping and dining by fields of cotton as we cruised down Highway 82. Soon, brown signs indicating Cooter's Pond and the boat ramp came into view. I hung back, but I could see the white blur of Matson's car up ahead. Just before the public park, he turned down a dirt road. I pulled over and cut the engine.

I didn't need to follow him down the road to know where it went. Everyone knew that the mayor's riverfront home was through these woods. In fact, everyone in town had been to this home at some point. Because the mayor held all his political parties here, as well as every spring's hosting of the annual high school graduation shindig. It was a local thing. Sort of a rite of passage for townsfolk. Graduate from high school and get to attend a huge party in your honor on the river. Food. Sun. Swimming.

I had attended this party a decade ago, and it was a night I'd never forget. Not because the festivities were so unforgettable, but that night with Ty had certainly left a permanent marker in my gray matter.

I swiveled my head around in search of other cars. Other than my huge, red beacon of metal, no one else was in sight. Should I go on foot up to the house and spy on Matson? Should I turn this car around and get to work before I got fired? I knew I was hanging on by a thread with Barry already. Or should I call Ty?

And say what? *Oh, hey, Ty, I was just following Matson Mills, and he's at his father's waterfront house when he should be on his way to work. What's that? He doesn't have a job because he's a rich brat. Well, I think you should come down here and check it out anyway.* Yeah, that didn't sound like a conversation worth starting. In fact, it made me look more than a little insane.

Against better judgment, my body began to move of its own accord. As a medical student, I knew this wasn't possible, but I managed to convince myself of it anyway. My hand opened the door, my feet swung off the floor mat, and my butt scooched off the seat. Soon after, my legs took over and began to propel me up the smooth dirt of the driveway.

About halfway up the drive, I began to wonder if I should ease off the shoulder and sneak up on the house via the cover of trees. Then I reassured myself that since I'd already decided to trespass, I might as well come in on my own terms.

Go all out. Get yourself arrested, why don't you?

Geez. Now I was talking to myself.

As I crested the top of the winding road, the beautiful home known as Mills Landing came into view. I'd always loved this property. It was so much more like home than their stuffy, pristine house over at Sugar Pines.

Matson's car was parked in front of the three-car garage bay. One of the bay doors was open, and a black SUV was inside. I heard the sound of voices. They were speaking loudly enough to travel from somewhere at the back of the property but not clearly enough for me to make out the words.

Now I decided to go into stealth mode. I hugged the edge of the house and slithered down the log-lined exterior. The voices were distinctly male. I assumed one of them was Matson, but I was unsure of the identity of the other voice.

My heartbeat picked up its gallop as I neared the far corner. If I were to just take a quick peek around the edge, would they see me? I should just forget this entire thing and get back to my car. This was ridiculous.

But I just knew they were discussing the body. I could feel it in my bones. I was closer now, but still unable to pick up on the discussion. If I could get a visual on who was speaking and on their location, I could make a move from here. Oh, what the heck. On the count of three.

One...

Two...

Three...

The sound of a car engine behind me froze me in place. I squatted behind the bushes. Perspiration had never been a real issue for me, but it had suddenly decided to present itself in the form of a shirt-wetting phenomenon. I could actually feel my shirt against my back as if it were a second skin.

A car door slammed and the sound of shoes on the front steps was followed by the front door slamming with some amount of force.

It was now or never.

I darted my head out from behind the bushes and around the side of the house.

There, down by the water's edge, stood Matson Mills and Officer Chubby.

What were *they* doing here together?

Before I could begin to consider the possibilities, the back door swung open with such force that it hit the exterior wall. I cringed as a booming voice followed the door crash.

"Are you insane? What the hell have you two done?"

From my vantage point, I could see none other than the mayor himself striding across the corner of the poolside, heading toward the open grass. He was moving at a fast clip, and his son and Mr. Jelly Donut had halted their conversation and watched his progress with open mouths.

"Dad..." Matson sounded childlike and pleading.

"Would either of you geniuses care to tell me what you've gotten us into?"

The geniuses stared at him. Neither offered up an immediate response. I wanted to laugh, but I was holding my breath. Waiting for a full confession.

If this had been a movie, I would have rubbed my hands together in utter glee.

But my elation was short-lived, as a strong hand clamped down on my shoulder.

I muffled a scream and nearly dove over the bushes and into the pool.

A large hand covered my mouth, sending my heart into the stratosphere. Only to be soothed by a deep but recognizable whisper: "You need to get out of here. The cops are on their way here, and something tells me that they'll recognize your big red car parked at the top of the driveway."

Colin.

I cut my eyes over at him, and he released his clamp on my mouth.

"What are you doing here?" I asked.

"You're asking *me* that?"

"Yes…" I tried to calm my panic and plan my next move. The mayor and the other two were still chatting at the riverside, but they were too far away to overhear.

"I was following the mayor this morning, and he had an unpleasant discovery waiting for him in his office chair when he got to work," Colin explained.

Did I dare ask? "What was it?"

"I'll tell you later."

"Colin?" I studied Colin's eyes. It was obvious that he was suppressing emotions, but I couldn't for the life of me figure out exactly what those emotions were. "Are you okay?" It was the first thing that popped into my mind.

"Don't worry about me. Worry about getting out of here and moving that car before your boyfriend shows up."

"He's not my boyfriend."

He raised his eyebrows at my response but didn't argue the point further.

"Let's go." He scuttled backward and motioned for me to do the same.

I dropped down onto all fours and followed him out of the bushes.

"What…you have an issue with chatting in the bushes on a hot summer's day?"

He didn't respond to my humorous ramblings. Instead he somehow had the ability to crab-walk out of there and still look both cool and *hot* at the same time. The man had training.

Just as we'd escaped the cover of the foliage, the sound of tires crunching down the gravel driveway caught my attention.

"Uh-oh—ahh." My words were cut off by the yank of Colin on my right arm. With one swift motion, he'd moved us into the wooded area just north of the drive and out of sight.

As the car rolled up to the circular drive to park behind the mayor's, we made our way out deeper into the woods. I tried to keep up the pace with Colin while watching the sleek black Mercedes wind its way down toward the house. The windows were tinted, and I was dying to know who was behind the wheel.

"*Where are we going?*" I whispered to my tour guide.

He didn't answer—just kept moving at a steady pace. Tree limbs swiped across my bare arms and leaves brushed against my face.

The sound of raised voices behind me tempted me to look back over my shoulder, but I couldn't manage that without losing my balance. One of the voices was female. I wondered if it was Mrs. Mills, or maybe Amika. Colin wove us to and fro, and I was sure that any moment we'd be lost in the forest with no breadcrumbs to lead us out.

"Why are we going this way? My car is over there—"

A beat later, we were standing at the passenger side of my car.

"Should I drive?" he asked, a grin on his face.

"No one drives Stella but me."

"Stella?"

"It's a long story."

"Sounds like we both have a story, but let's get a move on. I have a feeling that things are about to get a little hectic back there, and you need to be somewhere else."

For once, I didn't argue. I slipped into the driver's seat and leaned across to unlock his door. He slid in, and we were off, hightailing it back into town and away from the mayor's home on the Alabama River.

"What was Officer Chubby doing there, and who was in that Mercedes?" I asked.

"Officer Chubby?" He seemed to consider my words. "You mean Trask?"

"Yeah…I guess. What was he doing there chatting it up with Brat Boy?"

"He works for the mayor," Colin responded as he white-knuckled the door handle.

"I hate to state the obvious, but don't all cops work for the mayor?" I said.

"He's private security detail for the mayor during his off-duty hours."

"Ahh. So, what…they are gathering the troops to protect Mayor Mills now that his life is getting just a little more complicated this morning?"

He stretched back in a slightly more relaxed posture, his arm along the seatback. His eyes were studying me. I could feel it. "Don't freak out."

"I never freak out. Well, most of the time. I'm just not sure how you found me, and what is going on here. Can you bring me up to speed, please?"

"I mean, don't freak out; but you have something in your hair."

"What?" The car swerved as I turned the rearview mirror toward myself.

"Whoa…easy there." He reached over and guided the wheel back on track.

"I don't see anything. What are you—" But I was interrupted by a huge spider making his presence known by crawling over the top of my ear and sitting there with what can only be described as an evil grin.

"Ahhhhhhhh…what the—"

I hit the brakes and we both smashed forward. Colin caught himself with one hand and me with the other.

"It's not poisonous, Mandy. No reason to kill us both."

"Get it out. Get it out."

I jumped out of the car and ran around the back, shaking my head and flopping my hair forward and back in a wild, headbanger-like motion. I jumped on one foot and shook my head in a maneuver not unlike someone who was trying to remove water from their ear.

I caught sight of the evildoer as it hit the ground and scuttled away. Only then could I breathe. Colin stood outside the car, soaking in the scene, and a smile on his face the size of which I'd never seen before. A smile that both infuriated me and did something weird to my heart at the same time.

"I'm not sure what you're smiling at, but this was not funny."

He chuckled under his breath, and my heart did that weird thing again. Then Colin's smile faded, and he ducked down behind the car.

"What are you doing, exactly?"

A car swerved around the bend, wheels squealing as they slowed to survey the scene. As it drove past, behind the driver's window, I made full eyeball-on-eyeball contact with Ty Dempsey. He saw me, and he didn't look happy, but he didn't stop.

* * *

Twenty minutes later, Colin and I were parked outside the cable office. We sat in silence. I checked the time on my phone.

"I need to go clock in now. Are you gonna fill me in on the situation?"

Colin had been calm and quiet after the spider incident. His disappearing act as Ty had driven by intrigued me. What was the big secret, anyway? Surely it wasn't a crime for him to be with me on a public road. Well, a public road that just so happened to be only a few hundred feet from the mayor's property…but still.

"You don't have time. I'll be by later tonight."

He pulled the door latch, and I reached over and grabbed his left forearm. It was corded with muscles. He looked down at my hand as if it were a foreign object, and then met my eyes.

"Colin. What happened this morning? What was waiting on the mayor when he got to work?"

He looked down at my hand again, as if he'd forgotten how it had gotten there. I withdrew it. Maybe I shouldn't be so eager to accept his help. He was hiding from the cops, sneaking around outside of people's houses, and who knew what else?

Well, I was also sneaking around outside people's houses, but I glossed over that fact.

He stepped out of the car and swung the door closed. He took a step away from the car and then paused and looked back at me.

"It was him. My father. Someone killed him. Froze his body for years and then put the body in the mayor's office chair as some kind of statement or joke. He may not have been a perfect man, but he was my father, and I won't leave until I find out who was responsible for this."

"Oh, Colin...I'm..." The words caught in my throat, but he didn't wait for me to force them out. With three quick steps he was behind the building and out of sight.

He'd just disappeared. Again.

CHAPTER SEVENTEEN

———

The doorstep of a great house is slippery. –Irish Proverb

Coosada Road was one of my favorite places in Millbrook. The tree-lined street was shaded by overhanging limbs. The homes were preserved by the Historical Society, and their white columns stood steadfast and at attention as I drove past.

So many questions and so few answers.

If someone had removed Caden Brooks' body from the mayor's attic and then planted it in the mayor's office, it didn't make sense that the mayor himself was involved in the murder. Why would he set himself up to take the fall?

It had to be someone who had a beef with the mayor and yet still had access to his home and attic. Or maybe that was what the mayor wanted you to think. No, he wouldn't take that kind of risk—would he?

And what was going on at the mayor's waterfront home with Matson? Before I'd been scared out of my mind by Colin in the bushes, I'd heard Mayor Mills yelling at Trask and Matson. What had he said? Something about what they'd done? And who was the Mercedes-driving woman who'd joined in the fray when Colin and I were making our escape?

I just didn't have enough to go on. Trying to piece this together was making my head hurt. And speaking of headaches…

I turned down the moss-shaded lane, interestingly named Harm's Way. While it sounded ominous, it was actually named after Harmony Dempsey—Ty's late mother. When Barry had told me that I had a service call at the Dempsey compound, I'd felt both nostalgic and somewhat ill.

Now that I was here, the ill feeling took control, and all fond memories of childhood days spent on the farm dissipated. By the time I'd exited the vehicle, the cloud of dust I'd stirred up in the old van filled my lungs. Coughing and fanning my air space with my clipboard, I headed up the porch stairs. A screen door flew open in my face, and I jerked to a halt.

"Well, as I live and breathe..." Tate Dempsey stood before me in his muddied cowboy boots and jeans that were torn at the knee.

"Mr. Dempsey. How are you?"

He sized me up with his eyes, and somehow I didn't make the grade. "You back in town to stay?"

I cleared my throat as an image of Paget tiptoed across my brain. "For the time being."

He harrumphed. "Is what Penny wrote about you true? You accusing Dougie of murder?"

Penny was his adopted daughter, and she was the apple of this man's eye.

"I'm not sure that's exactly what she wrote, but...yes, I did find a body in the mayor's home. As I understand it, Ty is looking into it as we speak."

"That's not what I asked you, girl."

My face burned with either fury or embarrassment. I didn't know which. Somehow, this man had always been less than fond of me. I never understood why. Of course, then I'd gone and cemented the deal when I'd spilled the beans on the circumstances behind Penny's adoption. But his wife had adored me, and I'd grown up with both of his kids. Been around his home day in and day out for most of my life. But still, he'd always been less than nice to me. I'd always suspected it'd had something to do with his relationship with my father, but I'd never been able to pin it down. I could see that nothing had changed in my years of absence.

"I think I answered your question nonetheless, Mr. Dempsey. Are you having trouble with your cable?"

He seemed to want to say more. But he puffed up his chest instead. He motioned over his shoulder with a thumb.

"That box in there ain't working right. Barry said you'd have to take a look at it before they would order me a new one. I think some lightning came in on the line."

"Do you have a surge protector on it?"

To this, his eyes pierced me with another dose of distaste. "I don't know anything about that. I have whatever your boss installed. It's not my fault that it's broken, if that's what your insinuating."

I pasted on my best customer-service friendly smile. I gave a brief nod and entered the darkness of the family room, heading toward the custom-built entertainment center. Framed family photos and cross-stitched Bible verses filled the walls on both sides. A few minutes later, I had the cable up and running.

"All set, Mr. Dempsey."

He looked up from the morning paper in disbelief. "What was it?"

"Just needed to be rebooted. That happens sometimes. No one's fault." I extended my clipboard for his signature.

He took the clipboard and stared down at the work order.

"Mandy…" His voice was low and cracked slightly as my name wafted over his vocal cords.

I waited.

"Your folks would have been proud of you. What you've been doing up there at school. Penny told me that you're almost a real doctor now."

A small dose of embarrassment mixed with a large dose of pride swept through me. My throat wouldn't work for a moment. Mr. Dempsey hadn't said anything nice to me in…well…almost never.

"Uh…thank you." I managed to get the words out despite my surprise. I couldn't believe that Penny had been talking about me to him, much less in any sort of complimentary way.

"I don't know how long you're planning to stay…" His wrinkled, gnarled fingers scribbled down at the bottom of the triplicate paper. "But…just see if you can try not to cause any heartbreak while you're in town."

I thought his complimentary words had been surprising. But these…these words had me totally flabbergasted. "What? I'm sure I don't know what you mean, sir." My mind raced. "There's nothing going on between myself and Ty. I'm sure neither of us have even considered…" My memory flashed back to him driving by me earlier today. His eyes piercing me with both aggravation and concern. I knew he'd have something to say to me when I saw him again.

"I'm not talking about Ty." Mr. Dempsey's voice brought me back to the moment at hand.

I took the clipboard from his hand and watched his watery eyes as he pushed up from the table and faced me.

"I'm talking about Penny."

* * *

Penny had been adopted by the Dempsey family when she was only three months old. For a long time no one had known about the adoption other than Harmony and Tate Dempsey. They hadn't even told Ty about it. From what I understood, he was two years old when they'd brought Penny home, and he'd never remembered life without her.

Harmony had taken Penny from her sister, who was both addicted to narcotics and only sixteen at the time she had given birth. Harmony had gone home to Atlanta to stay with her sister during the latter part of her pregnancy and stayed for a few months afterwards. So it had been easy to convince the local gossips that the baby was hers. In fact, no one had ever seemed to question it. That is until years later, when Harmony's sister had come to visit.

Penny and I had been best friends at the time, and Ty and I were…well, we'd just reached the climax, so to speak, of our involvement.

One night I'd been staying over for Penny's birthday slumber party, and I'd overheard a fight between Mr. Dempsey and Harmony's sister. I'd heard all the sordid details, and she'd threatened to tell Penny the truth. Mr. Dempsey had bought her off, and she'd left the next day. Mrs. Dempsey passed away soon after from a rare case of ptomaine poisoning. I'd always wanted to blame the druggie sister, but nothing had come of it and I'd put the whole thing out of my overactive and hormonal teenaged mind—I'd never told Penny or anyone else about what I'd heard or suspected. Until…well…until Ty chose football over me, and when Penny didn't take my side despite my pregnancy fear, I'd spilled the all the sordid family-secret beans to her.

There hadn't really been a pregnancy, but they hadn't known that for sure. It had hurt me terribly when she'd turned her back on me, and I'd wanted to let her know that her family might not be worth standing up for after all, as they'd been lying to her since birth. Unfortunately, my timing was bad, and little had I known that the whole church was listening. We'd been at our church's Baccalaureate service the day after graduation and the backstage microphone had broadcasted the details all over church. I hadn't meant for it to go down that way, but it had. And I was still not even close to being back in the good graces of the Dempsey family. I wasn't sure I ever would be, but seeing how this still hurt Penny after all these years made me eager to try.

But that was a memory that I didn't have time to rehash at the moment. Right now, Barry was ringing in on my cell phone, and I had a work shift to complete.

* * *

My next stop was Boardwalk Apartments. It seemed like they called us in every other day or so. I guess it was because they always had tenants moving in or out, and there were always service starts and service disconnects to complete there. I didn't mind it, though. It was actually pretty simple. You just went to the switch box, more formally known as the network interface, and either flipped the switch on or flipped the switch off.

Ideally, if you were starting new service, you'd find the tenant home, and you could enter the premises and check to see if the signal was coming through clearly. If not, you could make adjustments, or better yet—if Barry had his druthers—bill them to install new wall wiring. I didn't like that part, but I did like checking the signal, because the more you could accomplish now, the less likely you'd have to revisit the same unit the following day. Re-ups—that's what we called it when we had to return to a prior work ticket to finish it up.

Probably the reason I'd been able to swing this job was because my father had been a telephone man for twenty-plus years before his death. I'd trailed along behind him on more than a few summertime work calls. The business of telephone and cable were quite similar, and Barry had been impressed that I'd been able to pick up the job solo after only a week of training with Shane. Of course, he hadn't been impressed with me so much this week. It might have had something to do with my little discovery at the Mills' house more than my technical skills, though.

Today, I was at the switch box for unit 10. I'd opened the metal box at the back of the unit, and I was rechecking my work order to be sure that I was turning on the signal for the correct unit. Unfortunately, someone had failed to number the switches with the correct unit numbers, and I was counting through them to try and figure out the right one when a shrill voice pulled my attention away from my task.

"I don't know what you are talking about, but it has nothing to do with you." The voice was raised three octaves above a screech. Though it sounded familiar, even at this high-pitched level.

I couldn't hear the recipient's voice and wondered if the screecher was on a phone call. The sound of clicking heels in the breezeway followed the voice, and I eased my head around the box's door to get a view.

Allyson Harlow.

I should have known. It had been, what, only a day since I'd been graced with her presence. I guessed I was due for another dose of humiliation and taunting. I eased my head back behind the box, hoping she was too distracted by her phone call to notice a lowly cable installer.

"I said that I *will* see whomever I choose. I'm a free woman. I don't get tied down to any man, and I don't dig jealous types." Her voice had bumped down from a screech to a slightly milder outcry as she fumbled with her large purse. She stood at the door to the last apartment on the left.

I assumed she was searching for a key. Meanwhile, I was beginning to bake as the sun reflected off the metal switch box and heated my face. But I stayed put; I just wasn't in the mood for more putdowns this morning. Besides, the fact that someone was giving her a hard time on the phone sent a jolt of jubilance through me, and I decided to keep eavesdropping.

In fact, now that I thought about it, maybe she was having a fight with Ty. She'd indicated that she was seeing him when I'd run into her at the station a couple days ago. But, then again, I didn't remember Ty as the jealous type.

"Look, they'll never find out. I promise. You were careful, weren't you, baby?" she said as I heard the key slide into the lock and the bolt slide free. "I'll see you later at O'Hannigan's, okay? We can chat about it then. Okay, Trasky-wasky?" She entered the apartment and closed the door.

Trasky-wasky?

Was she talking to Officer Chubby? As in *the* Officer Trask, as in the mayor's personal security? How many cops was she dating, anyway?

Another piece to the puzzle shimmied around in my head. But the final image was still out of reach. I finished my job and locked the box. I crept by her door and made my way to the second floor. I needed to see if the tenant was in and check the signal, and then I wanted to get the heck out of there. I had to finish my shift and then get home to meet with Colin.

'Cause the next step in my investigation had just dropped in my lap. Tonight I was visiting O'Hannigan's Pub, and I planned to go there in disguise.

* * *

Two hours, four static-filled screens, and a dozen dust bunnies later, I was done for the day. I parked the van at Flicks Vision and headed over to Stella. I couldn't wait another minute to get home and get changed. Washing this day off with a hot shower was just what the doctor ordered.

I'd called Ms. Lanier to check on Paget, and she'd asked how the investigation was going. I told her I'd fill her in later, and she suggested that I visit Mane Street Styles. She said that everything you ever wanted to know could be found out at the hair salon. Well, there or at a Service League meeting, but we didn't see them letting me into one of those anytime soon. Especially since Mrs. Mills was president of the local chapter.

But after news of the troubling discovery at the mayor's office and my impromptu surveillance of the Mills' river home, I needed a break from my mission—at least until tonight. And for that, I needed a plan. Maybe a little pedicure break at the salon was in order.

Of course, it didn't have anything to do with the fact that Colin was scheduled to appear this evening with an update and a lengthy explanation of all his cloak-and-dagger discoveries from earlier today and bearing more food—I could only hope.

I changed clothes, clocked out and hung my keys on the hook, and I was out the door. My beautiful Stella gleamed in the late afternoon sunlight. I paused as a flutter of white caught my attention. There was a note in the wipers. Had Ty left another note about stopping by the office?

A part of me hoped so. But was that part hoping to see Ty or hoping to find out more about the body discovery in the mayor's office? I wasn't so sure.

I snatched the note up and read.

We are watching you.

I surveyed the area around me and wondered about who the "we" might be. Seeing no suspicious characters in close proximity, I popped inside the car and shoved the key in the ignition.

Should I call Ty? Or save the note for my meeting with Colin tonight?

After a moment of consideration, I opted for the latter and cranked the car. A couple of blocks later, I pulled into the gravel drive of the Mane Street Styles. Where all the best hair in town is tamed. Or at least that was what their sign claimed. Given the number of hair crises I'd had over the past week, maybe I should have visited here sooner.

I exited the car and tromped up the wooden stairs. They were in need of repair, as was the door that pushed open without the need for a twist of the knob. The sounds of hair dryers, chatter, and pop music on the radio greeted me.

I stood just inside the door and surveyed the scene before me. Three hairdressers tended to their customers in swivel chairs. One teenage girl shampooed a head of hair as she smacked gum in time with her moving fingers. And one woman sat in the waiting area flipping through an issue of *Cute Cutz*.

One of the hairdressers caught sight of me and gave me a "one minute" sign with her finger before she started spraying what would turn out to be at least a half can of hairspray on her customer. The little old lady she was working on had her hair set in a mile-high grouping of curls. Her hair was stark white and her eyes were closed during the onslaught of spray. I wondered how she might be able to breathe under there and worried for her lung health.

While the cloud of spray settled, I decided to check out the menu of services tacked on the wall above the register. I'd be able to get a pedicure, but it was by appointment only. Darn. I could really use a new polish about right now. I hadn't exactly been taking care of my feet of late.

"What can I do for you?" The soft voice startled me. I hadn't heard her approach over the hair-dryer noise. I caught sight of the little old lady as she waddled out the door, her head looking to weigh more than her entire body, but I knew that her hair would hold in place until she returned next week. Not one single strand was moving on that baby.

"Uh, yes. I was hoping to get a pedicure, but I see that I should have planned ahead." I pointed to the sign.

"Ah, yeah. Gina does those and she only works on weekends. Sorry about that. Is there anything hair related I could help you with? I'm free for the next hour."

I started to shake my head, and then I thought about my plan to infiltrate O'Hannigan's tonight. If I was going to go incognito, I needed to hide my extremely noticeable red locks.

"Is there any way I can get a temporary look?"

She eyed me cautiously and then ran her fingers through my hair. "How temporary are we talking about?"

CHAPTER EIGHTEEN

———

There is not pain greater than the pain of rejection.
–Irish Proverb

One and a half hours later I stared at myself in the mirror and a dark brunette with cat-green eyes and ruby-red lips stared back at me. Who was this creature?

My venture into the salon had turned into more than I could have ever hoped for. Not only had I managed to snag a drastic new temporary hair color that was sure to help me blend in during Operation Hussy Takedown, but I'd also made a new friend. And both of those were at the top of my cool list.

Sundae Giddings was my new hairdresser, and she was a fast-talking hair whiz who knew how to relax and rejuvenate me with a few select hair products and a skilled hand at makeup application. I, literally, looked like a new woman.

Sundae had listened as I'd run down my current predicament, and she'd been more than willing to assist me in my pursuit of crime-solving information. But she'd made me promise that I'd come back soon and fill her in on the updated details. I was looking forward to chatting with her again already.

Now, as I stood in front of the full-length mirror in Aunt Patty's bedroom, I modeled several different outfits. I didn't have much to choose from, as I'd only packed a few things. I still had boxes of my stuff in storage, as I'd had to move out of my apartment and sublet it when I'd found out that I'd be home a while. As I didn't have time to make a run to Storage Binz of Deatsville tonight, I had it narrowed down to a pair of red jeans and a black cowl neck blouse or my blue maxi dress.

I tried on both and decided to go with the dress. I knew the jeans were more like what red-haired Mandy would wear.

Besides, this outfit made my dark hair look all the more dramatic, and that was exactly how I was feeling right now.

Dramatic.

It was almost as if I was escaping my life to take part in someone else's for a bit. And it was a nice feeling.

Paget was all set up with Ms. Lanier for the night, and I was waiting on Colin's arrival. I'd decided to take him with me on my O'Hannigan's excursion. I figured that parking big old Stella out there in the parking lot wouldn't be exactly flying under the radar. Plus, he seemed like the perfect accessory to the new me, and it never hurt to have backup.

Gosh, I was starting to sound like a cop.

I moved to the bathroom to double-check my makeup and realized that I was almost giddy with the thought of tonight's escapade. I wasn't sure what if anything we'd discover by watching an interaction between Allyson and Trask, but it was something to do.

A knock on the kitchen door sent my pulse into overdrive, and I dabbed on a little of my fave perfume before I made my way to greet my spy.

* * *

I sipped my second Cosmopolitan and continued to watch the room around us.

"Are you sure you don't want something to drink?" I felt a little awkward being the only one partaking of a cocktail—or two. But Colin was all business. A little more business than I would have liked in my current "new me" frame of mind.

He eyed me briefly before returning his watchful gaze to the bar's entrance. "No. I don't drink when I'm working."

"Are you really working, though? I mean, what exactly do you do for a living?" Might as well get it all out in the open. I hadn't been able to find out a single thing on him myself. And it was time for him to fess up some details.

"It is not something I'm really allowed to talk about."

"Colin…" I reached out and slipped my hand in his as it rested on the tabletop. He focused on me at the physical contact. "You have to give me something. Are you really a spy?"

The corner of his lip curled up slightly in what one might consider the start of a really great smile.

"We don't really call it that, but I can confirm that I work for the government in a certain covert operative capacity."

Aha! I knew it. He was a spy.

I was on a roll, so I kept pushing. "Okay so you can't tell me much about your job. I get that. But why isn't there any record of you living here? Why don't I know you or know *of* you at least?"

He let go of my hand and I suddenly felt lonely. He leaned back against the booth and crossed his arms. "Mandy, I don't really want to talk about this right now. You asked me to come and see if we could figure out the connection between Trask and Allyson Harlow. We've been here for over an hour and I haven't seen either one of them here."

"Yet," I said, taking another gulp of my cranberry and vodka goodness.

"What?" He zoned in on my lips as I pushed my cocktail cherry between my lips and then slipped it into my mouth.

"I said…we haven't seen them yet. I didn't exactly overhear what time they were meeting here, just that they were going to meet here. We could be here a while. Why not have some fun and learn something more about one another?" I offered a seductive smile. Or what I thought would pass for one.

"Mandy. I want to stay focused on figuring out who killed my father and who is behind all these games with moving his body around. I don't really want to chat about my childhood right now."

I shrugged. You couldn't make a man talk if he didn't want to. I knew this to be true—no surprise there.

"Okay, okay. I give up. For now. But what about this mysterious note from my windshield? What's that about?"

When he didn't answer, I looked up from my now-empty glass to see that his eyes were focused on the front door. I followed his gaze and saw Trask making his way to the bar— alone.

He took a stool and motioned for the bartender, who brought him a beer from the tap.

We stayed silent for a moment, just watching him gulp down the beer. He looked around the room and his eyes roamed my way. He focused in on me a moment, and I just knew I'd been made.

I ducked down, hiding my head under the table.

"Uh, Mandy. What are you doing?"

I shifted my head to look up into Colin's eyes. I basically had my head in his lap.

Oh, boy.

"Sorry." I sat back up. "Do you think he saw me?"

"No, but try to be a little less conspicuous. He is a cop and more likely to notice women who duck down under the table when he casts a glance in their direction." He grinned at me.

"Right. You know, this spy business is not as easy as you make it look. And now that I mention it—the one time I've worn a dress in weeks and you had to pick me up on a motorcycle? Come on."

He laughed. I felt warm all over.

"Tell me again what made you decide to change your hair color?"

"Ah, I don't know why I went through with it. But it is just temporary. Sundae said it would wash out in a few weeks." I gulped a little more drink. "Do you like it?"

"No."

Well, so much for my warm and fuzzy feeling.

"I'm more of a whisky fellow. Don't go in for the fruity drinks too often."

A little glee sprouted up. He was talking about my drink—not my hair.

"Now your hair, on the other hand…I don't think there is any possible way you could ever look bad."

Looked like my disguise was working in more ways than one.

"Wonder where the hussy is?" My voice slurred just a little on the word "hussy," making it sound like "hushy." It made me laugh.

Colin cut his eyes to me and then back to Officer Chubby. "Mandy, maybe you should switch to water for now."

"I'm fine. I'm fine. I'm just bored. I thought this was going to be more exciting. Isn't this super-secret-agent stuff more exciting than this usually?"

"Actually, no. It is a lot of waiting and watching."

"Well, this is not the night I had in mind. I mean, I want to see some action."

"Check this out," he said. And I broke out of my rant about boredom to see Myrna Mills stroll into the bar. She stopped just inside the entrance and seemed to be searching for something or someone.

"Wonder what she's doing here?" I asked the obvious question in an exaggerated whisper. As if anyone could hear me over the blaring music.

Mrs. Mills' eyes landed on someone at the bar, and she made her way through the crowd. She tapped Officer Trask on the shoulder.

"He does work for the mayor. Maybe they need him for some off-duty security business."

"Bored now." If the mayor's wife was here to let Trask know that he was needed for some mayoral business, then he wouldn't be here when Allyson showed up, and we wouldn't be able to listen in on their conversation.

Mrs. Mills was speaking quickly, and Trask was listening and trying to respond but not getting a word in edgewise. We couldn't hear the conversation, but it was obvious after a few beats that it was rather heated.

"I'm going to try to get a little closer and see what this is about." Colin ducked out of the booth and was gone before I could respond.

The waiter stopped by with a refill and I was momentarily distracted. I took another delicious sip of my yummy beverage and then refocused on the discussion between Mrs. Mills and Officer Trask. Just in time to see her slap him across the face.

Whoa.

* * *

I wasn't feeling too well. After Mrs. Mills had caused her little public scene and then stormed out of O'Hannigan's, I'd made my way to the ladies' room. I sat down on the floor and pressed my face against the cold tile wall.

Something was happening to me. The room swam, my face felt hot and I felt…weird. I didn't know how else to describe it. At first I thought it was just a little too much vodka, but my body was rapidly becoming numb. It wasn't a normal reaction to a couple of cocktails for me, and I began to try to tick off the symptoms in my mind.

Had someone slipped something in my drink? That last drink. Come to think of it. I hadn't ordered it. Had I?

If I could just close my eyes for just a moment. I needed to take a few deep breaths.

My lungs were burning. My stomach churning. Then, darkness.

CHAPTER NINETEEN

———

A dishonest woman can't be kept in and an honest woman won't. –Irish Proverb

"Mandy..." His voice was nice. It had a certain raspy quality to it. I wished he'd been more impressed with my makeover.

"Mandy..."

Oh yeah, what was I doing again? Why was my head so heavy? Gosh, I wondered how much my head weighed. An average human head constitutes about eight percent of a human's body weight. If you cut off the head of a cadaver, it weighed in at about five kilograms, or eleven pounds. That seemed like a lot, didn't it?

"Mandy, if you can hear me...I've got you. I'm taking you to the hospital. Hang in there."

The hospital. Yes, that was good. I felt like crap. What if I didn't make it? Who would take care of Paget now?

That last thought made me choke. I started coughing, and then tears welled up in my eyes. I closed them and felt the tears make a trail down my cheek and roll into my ear. That tickled. I heard a muffled voice coming from nearby, but couldn't make out the words.

I pressed my eyes closed and took a deep breath. *Slow your heart. Slow your heart.*

* * *

Bright white light hurt my eyelids.

"What happened here?" Voices chattered nearby.

"Can I get something for nausea?" Someone was speaking, and she sounded authoritative. "Twenty-five milligrams of promethazine, please."

Oh yeah, that was a good choice, but it might make me sleepy. I didn't want to be sleepy. I wanted to wake up.

"Make it hydroxyzine instead," I croaked out. *I* was the one barking orders. Go figure.

"She's waking up, Dr. Cavello," another voice responded.

My body still felt sluggish. I opened my eyes a crack and saw tubes running into my left arm. A standard IV drip and a banana bag. They were trying to regulate my body chemistry. Magnesium sulfate.

"Did you push the Romazicon?" Dr. C's voice sounded nearby.

"Yes, sir. She seems to be waking up now."

"Hello, Panda. How are we feeling?"

I opened my eyes a little more. They felt crusty.

Dr. C. peered down at me with concern. His eyes looked tired, and the dark circles beneath them were almost as dark as…eye shadow. Why would he be wearing eye shadow? I must be on narcotics.

"I'm sorry." The words came out of my mouth, although I wasn't quite sure what I meant by them.

"Shhh…no need for that. Do you know what happened? Who brought you here?"

"I have no idea." My brain seemed to be clear on all the medical ramifications of what was happening to me, but I had no idea how it had happened or what I'd been doing when it happened. "Why can't I remember?"

"It'll come back to you, Panda. Anterograde amnesia is common with Rohypnol ingestion."

I tried to sit up but he pushed me back down. "Easy now."

"Date-rape drug? How did that happen?" My skin was absolutely crawling at the thought. "Was I? Did I?" I swallowed back tears.

"No. No, Panda. We didn't find anything like that. Someone brought you in, but he didn't stay. I don't think anything like that happened to you—thank goodness for that."

"Paget?"

He rubbed my hand. Large, warm fingers pressed into the palm. I still felt cold.

"She's with Ms. Lanier. She's fine. It's you I'm worried about."

I smiled. "I'm not worried. You're the best doctor I know."

He smiled back and shook his head. "Liar."

I let out a small cough, followed by laughter, and his face lit up.

He looked back over his shoulder and lowered his voice. "Ty Dempsey is waiting outside for you, but I won't let him in unless you give the go-ahead."

I swallowed, and my throat was thick. "Can I have some water, please?"

He let go of my hand and took the small, pink plastic cup off the bedside table. He filled it halfway with water from a matching pitcher and inserted a straw. Holding it to my lips, I took a few small sips. The water tasted heavenly.

When I spoke, my voice came out all crackly. "Where's Colin?"

Dr. C. raised his eyebrows. "Colin who?"

I just stared at him blankly. Where had that come from?

"You know Colin?" The words sounded dumb even to my own ears, but I said them all the same.

"I'm not sure. Is that who you were with tonight? How do you know this Colin?" Dr. C. made a sour expression. "Mandy, we need to figure out who this man is and give the information to Ty. This is serious business."

Colin's face was on the periphery of my mind. He was there tonight. We'd gone to O'Hannigan's. That was clear in my mind, but I was forgetting something important. I knew he didn't have anything to do with this. I was pretty sure of it, at least. But what happened? How had I ended up drugged and in the hospital?

"I don't know what's going on, Dr. C., but I guess it will come back to me. I'm really tired. Can I stay here tonight since Paget is okay with Ms. Lanier?"

"Absolutely. I'll be back to see you in the morning, and I'm just a phone call away if you need anything else tonight. And speaking of Paget, I need to give you some information about care options for her. You didn't call me this morning, as we discussed you would."

My heart sped up at the mention of alternative care for Paget. I had asked him to look into it the last time we spoke, but I'd totally forgotten about the request. I'd also forgotten to call him. Too busy sneaking around and spying on the Mills. Speaking of spying, I guess my trip to O'Hannigan's hadn't been too productive. I really couldn't remember much about it. I knew I'd planned to eavesdrop on Allyson and Chubby, but what had happened after Colin and I had arrived there? That part was still sketchy.

"Wait. You found a place for Paget?" My head hurt, I was having trouble focusing.

"Let's discuss it later. There's a waiting list. It wouldn't be something immediate anyway."

I nodded, and the up-and-down motion made my skull throb.

He patted my arm. "Panda, let's just get you better and home. I'll check in on Ms. Lanier, and I'm sure Paget will be fine with her for tonight. I might let you go home later tomorrow. We'll see. One thing at a time. Okay?"

I forced a nod, and he turned to leave. "Dr. C.?"

He looked over his shoulder.

"Thank you for saving my life."

He gave me a tender pat on the head and then walked to the door. But before crossing the threshold, he turned back to me. "Oh, and Panda?"

"Yes?"

"I love the hair." He winked at me and then left.

I reached up and rubbed my head. I'd almost forgotten about my dark-haired makeover. In the end, it hadn't mattered much. No one had even paid that much attention to me at the bar.

And I hadn't really found out anything beneficial to solving this case.

But someone *had* noticed me and slipped me a roofie. Who could it have been and why? Was this the mysterious note sender who told me that they'd be watching me?

My life seemed to be racing downhill at a rapid pace. I didn't like feeling unorganized, and yet it seemed that the harder I tried to make things work, the worse my life was getting. It was time to get organized.

I pressed the bedside remote and waited for the nurse to answer.

"Yes…may I help you?" a bored voice came through the speaker.

"Could you ask the officer outside my room to come in? I'm ready to talk."

* * *

Ty appeared a few minutes later and sat in the corner chair, propping his booted feet on the foot of my bed.

I kicked out with my covered toes and made contact with the sole of his boots.

"How're you feeling?"

"I'm not sure yet. Confused, I guess. I'm not really clear on what happened. I know I was at O'Hannigan's but I don't know who or why someone would have slipped something into my drink."

"Mandy, what were you doing there and what happened to your hair?" He looked pained to have to ask the question. He let out a long pent-up breath and leaned back in the seat. We both remained silent for a few breaths.

"You don't like my hair?" Focusing on the most important things first.

"No, I don't. You're a good Irish girl—your hair shouldn't be that dark. And why are you wearing so much makeup? You don't need it."

I shrugged. My head had started to ache, and I felt a little queasy. I think that was his way of giving a compliment, but I wasn't sure. "I'm not feeling too well. But I'm trying to figure out what happened, and I could sure use your help."

"Oh, trust me, Mandy, if there is one thing I'm sure of it is that we will find the bastard who did this to you." He sat forward in the chair, moving his feet back to the floor.

"I don't want to think about that right now. I want to see if you'll share what you know, 'cause we may have to work together to solve the case of Colin's father. And—"

"Wait."

I stopped my train of thought as he interrupted, and my stomach gave a little gurgle that made my tongue swirl around in my mouth. I looked to my left and longed to have a sip of water.

"What? I'm not through talking," I managed to get out with my dry, parched, and now icky-tasting mouth.

"We are not going to be working together to solve any crime. And how do you know this Colin, and how do you know that his father is the body that you found?"

I was the one to let out a pent-up breath. "I know a lot of things, Ty. I'm not the same stupid high school girl that crushed on you all those years ago. I'm a doctor—well, almost a doctor, anyway. I'm older and smarter, and I know things. You don't need to worry about what I know. You need to worry about—"

He held up his hand, and despite my rant I stopped talking. I eyed the water pitcher again. The tray that held the water was just a tad out of my reach. Dammit. If I asked him for help, it would show weakness, and I was trying to make a stand here. Despite the fact that he continued to interrupt me.

"Mandy. Hold on a minute. Are you talking about Colin Brooks? Has he been in contact with you?"

I blinked heavily. My eyes felt so thick. Why did they feel so thick?

I was having a little bit of a hard time following the conversation. I was suddenly nauseated to the nth degree. I started to speak but felt a bit of burp surging from my stomach. This wasn't good.

Ty stood up and walked toward me. He sat on the edge of the bed and reached out to cup my chin in his warm hand. My heartbeat quickened, and I reached out to push him away from me. I swallowed down the sick feeling that was creeping up my throat.

"Is that what you were doing in the bar tonight? Some half-assed attempt at solving this case?"

This moment was rife with awkwardness, and my stomach still battled for attention.

I wanted to speak, but I didn't dare. I was just a breath or two away from tossing my cookies.

Ty cleared his throat in an obvious effort to get the conversation back on track.

"Mandy. Colin Brooks is a dangerous man. If he's been in contact with you there's something I need to tell you..."

I tried to process the words. An image of Colin sitting at my kitchen table and handing the box of chopsticks to my sister flashed through my head. I opened my mouth to speak, but instead...I threw up. All over Detective Ty Dempsey.

CHAPTER TWENTY

You can't put a wide head on young shoulders. –Irish Proverb

Two hours later, I was flipping through the channels on the hospital television. My stomach felt a lot better. I'd had a nice dose of anti-nausea medicine and had managed to eat a little dry toast on top of that. I was resting comfortably and thinking about Colin Brooks.

Ty had left in a bit of a hurry after the stomach interruptus situation, but the information about Colin that he'd shared with me had not been lost.

Was Colin really a dangerous man? And what had Ty needed to tell me about him? I had to admit that Colin was always sneaking around and popping up in the dark? Pulling his ghosting skills out whenever needed. He was there one minute, gone the next, and was only seen by whom he chose to be seen by. But he had been there when it counted. He may have saved my life tonight.

But tonight hadn't exactly gone as planned before my little drug-ingestion situation. Not only had I failed to really uncover any new information about the mystery at hand, all sorts of new questions had been raised.

He had admitted that he worked for a government agency, but which one? And in what capacity? Why did Ty think he was so dangerous? Mysterious, yes. Dangerous? I wasn't sure. I needed to talk with him either way.

My memories of this evening were slowly coming back to me. I'd gotten my hair dyed. I'd flirted with Colin. I'd had two too many Cosmos. Then, before I'd gotten sick, he'd moved in closer to see if he could overhear the conversation between Trask and Mrs. Mills. I remembered that much. But what happened after that?

I closed my eyes and curled up in the bed. A now somehow familiar scent reached my nose. Clean, warm linen with a hint of something slightly woodsy mixed in. I knew that scent. I smiled.

"Good to see you smiling." His voice made my eyes open...he was here.

"How do you *do* that?"

He shrugged as if he had no idea to what I was referring. "Do what?"

My face heated. I was feeling a little embarrassed about my behavior at the bar. For all intents and purposes, I'd come on to him and he'd rejected me.

"You just appear like that. Whenever I think of you. Whenever I need you. You're there."

His thick, heavy lashes caught my attention as he seemed to really take me in. "You really took this undercover operation seriously tonight when it came to disguise, huh?"

I let out a small chuckle. "Yeah, I think the hair thing might have been a mistake, but it was nice to get everything off my chest at the hair salon anyway. But, all that aside, I think I owe you my life, Colin."

He looked deep into my eyes. "Dr. Cavello saved your life. I just did the heavy lifting."

"Excuse me? *Heavy* lifting?"

This time he let out a laugh. A small dimple appeared on his left cheek. Something about him I hadn't noticed before. It made my heart race a little.

"Sorry about that. I just wanted to see how you were feeling. I can't stay. I'm checking into something." He looked over his shoulder.

"And what might that be?"

"Oh, I was able to snag your glass from the bar on our way out. I have a pal of mine running a trace on it."

I sat up a little straighter. "So you can find out who slipped me the Rohypnol?"

Something dark shone in his eyes. I'd never seen it before and I wasn't sure I liked it.

"Colin. What are you thinking?"

He shoved his hands in his pockets and backed toward the door a step. "I'm thinking you should get your rest and feel better soon. I'll see you tomorrow." And with that, he was gone.

Colin had an idea of who might have tried to drug me. He was going so far as to run prints on the glass, and I had no doubt that he'd figure this out. But it made me feel more than a bit anxious. The whole thing didn't make sense. How had someone known that was me so easily? I was there with Colin, and he wasn't exactly a well-known face around town. I'd dressed differently and I'd changed my hair and makeup—and yet someone had targeted me specifically and drugged me.

I was lucky that I'd only had a few sips of the drugged beverage.

But now what? Was this the work of the person who'd left the note on Stella earlier today? Maybe I should have been more wary of that. Maybe I should have told Ty about it. Was I really putting my life in the hands of a man I hadn't met until just a couple days ago?

I was missing something here. I just couldn't quite connect the dots. The dots? Oh yeah…

And where was Allyson tonight? Why hadn't she shown up for her rendezvous with Trasky-wasky? And why had Mrs. Mills shown up instead?

The image of Myrna Mills slapping the dickens out of Trask's chubby face replayed in my mind. My memory was back.

I closed my eyes again and replayed the scene. The waiter had come up on my left side, just as the big confrontation was going down bar side. I hadn't really made eye contact with him. In fact, as he'd placed the drink down, I'd been trying to see around him in order to watch the heated exchange in progress.

Something about that waiter tickled my memory like the wisp of a feather. What was it? He'd smelled like…perfume? A familiar perfume. Why would he smell like perfume and why did I recognize it?

My super-sniffer abilities might be another one of my superpowers, but I just couldn't quite place it at the moment. Maybe I just needed some rest.

Yes, that sounded good. I closed my eyes and drifted off.

* * *

I dreamed of the dark woods and Paget being lost in them. Only I knew, deep down, that it wasn't Paget who was lost, but me.

I awoke to sunlight creeping through the edges of the curtains and the sound of the overhead PA system paging some lost employee. I also awoke to a new day with new challenges that were suddenly my life, despite my desire to just go back to normal.

I needed to get out of here. I needed to get home. I needed to check on Paget and to get out of this skimpy hospital gown. I needed to brush my hair and my teeth. In the midst of all my thoughts, I suddenly had the realization that not one but two of the hottest guys I'd ever known had both seen me in this disheveled state. Oh my.

Ugh-a-riffic.

I pressed the nurse call button.

No one responded.

I pressed it again.

Still no response.

I managed to sit up in the bed and swing my legs out over the side of it. My head was a little woozy from the effort, but it was so good to stretch my back that I didn't mind.

I pushed the button again, and this time someone answered. "Yes, how may we help you?"

"Great. Sorry to bug you, but can you please page Dr. C.? I'd like to talk to him about being discharged."

There was a pause. "Oh, you've already been discharged. We're just waiting on transport."

"A transport? To where?"

"To jail."

CHAPTER TWENTY-ONE

———

You must crack the nuts before you can eat the kernel.
–Irish Proverb

Ten fingerprints, two mug shots, and a pat-down later, I sat in a small jail cell staring at the grungy floor. Had the pat-down really been necessary? I mean, come on. I'd been in a hospital gown. What was I gonna have on me?

I wondered if the State of Alabama would still issue me a license to practice medicine with a criminal record hanging over my head. The nausea that I'd fought off a few hours earlier was rearing its ugly head.

The fact that I sat in a jail cell was just my kind of luck. I was feeling more than a little sorry for myself. A yawn crept onto my lips, and I didn't hold back.

"You know what they say?"

I sat up a little straighter as the voice pulled me out of my nodding off.

"What's that?" I asked as I eyed the white-haired officer who strode up to the cell door.

"They say that a guilty person rests easy—knowing that he's already been caught, he has nothing more to worry about." He tapped the cell door with his ink pen before sliding it back into his pocket.

"Oh, really. Well, what do they say about citizens who are falsely arrested for a crime they didn't commit?"

He didn't miss a beat. "Rare."

I swallowed. This man, whoever he was, was out to get me.

"Who are you?"

"I'm the captain around here, and I also happen to be close personal friends with the Mills family. I didn't know you or your family before you left, off to doctor school. But I do know that we believe that filing a false police report should come with ramifications. I intend to see that this matter is settled in short order. I'll do anything to protect the good people of this community—particularly fine men like Dougie Mills. We don't like messes around here, Ms. Murrin." He stretched out the syllables of my last name, and I didn't like the way it sounded on his lips.

"And I guess I just poisoned myself and left threatening notes on my own car, too?"

"Well, stranger things have happened. As I understand it, you would once have done anything to gain the attention of our Detective Dempsey. Maybe this whole thing is some grand gesture of a lonely girl." He turned to leave. "Have a good rest now. Sleep tight."

What was this all about? Filing a false police report? They'd found the body, hadn't they? Alas, it wasn't where I'd said it would be, but that was no fault of my own. If this captain-whoever was determined to wrap this case up around blaming me, I might be in serious trouble. And now he thought I was some pathetic girl who'd set up my own drink tampering just to get the attention of Ty Dempsey?

I lay down on the bunk. For a second I wondered what kind of germs might be living on it, and then I decided to forget about germs for just a few minutes. I was still tired from my hospital stay, and I just couldn't focus. There was way too much espionage and estrogen flowing around in my brain.

"I see you're making yourself at home." The familiar voice sounded in my tired ears, and I didn't even stifle my second yawn at the sound of it. I wasn't just physically tired. I was tired of the whole darned case.

"What do you want, Ty? Want to cause more problems for me? Want to send me to prison so that you can be the big hero cop?"

He didn't take the bait, and instead reached in his pocket and extracted a key card that looked remarkably like a hotel room entry card. I saw that he'd changed clothes since the throw-up incident earlier. He was wearing a fresh pair of jeans that were clean but had seen better days. He had on a powder blue T-shirt that was tight fitting over his rather large, bulging biceps. Biceps that could lift a girl onto the hood of a car and...

Oh, Mandy, stop it already.

He slid the card down the crease of a black box and a green light and single beep followed. The door to the jail cell opened to the left, and Ty entered the cell.

"I'm here to take you home. I posted your bail. I know Judge Holley, and he owes me a favor. And I called Randall Jamison for you."

The name Randall Jamison stirred a little blood flow to my heart. He'd been best friends with my father once upon a time. He'd been one of the first on the scene when my parents had died. I sucked in a little breath and then shook my head, as if to erase the train of thought that was stirring up things better left buried deep inside me.

I stood up. Perhaps a little too suddenly, as I surprised both Ty and myself by wobbling a little. He leapt forward to steady me by placing his hand on my back.

I looked up into his face. There was stubble on his chin, and I had the sudden urge to run my fingers across it. I chewed the inside of my cheek. What was the matter with me?

"You okay?"

I swallowed. "I'm okay. Thanks for getting me out of here. Not a fan of this place."

He looked around the gray cell and smirked. "Let's get you home. You need some rest. Randall wants to see you tomorrow."

"Ty..."

He put his arm around my back and started walking me forward gingerly. "Yep."

"I didn't have anything to do with this case—other than finding the body. You know that, right?"

"I know that, Mand. There's something bigger than you and me going on here, and I intend to find out just what the hell it is."

I nodded. I felt better already. But I wasn't quite sure if it was because Ty believed me or because his arm was around me, and I liked it. A lot.

Well, la dee dammit!

* * *

I didn't argue when Ty helped me into the house and to Aunt Patty's bedroom. How he knew that I'd been sleeping in that room, I didn't know—and I didn't ask. I was too tired to even get into another discussion.

We'd stopped by Ms. Lanier's house for just a moment. Just long enough for me to get a timid hug from Paget, who looked more scared than I'd seen her since Aunt Patty's funeral. She stared at my darkened hair and then back and forth between me and Ty. She was out of sorts. She'd wanted to come home with me. She told me so, but then stayed with Ms. Lanier without putting up too much of a fight. Ms. Lanier had convinced her to spend one more night together to allow me a chance to rest.

She'd promised them that they could make cookies and play Monopoly. Both of these things rated at the top of Paget's list of favorite things to do.

Even though it was only lunchtime, I had such a need to rest that I melted into the pillows as Ty covered me with the oddball afghan and instructed Pickles to lie beside the bed rather than on it. The dog obeyed, but not before sniffing me for good measure.

My eyes were heavy and my spirit drooped. All of this was just too much. I didn't even want to talk about it anymore. I just wanted to make it all go away.

"I should have stayed with you, Mandy. Even though things turned out the way they did. I should have stayed. I got what I deserved."

"Hmmm?" What was he talking about now? My head was heavy. The pillow pulled me down deeper and deeper by the minute.

"That night. I should have handled the whole thing differently. You were scared and alone, and I was caught up in my own stuff. We never should have even done what we did. I was stupid. I'm sorry, Mand."

I heard the words, and they were the words that I'd wanted to hear for all these years. But, even now, I couldn't be sure I'd heard them. Maybe I was dreaming them.

But before the bedroom door clicked into place, I thought I heard him say something. Something like, "I'll make this right, Mand. Like I should have done before."

I tried to smile, but my face wouldn't cooperate. So I slept.

* * *

Some time later, I awoke to find Colin sitting in Aunt Patty's rocking chair, reading an issue of *Seventeen* magazine. I chuckled.

"What? They have some helpful tips in here," he said as he grinned at me and set the magazine down on the nearby dresser.

"What kind of tips? Like how to decorate your locker or the perfect lip gloss for the perfect date?"

He gave me a wink. "You never know when you'll need to think like a teenager."

"Do men ever really stop thinking like a teenager?"

"Touché."

I sat up slowly and stretched my arms over my head. He walked up to the edge of the bed and offered me his hand.

"You know. It might be considered weird in most situations."

"What's that?"

I took his hand and stood. "Waking up to find you in my room—not once but twice in the last day."

"Oh, that?" He shrugged it off. "That's just my way. Does it frighten you?"

I looked up into his drop-dead gorgeous face. "It should."

He smiled. I smiled back.

He let go as I made my way toward the kitchen and the smell of something mouth-watering. I was a woman on a mission, and my super sniffer rarely disappointed.

"Did you bring food?"

He didn't answer, but I could feel his grin behind me as we made our way down the hallway and into the kitchen.

Señor Drool lay on the floor beside his empty bowl. But he wasn't waiting to be fed—he was recovering from stuffing his huge body full of food. I could tell by the way his tongue lolled out of his mouth and made a sizable puddle of drool on the hardwood floor.

"I see you bribed my guard dog."

"Yes, we have an arrangement. It's a good thing you don't count on him for security—he's quite easy to bribe."

I laughed. There was something about being around Colin that was so easy. No pressure. No fear. No past.

Maybe that was all it took to make my life simpler. Just leaving my past behind. If only I could...

"I come bearing news and a full selection from the dinner menu at the café. I wasn't sure what you'd be in the mood for, so I brought one of everything."

My jaw dropped significantly lower than what was attractive, I was sure. But the kitchen table was covered end to end with to-go boxes. Some moist on top from the heat inside. Some bulging with contents unknown. But all filling my nose with promises of pure heaven to be consumed.

"You may just be the man of my dreams."

I turned to look at him, and could have sworn I saw him blush. But then it was gone. Maybe I was imagining things. Surely, uber-cool secret agent types didn't blush.

"Come on, then. Have a seat and eat. I'll talk."

Who was I to argue?

"So, I got the results back on your glass."

I shoved in mouthfuls of fried okra and glazed ham. I looked up at him to continue, but I was too busy chewing to chat.

He continued, "My trace guy found two sets of fingerprints on the glass. One was yours and the other was Matson Mills."

I swallowed down a clump of food and chased it with some sweet tea. "Matson Mills?" Damn. "I can't believe he was right there and I didn't even see his face. I wasn't even paying attention. I'd hoped that they would reveal some pertinent information about the case and give us a nudge in the right direction, but this is totally weird. Why would he want to spike my drink?"

"Honestly, from what I've seen of the kid, he doesn't seem smart enough for all this by a long shot."

"Yeah. I know what you mean, but we really don't know him that well. Maybe he has accomplices who are doing all the brainwork. I mean, I saw him and Trask chatting it up at Mills Landing. Do you think they could be in on this together?" I asked around a mouthful of banana pudding.

He leaned back in the chair, arms crossed. "You know, Trask and Matson are sort of brothers. They could be in on this together, and Trask had the perfect opportunity and easily the means to plant my father's body in the mayor's office."

I stopped my spoon midair. It was loaded with a follow-up bite of banana pudding, but this had my total attention. "What do you mean by 'sort of brothers'? You mean in a frat-house sort of way?"

He gave a quick grin with a flash of that captivating chin scar. "No. I mean, as in a stepbrother situation. You knew that Trask was Amika's son, right? She brought Trask with her to America when she came to work for the Mills. He grew up right alongside Matson. I hear they are quite close."

My eyes did a sort of bulging thing, and the bite of banana required two swallows to get it down. "Uh, no. I didn't know that useful bit of information. Thanks for mentioning it. I thought Amika was German or something—where did the name Trask come from?"

Trask and Matson? Amika was Chubby's mother? The matching set of crystal blue eyes danced a jig around my brain.

"I think I read that their real surname is Traskbauer. They shortened it, I guess."

"You read? Where did you read that?"

He gave a little hand rotation as if he was waving off the question. "I've seen some company files on them—from when they were non-citizens."

"Company files, huh?"

Company as in CIA?

He did a head tilt from side to side, but didn't respond. I decided to drop it for now. This was the most forthcoming he'd been with me to date.

"So, what would Trask's motive be? Is he jealous of not having a real father present, or is the mayor a real jerk of a boss, or what?"

"Well, he's always been a real jerk in my opinion, but I'm not sure it is a reason to frame him for murder. Although if the mayor himself killed my father…maybe someone is trying to shout it to the world. Hey, look here—this is who killed Caden Brooks."

His theory wasn't without merit, but it still all seemed a little juvenile somehow. "I'm sorry, Colin. I know all this must be hard for you. When my parents died it was a simple traffic accident. I cannot imagine all this complicated stuff going along with it. I'm just sorry that you have to go through this."

He reached out and ran a finger across my jawbone. And I gave my cornbread a healthy squeeze. "So, what now? Can you send the fingerprint evidence to Ty?"

"No. I'd rather not."

I shook my head, surprised by his answer. "But I thought we were going to take down whoever did this to me."

"My friend who ran the evidence might lose his job if he had to explain that he'd run the test outside the system and had given me confidential information. I'd rather work this my own way, if you don't mind."

I shrugged. "I guess so. Boy, the list of suspicious characters grows daily around here." I leaned forward, resting my forearms on the table and surveying the multitude of empty boxes. *Maybe I should stop eating now.* I checked with my bulging stomach, and it agreed.

"We need to start from the beginning and try to line up all the players."

"The beginning? You mean from when I found your father's body?"

"No, I mean from the night he died."

Gulp.

CHAPTER TWENTY-TWO

———

What I'm afraid to hear I'd better say first myself.
–Irish Proverb

The next morning Ty arrived to escort me to my appointment with Randall Jamison. I'd had a good night's sleep courtesy of the long chat I'd had with Colin, a scrumptious pancake breakfast courtesy of Ms. Lanier and Paget, and a long, hot shower courtesy of the City of Millbrook's water supply.

I greeted him with a grin as I met him on the porch and followed him down to his truck. He watched me inquisitively as he hurried to open the door for me then helped to hoist me up into the tall seat. Since I was in such a jovial mood, I didn't argue.

"I can't believe you're driving a truck. What happened to your Camaro?" I asked.

"Oh…" He paused as if thinking back with fond memories. "I switched to trucks a while back. More practical."

"Practical?" I gave him a dubious look. "Since when have you ever been practical?"

We remained silent for a time after that.

"What's going on with you? You seem unbelievably happy today."

I turned to observe his face. It was etched with worry. Dark circles under his eyes and downturned lips completed the picture.

"No, Ty. Just feeling better than I have in days."

He seemed to consider my words before he spoke again. "You seem strange. Not your usual…self."

I laughed. Ty shot me a sideways glance.

"I'm just ready to get this over with," I explained.

He reached over and turned the air up a notch. "You don't seem worried. You seem unbelievably calm for someone who is out on bond."

"Ty, you don't believe I had anything to do with this case other than that I found Caden Brooks' body and reported it, do you?"

"No."

"Thank you, Ty."

"For what?"

"Just…thank you for being here for me. For saving Paget. I never—" My voice failed for a moment.

He gave a quick nod and turned up the air another notch.

I changed the subject to something less emotional. "You're about to freeze me out of here. What are you so hot under the collar about?"

He didn't answer, but he turned the air back down again. "I just think the mayor and the captain are in on this whole thing together. I got to thinking about it. And I remember that, shortly before Caden Brooks disappeared, there had been a rumor that he was planning to run against the mayor and that the Mills would rather die than to let the Brooks rule this town."

Everyone knew that the Brooks and the Mills had once been the best of friends but had now been enemies for longer than they'd ever been friends. I wasn't sure exactly why, but I guess it didn't matter. What mattered was what happened that night.

"So, who all knew that Caden was going to run against him?"

"Well, not many—I'd guess. As far as the town knew, it was just a rumor. Caden went missing and the rumor died down."

I considered this a minute. "Why do you think the captain is in on it—well, other than these ridiculous charges that have been filed against me?"

Ty turned into a small parking lot outside a ranch-style home just off Grandview Road. A modest brass nameplate marked the door to announce that this was the office of Randall Jamison, attorney at law.

I waited for Ty's response.

He cut the engine and turned to face me. "Look, I'm not sure how involved in all this you should get, Mand. I don't want to see you or Paget get hurt."

The mention of Paget threw me for a little bit of a loop. What did she have to do with this?

"Ty, I'm already involved, wouldn't you say?"

He exhaled loudly. "Yes. You're involved."

I reached over and placed my hand atop his. The skin was warm, and I almost pulled back when a tingle shot up my arm at the contact. If he noticed the tingle, he didn't let on.

Instead, he flipped his hand over and held mine in his palm. "Mandy, Captain Owens and Mayor Mills have been tight for years. Owens moved here after you left town, and it is well known that Mills brought him in just for the job. Apparently they were old college buddies. They run this town inside and out. If the mayor is involved in something, the captain knows about it. And if the mayor's family was involved, the captain sure as hell will find a way to get them out of it. Whatever it takes, this will not fall on the mayor's head."

I squeezed his hand. "Okay, I don't necessarily trust the captain, but I don't see how that involves Paget."

"Well, I'm not sure that it involves Paget, but I know that she has been hanging out with Adam Owens a lot lately, and if there's one thing the captain protects more vigorously than the mayor, it is his son."

Adam Owens. Paget's new friend and day tender. The boy she was gaga over.

I pulled my hand away. I knew what it was like to get involved with the wrong guy. I was looking at him right now. Still had him in my life despite all the years and miles I'd put between us. When all was said and done, Ty was the reason I'd distanced myself from Millbrook.

"Should I be worried about this Adam Owens kid?"

Ty shook his head. "No, Mand. I don't think the kid would do anything to hurt Paget. He seems like a good kid. I just mean…well, if the captain wanted to make trouble for you, he could see that Paget was taken from your custody. Sent away to a foster parent or something like that. If he's trying to dig up dirt that you're irresponsible or an unfit guardian. Some kind of crap like that."

My brain did cartwheels and my heart raced to catch up. "Do you think he would do something like that?" A touch of panic set in. I hadn't even begun to think about anything like that happening. I had never thought of someone trying to take Paget away from me. I'd been the one trying to figure out who else could care for her. Guilt shot through me.

"I don't know, Mand. I was hoping Randall could give us some advice here."

"Isn't that what we're doing here?"

Ty nodded. "Yep, and I think it is my fault for not jumping on your report from minute one. He and the mayor had too much time to clean up the mess before we got involved."

"What do you mean? You don't actually think the captain tampered with the crime scene, do you?"

Ty's cell phone chirped in his pocket, and he ignored my question to retrieve it and check the display. "C'mon. Randall is waiting on us."

I didn't like that he'd avoided my question. But I followed him up to the office door and allowed him to hold the door for me.

I'd only been in this office once before. When Aunt Patty had come in to sign some paperwork after my parents' death. The head of a six-point deer stared down at me from the receptionist's desk and it gave me a weird set of chills. I'd never been into hunting, but most of the men in town lived by it. I always hated seeing the deer mounts, but you got used to it when you grew up around here. Of course, I'd been gone for years, and we didn't exactly have taxidermied animal heads hanging around the campus at UAB.

The receptionist silently motioned for us to enter the double wooden doors to our left, and I followed Ty.

"Well, look at you, little Mandy Murrin. You're all grown up and how lovely you are…" A booming, bear-sized voice greeted me as I entered a den of wildlife gone crazy. Randall Jamison, avid hunter, lived and worked in a still-life zoo. It was creepy. I couldn't imagine walking in here at night. It would be like the scene of a horror movie to me.

I stayed close to Ty. I may have been raised in the South, but that didn't mean that all the customs and traditions fit in my life.

Randall was dressed in khaki slacks and a Robert Trent Jones Golf Trail collared shirt in emerald green. His eyes were a warm brown, and he smelled of a soft hint of cigar smoke.

I reached out to shake his hand, and he grabbed it, pulling me into a warm embrace from which I thought I might choke.

"You are just beautiful, Mandy. Your father would be so proud of you. I understand that you are just weeks away from completing your medical degree. Is that right?"

I tried to nod, but he had me pinned under his substantial arm, and I was worried that if I nodded that I might wedge my head farther into his embrace, thus cutting off my air supply entirely. I just mumbled something like an "uh-huh" from underneath.

Randall finally released me and I took a couple of slow, deep breaths.

Randall continued to stare at me for a moment as if lost in time. "You look so much like your mother. I really loved your folks. I..." His steady, confident voice seemed to shake a little. I watched his face go through a series of emotions and then settle back into a soft smile. "I know they'd be proud as hell of you, girl. I try to check in on little Paget now and then. She's growing like a weed that one. Just as beautiful as you, too."

I returned his smile. "Yes, thank you, sir."

He waved his hand in the air. "Oh, sir schmir. Call me Randy."

I chanced a glance at Ty, and he was looking down at his boots, which were crisscrossed at the ankle.

"Well, I appreciate your help, Randy."

He sat down behind his tall, gleaming wood desk. It looked like it was built here in this room. It was way too large to have been brought in through the door. I cast a furtive glance at the door and caught sight of a fox watching me. And I wasn't referring to Ty, who kept staring down at his boots as if they were the most entertaining thing in the room.

I returned my attention to Randall.

"So, first things first…this drummed-up charge about you filing a false police report is pure nonsense. Mandy, it is just a tactic that the captain is using to buy the mayor some more time to come up with a legal defense of his own."

"But why would accusing me of filing a false report help the mayor?"

"Well, if the mayor's attorney can prove that you didn't really find the body in his home, then he can use the defense that if he'd been involved with the death that he never would have planted the body in his own office. In other words, he wouldn't have implicated himself."

"Right. Right. But haven't they done an autopsy yet? Can't they see that the body was frozen?" I leaned forward as I thought through the evidence at hand.

"You would think. Only, the entire case has been mismanaged since the get-go."

We both turned to look at Ty, and he was still studying his boots as if there would be an exam at the end of the hour.

"You see, when the body was picked up from the mayor's office, it was taken to the local mortuary, Ride-Outs. They froze the body in their crypt and waited for the forensics team from Birmingham to come in and take custody of the victim."

"Ahh…" I was so exasperated by this news. "If they re-froze the body, it would be impossible to tell what condition the body was in when it was found."

He nodded, cleared his throat, and then continued. "After that, the autopsy was handled by an outside, independent medical examiner at the request of the chief of police. He wanted this entire thing handled privately due the case's sensitive nature."

"Sensitive nature? You mean the fact that the mayor had his butt on the line?" I crossed my arms, frustration mounting inside me.

"Yes. You know how these politicians are. And the Brooks family is huge in state government. When the body was found and identified, they demanded the independent examination. The thing is…the forensic evidence contamination had already occurred."

"What was the cause of death?"

"Cause of death was blunt force trauma to the head. Now, despite the forensic evidence issues, they were able to determine that the blow to the head was most likely caused by a golf club. But seeing as how the mayor's house is located on the Sugar Pines course along with dozens of other residents, it is not exactly open and shut."

"Kind of like a swing and a miss, huh?"

The men stared at me. Had I said that out loud? Maybe that was a baseball metaphor anyway.

"They've searched both Mills' residences and haven't found any golf bags with missing clubs, but we are looking at a decade-old crime here. I doubt the murder weapon will be found anyway. And, of course, the freezer was never recovered, so that evidence is lost as well."

"Do you think there is a chance that the mayor could get away with this entire thing?"

Randall continued, "It is always a possibility, Mandy. Politics is huge in this state. But when it comes to the battle between the Brooks and the Mills, anything can happen."

"Why don't they go back to the beginning and trace the events of the night that Caden Brooks went missing?"

"They are, Mandy, but it is all a bunch of supposition. No one seems to know what happened that night and if they do—they aren't talking." Ty finally chimed in on the conversation. I guessed that he'd finally lost interest in his boots.

"But wasn't the mayor supposed to meet with Caden Brooks the night he disappeared?"

"How did you hear that?" Randall propped his elbows on his desk and surged forward.

"From his son—"

At this revelation, both men fell silent—all eyes were on me.

Ooops.

"Mandy, are you confirming that you are indeed in contact with Colin Brooks?" Ty was sitting forward in his chair now, hands on knees, staring at me with no shortage of concern on his face.

I looked back and forth between him and Randall, who had no less concern on his face.

"Well...I..."

I wasn't sure how much to tell them. Colin had never necessarily come out and told me that I couldn't reveal our connection to anyone, but I'd somehow known from the beginning that it wouldn't be a good idea. Even after I'd found out about him being a secret agent of the government, I guess the truth was that I'd just liked keeping him all to myself. It may not have been smart, but I'd just taken the word "covert" to heart and was kind of keeping him under wraps.

"Mandy, when have you had the occasion to speak with Colin Brooks about this case?" Randall asked.

I cleared my throat and took a moment to pull my hair off my shoulders and twist it up in a makeshift ponytail. Somehow, I felt oddly protective of Colin right now. Maybe it was because of the fact that this case revolved around his father. Maybe it was because I knew what it was like to lose my father and that I wanted so terribly for him to find justice—in a way that I'd never been able to find. I told myself it was for sure *not* because I was starting to care for him in a way that had nothing to do with this case.

I blew my breath out in an upward stream that made my side bangs flutter to and fro.

The men stared at me and waited. Randall was patient. As if he had all day. But Ty...I could feel the impatience radiating off him like the sun radiates off a sandy Gulf Shores beach.

"Look, he approached me a while back, after he overheard that I'd found the body. He showed me a newspaper article about his father's disappearance, and he asked me some questions. That's all."

Mostly.

Ty shook his head. He knew me. He knew I was holding back. And he wasn't happy.

"You can't trust him, Mandy."

"Mandy, I hate to say it, but Ty's right. His mother was Caden Brooks' first wife. She had some sort of mental issues. She left town with Colin when he was very young. Caden had always surmised that Colin had inherited the same problems. He sent a private investigator after them, but they'd just seemed to disappear off the face of the earth."

"So you all just took Caden Brooks' word for it? Everyone just jumped on the political bandwagon and assumed that the kid was bad and the mother was crazy? Because surely a politician has *never* lied about anything before." I couldn't hold back the sarcasm in my voice any longer.

At least they had the courtesy to look a tiny bit contrite about my theory. While my mind swarmed with curiosity. Was there more to my spy than met the eye? And what kind of mental issues had his mother suffered from? Was that why he was so naturally good with Paget?

"Well, he and his mother have been presumed dead for years. In fact, Caden had them declared dead not long after they disappeared," Randall said.

I took this moment of pause to cast a furtive glance at Ty. He was still staring at me, his eyes squinted and his breathing shallow. Something about my revelation of seeing and speaking with Colin Brooks had really sent him into a mood. Was it protectiveness or jealousy? I couldn't tell for sure.

Randall cleared his throat and continued, "He was never seen or heard from again, that is…until…well…when exactly did you meet him and are we really sure this is even Colin Brooks?"

"I guess I have just taken his word for it." My curiosity was extremely peaked now. I'd searched the web left and right and hadn't found out anything about Colin. Randall's story explained why—sort of.

"Can you set up a meeting between us?" Ty's voice was surprisingly steady.

"He doesn't really set up meetings, per se." I tried to imagine setting up a sit-down between Ty and Colin. I couldn't even imagine how that would go over.

"Mandy, this is serious business. We need to get to the bottom of this. For all we know, he could be responsible for his father's death." Ty spoke and Randall and I watched as he stood up and walked to the window, looking out into the woods beyond the office walls.

I couldn't say that the thought hadn't crossed my mind a time or two. But I'd grown to trust Colin. Despite his mysterious past, I believed him and I wanted to help him figure out what really happened to his father.

"I'll ask him." It was all I could offer.

Ty started laughing.

I squinted at him. "Why are you laughing, pray tell?"

"Isn't it obvious what happened to Caden Brooks? The whole feud between the Brooks and Mills has nothing to do with anything. It is just incidental."

"How do you mean?" Randall leaned back again and propped his feet on the corner of his desk.

"That no-good Colin Brooks killed his own father and tried to blame it on the mayor. He hid the body there, and only when Mandy found it did he miraculously reappear in town. Now he's here to see that the mayor goes down for it, and then he'll disappear again."

I stood there, staring into the eyes of a…well, I wasn't sure what it was…some sort of raccoon mixed with a cat—a cacoon? I shuddered. This taxidermy paradise was giving me hives.

Ty's theory made some sense, but I knew Colin. At least, I felt like I knew him enough to know that he was tormented by the finding of his father's body. He wasn't a part of that. I just knew it deep down. "I don't believe it."

Ty eyed me from across the room and shook his head. "Whatever, Mandy. The whole point is that we need to find him and question him officially."

I understood where he was coming from, but getting Colin to agree to it was a totally different matter altogether. With the way he ghosted in and out of the room, I doubted he made appearances anywhere he didn't want to be.

Randall continued, "That's fine. Look, we won't settle all this today. There's still the question of why the captain has it out for you, Mandy. I think this posturing with the ridiculous charges is all a bunch of hogwash to try and throw the bad press off the mayor. We have a hearing set for Monday and I'll get this whole thing thrown out. Until then, see if you can work with Ty to bring this man who claims to be Colin brought in for questioning."

I grabbed my purse from under the chair and headed toward the door. A now-quiet Ty following along behind me.

I pushed through the office door and into the reception area, but I heard Ty speak to Randall as I departed.

"We need to talk about it later, Randy. But this may be a problem."

CHAPTER TWENTY-THREE

———

You'll never plow a field by turning it over in your mind.
–Irish Proverb

I stared out the window as we rode home in silence. We passed a sign for The Millbrook Players near the elementary school. Huh, since when did we have a live theatre here in town? Maybe I could take Ms. Maimie to see their rendition of *Hello, Golly* as, given her history in "performing arts," she'd be sure to enjoy that. I smiled internally at the thought.

Despite the tension between us, Ty remained surprisingly quiet during the ride. But when he cut the engine in front of my house and turned to face me, my heartbeat tapped a worried rhythm.

"I don't want to talk about it," I pre-empted.

"Well, it looks like we have to, Mandy."

I shook my head and stared down at my white New Balance shoes that had a bit of a rust-colored stain on one toe. Hard to keep new shoes clean.

"Mandy, you don't even know who this man is. How can you trust him? How can you believe him? And, worse yet, even if he really is Colin Brooks, you don't know what this man is capable of. Maybe even murder."

"Okay, Ty. I hear you. I understand."

"I don't think you do." His voice rose an octave.

I sat there. Words failed me. I knew he was right and yet I knew what my gut told me about Colin. I wasn't ready to just turn him in and let the chips fall where they might. I needed to see this through.

Ty spoke again before I could formulate my thoughts further. "Look. I'm sorry I didn't believe you. I'm sorry I chose my future over you. I'm sorry. I'm sorry. I'm sorry." He sighed loudly, frustration evident.

There was the apology I'd waited all these years to hear. But, surprisingly, it didn't really make anything better. It just took me back to yet another painful time in my life.

That night of the graduation party was the night that I'd told Ty I was pregnant. We'd only done it that one time—*on* his car, not *in* his car—and it wasn't exactly the stuff that dreams are made of. But I'd naively thought that our one night together meant that we'd be together forever. When he'd announced, at the party, his decision to play football at Auburn, I'd been overcome with jealousy. I wanted him with me—at the University of Alabama some 160 miles away. I, too, had a scholarship—mine academic, of course. I couldn't wait to get out of this town, and I'd thought he'd come with me. We'd be together and everything would be right. I was wrong.

My mind blurred with images of that night, after the party. Our close-knit group at the football stadium running around in the rain—my tears mixed with the rain. The thoughts were making me feel a little sick to the stomach. So I cleared them from my mind like a hand on a dry-erase board.

"As I've said before, I was jealous, desperate…I loved you. I thought if I said I was pregnant that you'd stay—that you'd go with me instead. So it was a lie, but it didn't matter anyway. You walked away. You left me, not knowing if it was the truth or not. What if it had been true? You'd have been the jerk that walked away. As it turned out, you were just the jerk who took my virginity and walked away."

We sat in silence for a few moments.

"Mandy, I was immature. All these colleges were fighting over me. It was my chance to get out of Millbrook. To not have to follow in the Dempsey family tradition of getting married, having babies, and becoming a cop. It was all I could do to wait until graduation to announce my choice of colleges. Then you drop that news on me behind the stadium…in the rain. You looked so beautiful and so helpless. I knew that if I stayed that I'd give in and marry you. When I got to spring training and blew out my knee—I blamed you. I know it wasn't right, but I had to blame someone, and I thought it was you and the distraction of wondering what you were going to do. Wondering if you were going to raise that baby all by yourself."

"And then you found out there was no baby."

"And then Penny tells me that you revealed our family's dirty little secret about my druggie aunt and Penny's adoption. My mom died, and everything seemed to come back to you. Penny hated you, and I jumped on the bandwagon." He took a deep breath and looked out the window. We both stared at Ms. Lanier, who was in her backyard, hanging out laundry.

"I'm sorry too, Ty. I've said it before, but I really mean it. I was immature too. But you have to stop blaming me for everything. We have to let the past go. Our present is in one heck of a mess right now. Let's just focus on that, shall we?"

He blew out a breath and turned to me. "Okay, Mandy. Okay."

I'd thanked him again for the ride, the bail, and the help with the visit to Randall's office. Now I'd reached Ms. Lanier's front door, and when I looked back over my shoulder, he was still sitting in the truck watching me.

He looked deeply troubled. It was something I hadn't seen in his face for a long time, but I knew it when I saw it. Ty Dempsey was worried about me.

* * *

All that reminiscing had worked up my appetite. Ms. Lanier offered up a tasty lunch of pimento cheese sandwiches, homemade cucumber pickles, and her famous sweet iced tea (also known as syrup in a glass). I felt a little better now. Ty and I had reached some sort of stalemate when it came to our relationship, and that was progress for us. If only Penny and I could do the same.

Ms. Lanier spent the entire lunch filling me in on how wonderful Paget was doing in her summer school and how Adam Owens walked her home every day and spent time with her right here at the dining room table and was the perfect gentleman.

I still wasn't sure about the arrangement, but with Paget's full-time school still two weeks away, I needed all the help I could get to keep up with Paget. It was a little irksome that a high school quarterback and an elderly neighbor were doing a better job of caring for my sister than I had been.

"What have you found out about our little mystery?" Ms. Lanier asked in her version of a low voice, but which was still about standard volume to those of us who could still hear out of both ears.

I gave her a quick rundown of the details of my arrest and the recount of Mrs. Mills slapping Officer Trask at the pub.

She smirked at the mention of Myrna Mills. "I knew she was involved in this in some way. I've never trusted that woman since the day she stole my idea about the church's Easter Eggs-travaganza. You simply cannot trust a woman who steals your idea for a charity event."

I cracked up at her line of reasoning. The mayor's wife was definitely starting to look suspicious, and I hadn't crossed the housekeeper—or Allyson, or Trask, or Matson—off my list either.

"So, will you be over for supper, then?" Ms. Lanier said.

I looked up to find my neighbor and friend twirling a dishtowel around in her bony hand.

"Umm…well…no. Uh, I think I should be able to cook dinner for Paget tonight. It will be a good time for us to hang out and get caught up on things."

A whiff of disappointment wafted through the air, but Ms. Lanier covered it up with a soft smile. "All right then, dear. You two girls just let me know if you need anything. I'll send her home after Adam leaves today. That be okay?"

I started to object. He didn't need to spend every afternoon with her, did he? But as soon as the thoughts joined my mind, I knew that what I was feeling was jealousy. I was jealous of a teenage boy because he loved and cared for my sister. Something was wrong with my way of thinking. I hugged Ms. Lanier, thanked her for the food, and started to make my departure via the side porch door.

"Oh, Mandy…just a second…" Ms. Lanier headed my way with an exaggerated limp.

I looked down at her foot and saw that she'd made the hole in the left toe of her slipper slightly larger than it had been when I'd last seen it.

I bit my lip in fear of what was coming.

"I have this ingrown toenail situation. Would you be a sweetheart and take a look at it before you take off?"

Sis boom blah.

* * *

Having survived the toenail ordeal—barely—I made my hasty exit, in need of checking on Pickles and with a little hope of squeezing in a short nap before Paget got home.

As I traipsed across the lawn, lost in my thoughts, I almost ran into the car that blocked my path. A brand-new Lexus with shiny rims and a hand-wax job to die for. I knew the car and its owner.

Dr. Sharona Sewell sat in the large wooden rocker on my front porch looking extremely bored, but more relaxed than I could ever remember seeing her.

"Well if it isn't the Mighty Dr. Murrin."

I tried to emit happiness, but a few small tears threatened to beat a path to the front of my eyeballs at the mention of her nickname for me.

"Yep. Here I am. What are you doing here?"

She opened her mouth in mock horror. "What? I can't take a little drive south just to catch up with my favorite protégée? That's not much of a welcome."

I laughed and opened the door to the house, ushering her inside past a drooling, hungry Pickles, who eyed her with nothing more than minimum interest. I showed her into the den area and plopped down on the sofa.

Sharona Sewell was my residency advisor, and she was a brilliant teacher. She was also a good friend, and I had missed her desperately.

She came and sat by me on the sofa and touched my arm with a soft hand. I always wondered how she kept her hands so darned soft after washing them so many times in a day. I washed mine the same way, and my fingers could trick a gator into submission with all the scales.

"I guess I know why you're here." I watched her face and tried to keep my face stoic. Although seeing her here made me want to grab my bag, jump in the Mercedes, and hot wheel it back to the Magic City faster than green grass through a goose. I knew that I wouldn't be leaving Millbrook today or in the next few days, weeks, or months to come.

"Did you get the letter from the registrar's office?"

I thought of the crumpled-up envelope and wondered about its whereabouts. My best guess was in my dirty coveralls still hanging in my locker at Flicks Vision. Speaking of which, maybe I should check in with Barry as soon as Sharona left.

"I got it. Didn't open it."

"Why not?" She let go of my arm and pulled on her earlobe, a habit I'd seen her do in class more times than I could count.

"I just haven't had the time." *Been locked up in jail, seeing my attorney, trying to figure out why I'm suddenly involved in a decade-old murder.*

She gave me an instructor-like head tilt, her expression a mixture of frustration and sadness.

"Look, Mandy. I know you're working things out with your sister's care. And, again, I'm sorry about the loss of your aunt. But you can't let all these years go to waste. All your hard work. You're a brilliant physician, and your spot in the residency program is not going to wait on you forever. I don't want you to lose it. I *need* you to take it."

I smiled, but there was no mirth behind it and Sharona saw it—or the lack thereof.

"I can't. I wish I could—but I can't. I'm stuck right now. I'm just stuck." Never had a word been truer than this one. In all the ways I could be stuck, I was stuck. Not the least of which was that I couldn't leave the county while out on bond. Well, I could leave, but then Ty might lose his house since he'd put up the bail and, well, then I'd also have to go back to jail. I put on a brave face for my friend and mentor.

"Is this just about your sister? 'Cause we can work something out for her. Just come on back with me and we'll figure it all out. You need to be back by Monday."

"Monday?" I had to stop and think about the day. I'd lost all track of days lately.

"Yes, three days from now. That's why I took off early this afternoon and drove down. I wanted to see if I could convince you to let us move you back home this weekend. Bring your sister and your dog." Pickles lifted his head from my thigh, where it had been resting since the moment I sat down. He wanted attention. Well, he wanted food, but that was his version of attention.

He'd heard the word "dog," but when it wasn't followed by any movement to head toward the kitchen, he returned it to my thigh and added to the stream of drool that was already moistening my leg.

"You don't know how much I'd love to take you up on that offer, Sharona. You really have no idea how much I want to. But things are complicated for me right now. I need to stay here and figure things out and then…then…maybe I can reapply. Maybe after the holidays." My voice sounded hopeful—even to my ears. But as I spoke the words, I knew they were a lie. I was stuck here for the foreseeable future. There was little doubt that the holiday season would bring no relief to my situation.

I almost caught my breath at the realization of what I was saying. I was officially dropping out of med school. With less than a semester to go, I was giving up my dream. It stabbed me. The thought stabbed me like a knife, and my throat went suddenly dry.

"Is there anything I can do to change your mind? Anything I can do to help? Money?"

I reached over and took her hand. I squeezed it. "You are a wonderful friend and a wonderful teacher. I won't forget that. But no. I can't accept it. I have to take a little detour in my life right now. I need to do this right. If this was a matter of just this one semester, I could probably swing it. But Sharona, we're looking at residency—four-plus years depending on my specialty. That's a long time with little money coming in, and I'm already stretched thin on student loans. Endless hours on call and all that stress, I just know I wouldn't have time for much else. I need to take care of what really matters right now, and that's just not my education."

She squeezed back and then stood, straightening out her knee-length white suit skirt and trying not to flinch at the fact that Pickles' hair was now matted to the side of it.

"Those are big words, Mandy Murrin. But I know you can do this. You are one of the strongest women I've ever met. You'll handle this, and then you'll get back to the program. And, when that time comes, I'll do whatever I can to make it happen. Okay?"

I nodded. Words failed me as a wave of nausea crept up my esophagus and I tried to tamp it down. I'd just given up my medical career. It was gone like the seed hair on a dandelion. Blown into the wind with one strong gust. Just gone.

"Now, where do I get some food around this place?" Sharona grinned as Pickles' head shot up at the word "food."

CHAPTER TWENTY-FOUR

Watching is a part of good play. –Irish Proverb

An hour later, Dr. Sharona Sewell left Millbrook and took my medical career with her. I'd promised to return the withdrawal form as soon as I found it and signed it, but she'd agreed to turn in my verbal consent to release my spot in the program that was to start in just a few weeks.

It was hard to believe that I'd been home long enough to use up the allowed medical leave. Apparently, the school was only required by law to allow a short amount of time away from the program before they could release my place to another student. The last week of Patty's life combined with the last few weeks where I'd been trying to make ends meet for me and Paget had used up all of the program's good will, as far as this missing-in-action student was concerned.

There was nothing else Sharona could do to hold off the powers that be, and I'd known this moment was coming the very second I'd gotten the call about Patty. I'd only been dreaming of the day I could return to my real life—for now, this was my real life. I stared into the empty fridge.

I'd given all the leftovers, courtesy of my mystery man, to Sharona so that she could sit and chat with me before she had to take off. Luckily, she'd shared with Pickles, and after a quick run—well, *run* was a bit of an exaggeration where Pickles was concerned—in the yard, he had disappeared back to Aunt Patty's bedroom for a nap.

If I was going to cook for myself and Paget, I needed groceries.

Grabbing my purse and slipping on my rhinestone covered flip-flops, I headed out to Stella. But stopped short when

I realized that Stella was missing. I closed my eyes and rubbed them and then looked again. Still no Stella.

What? How? When?

Where was my Stella?

I pulled my cell phone out of my pocket and dialed the station.

"Millbrook Police Department, Officer Trask."

Oh, joy. I wanted to ask him if his face was still stinging after his little fisticuffs with Mrs. Mills, but I figured this wasn't exactly the time to bring it up.

"Is Detective Dempsey there, please?"

"No, honey, he sure isn't. Is there something I can assist you with?"

Honey? Could he be any more unprofessional?

I wanted to report my car stolen, but I didn't want to get him involved. I just didn't trust this guy.

"Uh, okay. How about Officer Prentiss?"

There was a pause on the line. Was he getting suspicious?

"Is this Ms. Murrin?"

Crap. How did he know that?

"Ye-yes. How did you know that?"

He chuckled. "Well, this may be little old Millbrook, but we have a 911 enhanced caller ID here at the station, missy. And why exactly can't I assist you with your problem today?"

'Cause I think you might be involved?

"All right, then. I think my car has been stolen."

Silence met me on the other end of the line. One beat. Two beats.

"You *think* it has been stolen?"

"Yes, well, I was in the hospital and then I was in jail—briefly, and I haven't really needed to use it in the last day or more. I keep it parked behind the house and, well—I just now noticed it was gone."

Again, silence.

"Well, I'll need to you come down to the station and fill out a report. That is…if this is a real report. I mean, maybe the ghost of that dead body you found drove it down here? Or maybe the mayor himself stole it?" His laughter barely enabled him to get that last sentence out, but then his coughing started up.

Just like I'd thought—this wasn't the person to report anything to.

"Thanks for your help, Officer Chub—I mean Trask. Could you just have Detective Dempsey phone me when he returns to the station?"

His coughing mixed with laughing was the only response I got as I ended the call.

I'd heard the phrase "getting your hackles raised" all my life and suddenly I knew exactly what it felt like. My temper was flaring. I'd had enough of all these games. The redheaded Irish girl was ready for a fight. Well, I might currently be a brunette but I was always a redhead at heart.

If only Colin were here to give me a hand.

Think, Mandy. Think.

I walked over to Ms. Lanier's house and filled her in on the details.

"Did you see anyone at the house? Near my car?"

Ms. Lanier looked at me with some manner of suspicion. "Just you, dear. This morning."

"Me? No, Ty picked me up this morning and we went to Randall's office. Then he brought me home. Remember?"

Ms. Lanier paced around the kitchen and kept returning to the window over her sink and looking out. From there, she had the perfect view of where I parked Stella.

"Ms. Lanier? Did you see someone take Stella?"

She turned around and looked at me. Fear and uncertainty in her eyes. "Yes. I saw you drive off in it early this morning."

What in the world was going on?

* * *

"Uh, that wasn't me."

"Well, you know my distance vision isn't all that great. But it was a woman with red hair. And she got in the car and drove off."

My mind whirred.

"Wait a minute. Red hair?"

"Yes, Mandy. I could see that much." She waved her hand at me as if I needed to catch up to the story more quickly.

I reached up and ran my fingers through my long, dark hair. Newly colored and not currently red as of this morning.

It finally sank in to Ms. Lanier and she put her hand over her mouth. "Oh, dearie. I'm so sorry. That wasn't you. You've had your hair colored. And I stood here and watched someone steal your car!"

She trembled slightly and began to sway. I went to her, wrapping her in my arms. "It's okay. Don't worry. I'll figure this out."

But I had one suspicion of who the red-haired culprit might be. If I only knew the why.

First things first: I needed a set of wheels.

"Ms. Lanier, can I borrow your car?"

She was sniffling into a crumpled Kleenex. "Sure. Sure. It's a little rusty and temperamental, but you're welcome to take it." She opened a drawer by the sink and handed me the key. "You know, I don't drive much anymore. My vision and my hearing are just not what they used to be."

"That's smart of you to be aware of that and to take precautions." I gave her a hug and then took off through her back door and into her garage.

There, was Ms. Lanier's 1958 Cadillac Eldorado Seville. It wasn't in the best condition I'd ever seen, but it looked pretty good considering the fact that it was the only car she'd ever owned. Her husband had left it to her when he'd passed away many years ago. I remembered that it was only then that she'd learned how to drive, and she took Aunt Patty everywhere with her, as Aunt Patty never drove. After she lost her brother—my dad—in the accident, she put Stella aside for me and never drove again.

It didn't seem practical, but it was her way of dealing with his death. I guess.

I shuffled through the messy garage and lifted the garage door. It rolled up with a few creaks and groans. Then I made my way around to the driver's side. I saw what she meant by rusty when I tried to pry the door open. It was a bear to move, but I finally made it inside. Now, if only this sucker would crank.

I closed my eyes and turned the key. A few whirs and clicks and then the engine turned over.

Woot!

I couldn't believe it. You absolutely cannot kill a Cadillac—the old slogan was right.

I pulled the beast out of the garage door and turned to wave at Ms. Lanier, who was watching from the front porch.

Stella, I'm coming to get you.

CHAPTER TWENTY-FIVE

———

The waiting man thinks the time long. –Irish Proverb

I drove around town looking for Stella, with no such luck. Finally, I stopped to get some gas and a snack at the Thrifty Mart. As I pumped the gas, I reviewed my options.

I could go down to the station and file a report, but the thought of doing things the "official way" had lost its appeal to me. After all, I'd tried that with the body discovery, and look where it had gotten me.

Now someone had stolen my car, and I had an idea that it might be Allyson. She wasn't exactly red-haired, but her strawberry blonde might pass for red at a distance. But I couldn't figure out why or what she'd want with my car. I knew that she was involved with Trask and I knew that he was tied up in this mess somehow. Why else would Mrs. Mills have had it out with him at O'Hannigan's? I also knew that Matson had tried to poison me, but why?

Why was everyone messing around with me? Why was I suddenly so important when it came to this case?

Could it be just like Randall Jamison had said? Could they simply be trying to take the focus off the mayor by making me look crazy?

"How're you liking the hair?" A soft and somewhat familiar voice caught my attention, and I looked up to see my new friend Sundae Giddings approaching.

I smiled and she returned it with one of her own.

"Well, I like the hair but I've been having a bit of a bad time since my makeover."

And that was putting it mildly.

She gave a little pout and then came to stand by me and the Caddy. "So, did you figure out everything you needed to figure out yet?"

I shrugged. "Ah, no. Actually, things keep getting more and more complicated by the minute. I just can't seem to get it all together."

Sundae tapped her finger on her lips. "Well, you know what they say…if you want to solve all your problems, ask the women in a beauty shop."

"Ha! Ms. Lanier said the same thing a few days ago." I smiled, despite my current predicament.

Sundae blew a bubble with her chewing gum and gave me a head tilt. "You've got all these people and all this stuff happening, right?"

"Yep. That about sums it up."

"Well, just gather all the folks together and let it work itself out."

Now, wouldn't that be interesting? All those people in one place just hashing it out. I let out a bark of laughter. "Thanks for the idea. I'm not sure if I can swing it, but I'll keep it in mind."

She stepped back and slipped her hands into her back pockets. She seemed to be considering something. "You know. Allyson Harlow was at the beauty shop that same day after you had your makeover."

"She was?" This caught my attention. "She didn't have her hair dyed red, did she?"

Sundae widened her eyes at the thought. "No. She didn't do that, but she did see your photo up on the makeover wall. Remember how we took your picture before you left?"

Scrabble tiles were lining up in my mind, but they couldn't quite complete the full word.

Before I could finish the thought, Sundae said, "Speaking of red, this isn't your car, is it? I thought you drove a big red one."

"Oh, I do. But I had to borrow this from my neighbor. Seems as if someone has stolen my car."

Her eyes widened again. "Really? Wow. I thought I just saw your car over by the high school. Should you call the cops and tell them that?"

"The high school?"

She nodded.

I returned the nozzle to the pump. I was done pumping gas, but my heart took over pumping blood at a heightened pace.

"We almost never have stuff like that happen around here. Things have sure been odd over the last few days. It is almost as if the town has gone crazy or something." Sundae continued to talk, but my mind was screaming one thing.

Paget.

"Listen, Sundae. Can you do me a favor?"

* * *

I'd sent Sundae off in search of Ty. I needed his help and I had no idea how to find Colin. I wondered what his version of a Bat-Signal would be? Maybe he would sense that I was starving and he'd show up with food.

When Sundae had mentioned that she'd seen my car by the high school, I'd gone into crisis mode. But I feared that going by the police station to report this was a waste of time. Someone was messing with my life and now…if they'd gotten to Paget…

No, I couldn't go there right now.

I had to get to the high school before summer school dismissed for the day. I looked down at the time on my cell phone and then pressed the accelerator. Football practice would be letting out soon, and Adam would be escorting Paget to the house.

With one more mile to go, my cell phone rang.

"Hello…" I clutched the cell phone between my shoulder and ear as I chugged through town.

"Yes, this is Penny Dempsey calling from the *Main Street Mile*. I'd like to see if you care to make a statement about your recent incarceration?"

The skin of my forehead seemed to stretch a little tighter as my old "friend" mocked me with her words. Hey, maybe moving back to your hometown would be the next new thing in cosmetic surgery—or a way to avoid it, at least. Just allow people to mock you and frustrate you to the point of insanity, and your forehead would stretch accordingly—thereby removing the need for Botox.

Note to self: see if this method has already been patented.

"Penny, there's no need for you to act all official. You good and well know that you'll post an article whether I talk to you or not, and, frankly, I don't have time to chat just now."

I rolled up to the one traffic light on all of Main Street and, of course, I'd caught the red. There was absolutely no traffic coming across from Coosada Road. But still, I'd caught the red.

"Maybe I will, and maybe I won't." Her voice sounded just a tad nicer than it had moments ago.

"Look, go ahead and write whatever you want. There is little I can do to keep this from spreading it all over town—if it hasn't already, and it is by far the least of my worries today."

Penny grunted. "Oh, yeah. What is worrying you now? How you're going to change your hair color back?"

"Whatever, Penny. Look, I've got to go." The light changed to green and I put the pedal to the metal. Only the car barely scuttled forward up the hill. "Oh, and can you try to track down your brother for me? I could really use his help right about now."

"Yeah, right. And what makes you think he'd help you?" Penny tried to sound tough, but her voice had lost almost all of its vehemence.

"He's the one who bailed me out of jail, didn't you know? So at least he believes in me."

The line went silent. She hadn't known. She hadn't known that Ty had bailed me out. That he was in contact with me and obviously knew I was innocent and had made a huge statement by putting his name and his assets at risk.

"So, you didn't know. You should really check your sources better than that, Penny. I mean, you've been working at that paper for, what? Going on fifteen years now? Since we started high school?"

The line remained silent. I hadn't been able to keep the smart-aleck tone out of my words. We both knew that I was referring to the fact that she'd never left town, never gone to college, and hadn't aspired to do anything other than work for that paper. I would be lying if I said that I didn't feel a little bad about pointing that out to her right now. But I was beyond worrying about her feelings. She'd made this call—she'd called just to taunt me. And I wasn't in the mood for it.

"No. You're right. I had no idea that you'd already caught my brother back in your web. Guess I should have known that he still had feelings for you. He was always a big idiot where you were concerned."

Ouch.

"I don't know what you're talking about. There is nothing going on between me and Ty. He bailed me out because he knows these charges are bogus. It sure would be nice if my lifelong friend felt the same way."

Now she laughed. "Lifelong friend? Friends don't destroy their best friend's family by revealing secrets just to spite her brother, leave town when their friend's mother is on her death bed, and, most of all, friends don't leave friends to pick up the pieces of their lives alone."

She didn't have to say these words. I knew them all, and they were true.

"Penny, maybe we should sit down and talk about it. You know…later." *Yeah, later, when I'm not a quarter-mile from the high school and frantic about the wellbeing of my sister.*

"Oh, it's more than too late, Mandy. I just want you to know that I'm going to do everything in my power to make your return home as miserable as possible. Just try and see what good all your fancy degrees will do for you when you're not welcome anywhere in this town."

Arguing the point any further was a waste of time. "Okay, Penny. Do what you need to do. The newspaper is seriously not on my mind right now. Look, I've got to go. But thanks for the call."

I pulled the Caddy into the parking lot and searched through the faces of students who were milling about near the back of the stadium. The coincidence that I was having this conversation with Penny as I sat behind the stadium wasn't lost on me.

"Okay. Okay. But I just thought you'd like to know about tomorrow's article, and if you haven't had time to check out today's article, you should definitely do that."

I opened the car door and stepped out. Elbowing my way through the barrage of football players, cheerleaders, and band members who had all been on campus for their summer camp practices. "Okay, Penny. If that's what you think you need to do." I was only half listening to her now. Where was Paget?

"Oh, I don't need to do anything. I *want* to. And by the way, good luck getting a job in town after tomorrow."

She was starting to get on my nerves now. "Uh, Penny, I already have a job. A crappy one, but I already have one nonetheless." I suddenly felt a burst of pride for my job at Flicks Vision. I truly must be losing it.

She cackled back at me as I spotted Adam Owens standing near the gym doors. Football helmet in hand as he chatted with a shorthaired blonde cheerleader who was wearing way-too-short shorts.

"Oh, you don't know? How priceless. I'm glad I get to be the bearer of bad news, then. You've been let go from Flicks. Yeah, it's in today's paper. A nice quote from your boss, Barry. Apparently, it is against corporate policy to employ felons."

The call ended as I caught Adam's eye.

Va va va boom.

* * *

"Oh, hi, Ms. Murrin. How are you today?" Adam grinned his all-American boy smile, but I wasn't in the mood for pleasantries at the moment.

"Adam, have you seen Paget?"

He looked at me, and then over my head back at the parking lot, and then back at me.

"Uh, well, I thought I saw her get in the car with you earlier." His eyes muddled.

"That wasn't me. Do you know where they went?" I heard my voice speak the words, but I wasn't sure how, as my throat was rapidly constricting with fear.

He stepped forward and touched my shoulder. "No, ma'am, but I'd like to help you find her. Let me call my dad."

"Uh, no." That was just what I needed. Captain White Hair back in my business again.

"But why not? Do you think that someone has taken her?"

Taken her? As in kidnapped?

All of a sudden I felt the impact of it hit me in the face and I grabbed Adam's arm in response. Little dots of light hit me in the face and a moment of dizziness took control. It was almost like I'd felt right after I'd been drugged.

Just then, a siren sounded in the distance and we both looked up to see an unmarked car pull into the lot. It was Ty.

Adam and I walked over to meet him, and he jumped out of the car. His face was unreadable, but his presence spilled a dose of calmness over me that I couldn't explain.

"What's going on, Mandy? Sundae Giddings tells me that your car has been stolen and that she saw it near here earlier. Is something going on with Paget?" He eyed Adam and gave him a nod. "Adam Owens, what's the deal?"

I clenched my stomach and bent over at the waist. It was all hitting me now.

"Come on. Sit here." Ty pushed me down on the seat of his car.

"I saw her get in Ms. Murrin's car just about half an hour ago. It was weird because she didn't tell me that she was leaving. But we were running laps, just like we have to do at the end of practice, and she was all the way up there at the top of the hill. There was a woman driving it, and she had a scarf thingy tied around her head. That's all I could see from here. But I thought it was Ms. Murrin and figured that she'd picked her up today instead."

Ty looked at me. I was at a loss for words. My throat just wouldn't work.

"Mandy, when was your car stolen?"

I shook my head. Tears spilled down my face.

"Mandy. I need you to pull it together for a minute. We need to find Paget."

I coughed and then drew in a deep breath. *Come on, doctor, pull yourself up.*

"Ms. Lanier saw someone take it from my house earlier today. She thought it was me because she had red hair. And, well…" I motioned to my new dark-haired 'do. Ty nodded. "And now Adam says she was wearing a scarf on her head…and that sounds just like…"

"Allyson Harlow," Ty said. "But what would she be doing stealing your car and picking up Paget?"

"I don't know exactly, but I know she's involved with Officer Trask, and I know he's involved in this case somehow."

"This case? You mean the Caden Brooks case?"

I nodded and then wiped my face with the back of my hand. I watched as his eyes narrowed and his jaw clenched.

"Mandy, if one of my officers is involved in this mess then why didn't you tell me before now?"

"I don't know." I swallowed, and my throat felt absolutely swollen shut.

"You don't know?" He sounded incredulous.

"Colin and I have been trying to figure this out, but—"

"You and Colin? Geez, Mandy!" He stepped back and looked down at the ground. His hand went to the butt of his gun, which was attached to a hip holster on his belt.

"Don't yell at me," I said. Tears threatened the back of my eyes again.

"Uh, Detective Dempsey." Adam's voice sounded from nearby, but neither of us looked his way. We were too busy glaring at each other.

"Detective Dempsey." This time Adam's voice was a little louder.

"What is it, Adam?" Ty broke our stare-down to acknowledge the boy.

"Isn't that Ms. Murrin's car right there?" Adam pointed to Main Street, which ran just above the school.

I jumped up out of the car and we both focused on a Hollon Brothers' tow truck as it slowly made its way down the street. Its yellow light was flashing on top and Stella was chained to the back end. Stella's front end was smashed.

I screamed.

CHAPTER TWENTY-SIX

———

The tongue ties knots that the teeth cannot loosen.
–Irish Proverb

Paget was missing. Stella was wrecked. And I was a bundle of raw nerves and energy. So I spent the remainder of the evening cleaning the house. The thing is…I never clean. Unless I'm frustrated. When something is bothering me, I clean. The real kind of cleaning that people do about once a decade. The "crawling around on the floor and scrubbing" kind of cleaning. The "polishing the tile's grout with a toothbrush" kind of cleaning.

I was worried, frustrated, and more than a little bit pissed off. I wanted to blame someone, and the more I scrubbed, the more I wanted to find Allyson Harlow and punch her face in. What kind of dangerous games was that hussy playing?

I'd skipped dinner, and that was serious business. Ty had all but forced me to go home after we'd stopped the Hollon Brothers' truck and asked about how they'd come into possession of Stella. Apparently, Stella had been driven into a tree just blocks away from the school, and they'd gotten a call from the mailman when it had blocked his way in finishing his afternoon route. No one had seen the driver, and no one had seen Paget.

We were back at square one. And even though Ty and I suspected Allyson, we didn't have any hard proof that she was the one who'd picked up Paget. At my insistence, we'd driven by her apartment, but she hadn't been there. Ty had asked me to go home while he checked on her whereabouts and put together a search team for Paget. And he was going to question both Officer Trask and Matson Mills.

I'd gone ahead and spilled the beans about his fingerprints being on my drugged-up cocktail glass at O'Hannigan's. Ty had given me another deep frown and scolding headshake when I'd told him how I'd come into the information. He'd told me that the evidence would never stand up in court because of how it was illegally obtained and the fact that the chain of evidence was nonexistent.

I'd shrugged. I didn't really care about that. I didn't care about this stupid case. I only cared that Paget was found safe and sound. I wanted my sister back.

He'd taken me home, and Adam had agreed to drive Ms. Lanier's Caddy back to her. Ty had told me that he had to get the captain and the chief involved at this point. I didn't trust them, but he'd told me that procedure was procedure and that my opinions of the captain were a moot point.

I wanted to be the one out there searching, but he'd told me that being at home where she could find me was the best thing. I'd argued but had finally admitted he was right. When he'd mentioned that I should remain alert for a ransom notice, I'd crumbled into his arms.

The thought had been sobering and terrifying. I'd come home and turned into a cleaning, non-eating machine while I waited for news—hopefully good news—from Ty.

I tried not to panic. Paget had gone missing many times before. But the nefarious way in which she was picked up at school and my wrecked car left me feeling wrung out.

Half an hour, a phone call from Ms. Lanier, and two more clean rooms later, and I was bent over the side of the tub, trying to make the screw in the drain cover fit back in when a voice sounded behind me—almost making me fall headfirst inside.

"Very nice."

I slipped forward and dropped the screwdriver, making a loud clanging sound as I saw the inside of the tub rushing toward my face.

"Whoa…" A strong hand grabbed my arm and set me to rights before slowly lifting me backwards and helping me regain my balance.

I turned to look into the eyes—well, the toned abdomen—of Colin Brooks.

Heat flooded my face at the sight of him, and words started to spew forth.

"You. You are the person to blame here."

He took a step back, obviously caught off guard by my sudden mood swing.

"What are you doing here, anyway? Here to drop some more mysterious hints about things and then disappear? Here to bring me food and then take off when the cops get here—you're really good at avoiding them. Or…or…what are you here for? How do I even know that you *are* Colin Brooks? Maybe they were right. Maybe you are crazy like your mother. Maybe you killed Caden Brooks and you've just been sending me on a wild goose chase all week." I started running out of steam by this point in my rant, but something in his face had changed.

His face tightened, eyes locked with mine. A vein throbbed at his temple, and the scar I'd thought was charming before seemed to scream trouble at me. He was all business, and I hadn't seen this look in all the time I'd known him. It was downright scary, and I was suddenly more than a little afraid.

Oh, good job, Mandy. Go ahead and accuse him of being a murderer while you are here alone in the house with him and you're down on your knees with no weapon in sight. Brilliant!

He reached for me then, and I flinched. He stopped and then reached out again and helped me to my feet.

Now, face to face, I smelled his scent of clean linen and something spicy…just a little spicy…like…like…spiced orange…nutmeg and…a cup of warm tea that I wanted to snuggle up with? Oh, good grief. I was just plain starving again, but this man smelled amazing and my moments-ago fear had turned into…something entirely different.

His eyes softened, the thumb of his left hand traced the line of my jawbone, and his eyes searched mine.

I opened my mouth to speak, but he pressed his thumb over my lips and shook his head. He leaned forward as if to kiss me.

Did I want to be kissed by this man?

I didn't really know him. He was full of this mysterious past. He liked to disappear. He was mysteriously employed by the government. He may have been involved in his father's murder. He brought me food…he knew how to communicate with my sister…he looked and smelled just great…he was…

Not going to kiss me. I realized this just as I closed my eyes and felt the tip of his finger brush against my upper lip. Sort of a flicking-scooping-type motion.

I slowly opened one eye and then the other. He stared down at his finger, where a smudge of gray goop sat upon the tip. He lifted it to his nose and sniffed it. I tried to think of a way to inconspicuously crawl under the bathroom counter.

He looked up at me. "Caulking?" I nodded, and he shrugged. "You've been busy." He reached over and snatched a single square of toilet tissue off the roll and cleaned off his finger before tossing it in the trashcan.

I remained speechless and mortified.

Thankfully, he broke the silence. "How much do you want to know about me?"

Miraculously, my voice decided to work despite the fool I'd just made of myself. I waved my hand in front of me. "Everything."

He raised his eyebrows.

"Well…more than I know now, anyway."

He nodded. "Let me show you something." He reached down into the waistband of his jeans. I drew in a sharp intake of breath. What exactly was he going to show me?

He stopped moving at my reaction and then made eye contact with me. He smiled, and I blushed. He must think I was some desperate chick who craved male attention.

He was at least half right. Which half, I wasn't sure at the moment.

He continued his search and soon revealed a four-by-six photograph. I wondered if hiding pictures in the waistband of your jeans was some special trick they taught him at spy school.

As he lifted it up between us, there was a photo of a younger Caden Brooks, the same gray eyes as Colin, a beautiful blonde woman, and a toddler with a mischievous grin on his face.

I knew that grin. I'd just seen it right in front of me.

* * *

I took the photo and held it in front of me, studying it carefully. Something about the image haunted me, but I couldn't exactly figure out what it was. I flipped it over and read the back. *Caden, Maggie, and Colin on Christmas Day.*

"This is you and your parents?" It came out as a question, but I already knew the answer.

"Yes. This was the last time we were all together. Shortly after that, my father started hitting my mother. She threatened to go to the police. He threatened to declare she was crazy and have her locked up. She took me and left town, and he made sure that all traces of us were erased."

"Wow. That's one way to tell your life story. Abbreviate much?"

"Mandy, it is not something I like to talk about much, but my father was not a good man. I never really got to know him, but there were times when I wanted to. Shortly before he was killed, I made contact with him. I wanted to seek him out. I needed to."

I reached out and took his hand. He gave it a short squeeze.

"Come on. Let's go to the kitchen. I brought you something," he said.

I tossed the screwdriver on the counter and looked at myself in the mirror. My hair was frayed around the edges and partially loose from my effort at a pissed-off ponytail. My makeup was smeared, but at least my face was now sans the caulking paste. Then I lost sight of myself as he pulled me into the hallway.

When we arrived in the kitchen, I found Pickles lying there at his feet, chewing on a very large stick of something that looked like beef jerky. He grunted at me as I passed him. "You are so easily bought off." He grunted again.

A box of orange Tic Tacs sat at my place at the kitchen table.

I exhaled. This man may be full of mystery, a big fat snoop, a liar, a criminal. Heck, I had no idea what or who this man really was—but he knew how to make a girl happy. He knew how to make girls *and* dogs happy. He paid attention to things—the details. That's what he was—a detail man. If I only knew what the heck he was up to, he could very well be the man of my dreams.

He made his way to the counter. "I brought you one of the strawberry pies from the Back Porch. Ms. Maimie said it was one of your favorites."

"You spoke to Ms. Maimie about me?"

He pulled a knife from the drawer and started to slice up the pie. "Yes, when I heard about Paget…I knew you'd need a little something. Do you want one or two pieces?"

I sat down. I should feel insulted or embarrassed that he thought I would pig out on two pieces, but… "This feels like a two-piece kind of situation."

He grinned as he set down the plate in front of me. He was so infuriating…but cute. Insanely cute. At least something good could come out of this day. A hot guy serving me pie.

"Thank you."

"Mind if I join you?" Colin stood above with his piece of pie.

"Yeah. Yeah. Obviously you just come and go at will. What did you hear about Paget and why weren't you here when I needed you?"

He bit the inside of his cheek at my comment. I hadn't really meant to say it out loud, but the thought had been there and my filters weren't exactly working right today.

He sank into the chair and scooped up a bite of pie before responding. "I'm sorry about that, Mandy. Ty and his guys are out looking for her and I didn't think it was a good idea for me to stick my head into it right now. But if you want me to…just say the word."

"Not right now. I don't want to be alone. And, frankly, if you don't distract me here, I'll be out there searching for her with my Maglite." It had gotten dark outside and I wondered if Paget was alone or scared or hurt.

That was when I caught it—the look on his face. The first time I'd been able to read emotion on his face. I was actually seeing him for the first time, and it kind of felt good. It was only there for a second, and then it was gone. I had a feeling that he didn't get caught off guard too often.

"But I might need you to meet with Ty at some point."

His eyes bored into mine. He was the type of man that was rarely surprised—he had a knack for surprising everyone else, but he rarely had someone come at him, I could tell.

He placed the photo on the table and took a bite of pie. "Now why would I want to do that?"

"Colin, why me? Why did you come to me to help you with your father's case? How did you know that it was him—just based on overhearing my conversation with Penny that day? And why come back now?"

I didn't believe that Colin had anything to do with his father's death, but I wasn't one hundred percent sure of it. I did think that he knew more than he'd shared with me, and I intended on finding out what. Tonight.

"Mandy…" He leaned back in the chair and crossed his arms. I noticed the muscles in his forearms. It hadn't been the first time I'd noticed his arms and their attractiveness, but this time I followed them up to his throat, and I swore I could make out his steady pulse at the base of his neck.

I almost made a move to touch him. To let him know that I was there, but I took a huge bite of pie instead.

Some detail was niggling its way to the front of my brain. I tapped my fork on the edge of my plate and then speared another fat strawberry onto it. I was waiting. It was his turn to talk.

Just when I thought he was going to ghost out of there without saying any more, he started to talk.

"I've always used my sources to keep up with my family. A few years ago, I heard that my grandfather was on his death bed and I decided to come and see him."

"How'd that go over?"

"Surprisingly well. He was happy to see me. He apologized for my father's actions and asked me to check into the case of my father's disappearance. He said that he'd just known that the Mills were responsible."

"Why'd he think that?" I asked.

"Yeah, well, you know how it has always been between the Brooks and the Mills. I really thought these were just more crazy ramblings of the old man. You know, get one more jab in before died."

I swallowed down a clump of whipped cream and crust. "But?"

"But it played on my mind and I couldn't let it go. When I saw that he'd kind of silently claimed me in his obituary, it meant a lot to me."

"Yeah, I saw that."

He raised his eyebrows.

"You aren't the only one that can investigate stuff and keep secrets." I smiled. He reached over and wiped a smear of whipped cream off my chin and then stuck his finger in his mouth.

Grrr.

"Anyway, one day, I called the mayor. I just decided to go right to the source. I told him who I was and asked him if he knew anything about my father's disappearance. He basically told me to buzz off and that my father had just been skirt chasing, as was usually the case. And that he probably got himself killed by some jealous husband."

"Needless to say, that pissed you off?"

He ran his tongue over his top two teeth and leaned back in the chair again. "Just a little bit."

"I can see how it might. Then what?"

"Then I got a call out of the blue from Mrs. Mills."

I stopped eating for a moment. "You got a call from Myrna Mills? Why am I just now hearing this?"

He held up his hands in an "I surrender" display. "She told me that she'd overheard my phone call with the mayor and she wanted to set up a meeting with me. I planned to meet her last week, but she never showed up. I decided to stick around and see if I could catch up to her and coax this information out of her. I figured she'd gotten cold feet or that the mayor had found out what she planned to do and put the big hush on it."

My brain was starting to catch up. "And so, then you just happened to overhear my conversation with Penny and you took a wild guess that something was going down around here?"

He stood up and began to pace the room. "Only things have been going a bit crazy since then, and I can't help but wonder if I've put you and Paget in a bad situation by asking you to help me figure this out."

"Hey…" A tiny trickle of fear came over me, but I shook it off. I had a lifetime of guilt over not being the best big sister in the world, and tonight I was certainly feeling the heat, but being hysterical wasn't going to solve anything—I needed to focus on something else for a bit. "Look. We just need to line up all the details and work the equation."

This seemed to amuse him, and he grinned at me, which just made me hungrier, so I ate a huge bite of pie in response.

"Well, to start…someone killed my father, and I've thought it was the mayor all these years. But since you found his body and someone is after you to stop snooping around, I think there is something more going on here than we originally thought. I can't quite put my finger on it—but you are personally connected to this. Will you help me? Will you trust me—just for a little bit longer?"

I stopped mid-chew. "Who said I ever trusted you to begin with?"

"You've never called the cops on me despite the fact that I've all but broken into both your car and your home several times now. You've eaten every single thing I've brought you to eat despite the fact that I could have poisoned any of it—and you haven't even hesitated to wolf it down."

I set my fork down.

"And you've seen me with your sister, and we both know that she would be a damned easy target for me if I wanted to hurt you or manipulate you in some way. Yet you seem fine with me interacting with her."

I stood up from the table. My legs were a little shaky, so I held on to the table's edge. He made a good point—too good of a point.

"Are you saying that I should be afraid of you? Are you really an agent for the government, or are you just some shadow man that goes around breaking the law and living under the radar? And you didn't have anything to do with Paget's disappearance, did you?"

"No, Mandy." He walked to me and took my shoulders in his hands. "No."

We stared into each other's eyes for what seemed like forever.

"I'm saying that despite all my training to the contrary, I need you, Mandy Murrin, one of the smartest, most beautiful women I've ever met. I need you to help me solve the murder of my father so that I can—finally—put this part of my life behind me."

I didn't hear much after *most beautiful woman he'd ever met*, but I did hear enough to know that this man was in pain and he needed me to help him. Wasn't that what I did? Help others with their pain?

"Okay, Colin." I tried to cross my arms with confidence, but failed miserably when my lower lip trembled, proving just how tough I wasn't. "I'll help you figure this out, but you have to tell me more. You can't leave me in the dark and expect me to solve your problems. I have problems of my own. No car, no money, no job, and oh yeah—my sister is missing and I'm out on bail."

He leaned forward and kissed me on the cheek. His lips were soft and I felt a little woozy.

I sighed, then said, "I'm going to need a lot more Tic Tacs."

He grinned.

* * *

An hour later, we'd finished off the pie. Oh, okay, I'd finished off the pie. Still no word on Paget, and I'd called Ty at least a half-dozen times. After each call, Colin would jump right back into our discussion and try to pull my attention off my current crisis.

As a result, we now had one empty pie plate and one very long list of suspects. Colin had explained that for a crime to be committed, you needed motive, means, and opportunity.

There were a lot of folks on our list and all of them had one of the above, but we were having a hard time fusing it all together.

"We have Mayor Mills, but he's such an obvious suspect. And there's the part about him moving the body to his own office. I just don't get it." I tried to work through it from the top, one more time.

We sat there staring at our suspect list, and Colin tapped the pen on the notepad in a staccato rhythm. "We can't totally rule him out. He had it in for my father, and somehow my dad ended up in the mayor's attic."

"Okay, moving on to Mrs. Mills. She was definitely ready to spit nails when the cops were searching the house, but that may not be reason enough to accuse her. Any woman would be irritated about that kind of intrusion. Plus, I know she was hanging out with Allyson at the club for brunch earlier this week. Do you think those two could be in cahoots?"

"I think that family is connected to everyone in this town in one way or another," he said.

"But she did contact you after she overheard your conversation with the mayor. Do you think she wanted to confess to you?"

"Maybe. I couldn't get her to reach out to me again after she stood me up for our meeting. And don't forget that she showed up at the pub and had some kind of heated discussion with Trask. Something was going on there. I followed her briefly after that and couldn't garner any more information, but I did confirm one thing."

"What was that?" I sat up a little straighter, but my full tummy protested.

"She drives a Mercedes, just like the one that rolled up at the river house the day that you were crawling around in the bushes."

"I was not crawling around in the bushes. I was tailing a suspect." I'd done a good job, too. I raised my chin slightly. "Anyway, big deal. She showed up at her own house."

He looked amused. "Well, what are the odds that she'd pull up to the house at that very moment? When Mills, Matson, and Trask are there arguing over the unpleasant discovery in Mills' office."

I scrunched up my nose. "That's a little weak."

"Speaking of Matson, that little twerp has to be involved somehow." Colin switched gears.

"Well, yeah, he poisoned me with Rohypnol. That little twit is definitely on my radar. He pops up everywhere. He was there the morning I found the body. He was at the country club when I had it out with Allyson. And he was at Mills Landing having a chat with Trask when the mayor showed up in his heated rage. He's definitely up to something, but he's a bit younger than me. Wasn't he something like twelve years old when your father went missing?"

Colin rubbed his chin. "I think he's the type that is easily manipulated into anything. It just takes the right person to pull his strings. I wonder if that puppeteer is Trask. What about this housekeeper you mentioned? How long has she been working there?"

"That's a great question. I think I remember her from way back when we had a graduation party at Mills Landing. Yes, now that I think of it, I'm pretty sure she's been around almost forever. You mentioned that she brought Trask to the states when he was a baby. He's not too much older than I am, and I'll bet they've been with the Mills this whole time."

"Yeah, the file stated that the mayor actually sponsored her for U.S. citizenship. So, she's been a loyal member of the family for quite a while."

"Ha, loyal member? I have it on good authority that she and the mayor have been up to the hanky-panky biz for years." I scrunched up my nose at the image.

"On good authority? Whose good authority?" He sounded amused.

"Ms. Lanier's authority."

He gave me a comical eye roll. I smiled. But then I thought of Paget again and reached for my cell phone. He stopped my hand.

"Let Ty do his job. He'll find her. Let's keep going."

I attempted a deep, cleansing breath, but it caught in my tight chest.

Okay, I can do this. She's going to be fine.

"Amika was also there the day I found the body. And then she followed me at some point later that day. We had a disturbing little confrontation at the Thrifty Mart. I'm not sure if she was threatening me or warning me."

He stood up and ran his hand through his hair as he started his favorite pacing.

I stood up too, but made my way to the fridge to see if there was any Coke left over. I needed something to wash down all that pie, and since I'd never made it out to get groceries, I doubted there was any milk there. I found the soft drink and held it up to Colin, but was relieved when he waved off the offer. There was just enough for one glass, anyway, and I was parched.

Since there was a lull in our detective work, I grabbed a bag of marshmallows from the cabinet and stuffed one in my mouth. It wasn't exactly a healthy dinner, but the hour was growing late and all this detective work was helping to keep my mind off Paget's disappearance. Sort of.

Thinking of marshmallows made me think of Allyson. "Allyson Harlow. She's close with the Mills family and she's involved in all this somehow. I'd bet this bag of cloud-shaped delights on it."

He stretched his arms in front of him. "I know you don't like her, but the only thing we really have on her is that she has some secret with Trask, and possibly a relationship. And now possibly this business with your car and Paget, of course. But what does any of that have to do with the murder case?"

I stuck another marshmallow in my cheek and munched harder. "Owwifer Chooby," I managed to squeeze out.

"Who?" He leaned back against the counter and crossed his legs at the ankle.

"Chubby," I said.

"Trask, yes. He does seem to keep popping up. I need to check into him. I know that Captain Owens hired a whole new police force with the exception of Dempsey and Trask when he arrived here. My understanding is that Dempsey is a third- or fourth-generation cop and we are certain that Trask is sort of 'one of the family' when it comes to the Mills. Trask certainly could be involved in a cover-up and would have had the means and opportunity to move the body. But the why of the matter is really hanging me up here."

I remembered the way Captain Owens had taunted me at the jail. I didn't like the guy, but maybe we'd just gotten off on the wrong foot. "And therein lies another connection…Captain Owens and Douglas Mills. Old college buddies. The mayor gives him his job, and who's to say that he didn't bring him in specifically to hide this crime?"

I twirled a strand of my hair around my finger.

"Your sister does that, too." His voice interrupted my concentration.

"What?"

"Your sister twirls her hair like that."

I cut my eyes over to the strand of hair wrapped around my finger and then released the hair. "It's a terrible habit." My eyes started to tear up, but I shook it off.

"So, who else is on the list?" He got back to business.

"We're forgetting at least one more suspect here."

Colin gazed at me. "And that would be?"

"Well, *you*."

He pushed away from the counter and walked toward me. Stopping just inches in front of me, he reached out and ran his fingertips down the previously twirled strand of hair and then returned it to its place behind my shoulder.

My breath caught in my throat. "I don't mean—"

"Of course you're right," he said, interrupting me.

"I am?" I yelped. His close proximity suddenly made me very nervous.

"Yes, they'd gladly pin this on me, if they could. And I understand why they accused me. It's easy to accuse someone you don't know. Someone that is a stranger. Someone that disappeared so easily and left no trace behind. They could say that I was the black sheep of the family with a vendetta against my father. The Mills have hated the Brooks, and vice versa, for a long time—so why not? And that opens up a can of worms about my mother. And, well, I can't talk to her about any of this. She cut off contact with me when she found out I came to see my grandfather." He paused, seeming thoughtful.

"I'm sorry, Colin."

"The thing is…our minds are full of all these suspects with all these seemingly extraneous motives. But it's as if…there is more than one plot going on here." He switched gears faster than a professional drag racer.

Wc locked eyes. "I think you're right." I managed the words. But all I could focus on were his lips.

"Mandy, I think we're looking at multiple conspiracies here. Now we just have to figure out how to prove it."

A heartbeat passed…and then two. I held my breath.

"Maybe we should call it a night. You seem tired."

His words felt like he'd ripped off a Band-Aid when I wasn't ready.

The moment was gone…almost.

"Can you stay with me until I hear something about Paget?" The question surprised even me.

He touched my face. I reached up and touched the scar on his chin.

I jumped when a knock sounded on the kitchen door. I spun around, took the few steps to the door, and snatched it open without a breath's hesitation.

And there, in the shadows of the porch light, was Adam Owens with my sister in his arms.

CHAPTER TWENTY-SEVEN

There is no thing wickeder than a woman of evil temper.
–Irish Proverb

The phone woke me from a deep sleep, and it took me a moment to realize that I hadn't been dreaming the nightmare about Paget. I bolted upright and then realized my phone was crammed in my pocket. I wedged it out to answer it with a frantic, "Hello."

"Mandy, we found Allyson. She has a solid alibi. I don't think she took your car." Ty's voice met my ears as I watched Paget snoozing in bed.

"Huh, yeah. Well, I'd like to hear more about this solid alibi. 'Cause I have reason to believe she was involved." I squeezed my left hand tightly, feeling the soft object curled up inside.

"Look, just because you two have hated each other for your entire lives…that doesn't mean she is out to get you at every turn." Ty was trying to convince me, but to no avail.

"Really? I beg to differ. She's just moved up to a larger scale than name calling and boyfriend stealing is all that's changed, Ty."

I bit the inside of my cheek as I tried to rein in my temper. I stood and started pacing the room.

"How's she doing?" Ty's voice changed tone as he inquired about my sister.

I walked to her bedside and watched her slow and steady breathing under the purple and green afghan. I'd wrapped it around her after I'd bathed and dressed her. She'd slept peacefully after Dr. C. had come by to check her out. He'd administered a shot of a strong sedative to ensure her calmness.

"She's okay, Ty. But…it was lucky that Adam thought to go back to the high school to look for her. It was smart of him to think about doing that on his own."

"Yeah, he's a good kid, Mandy. He's responsible. His parents have done a good job with him."

I turned to look out the window at the early-morning sun. I wasn't so sure about his father. For all I knew, he was involved in this whole murder cover-up. Although I did have to agree with Ty on this point: Adam seemed to be a smart, responsible kid in every way that mattered.

"What now, Ty? Any new information on what happened with Stella? I mean, you said you were going to question Trask and Matson. Were they involved somehow?"

I tried to picture Matson wearing a red wig and stealing my car in broad daylight. The image was beyond laughable. And Trask? Well, I didn't see that happening. Now that I thought about it, though, he hadn't seemed all that shocked when I'd reported Stella stolen, now, had he?

"The Mills are locked up tight by their attorney. He wouldn't let me get even five minutes with Matson. And, honestly, we have absolutely nothing tying him to the car theft or the Paget situation. I did try to push him on your drink tampering, but again…we have nothing official for me to work with there." He paused and cleared his throat. I knew that sound. It was something he did when he was trying to get his own temper under control.

He was, of course, referring to Colin's little behind-the-scenes fingerprint gathering. Colin had helped me get Paget in the house last night and his presence had seemed to soothe her. That fact had not gone unnoticed. He'd slipped out somewhere between Dr. C. arriving and Ms. Lanier stopping by to check on us. I'd found a note on my pillow when I'd gone in to retrieve the afghan for Paget. He'd told me to meet him at the café at noon.

I was looking forward to seeing him again, but I had business to take care of first.

"And Traskbauer?" I used Trask's real last name.

He remained silent for a moment. "Yeah, well…sounds like you've been doing a little checking up on him. But the fact that you think he's involved with Allyson and your account of

Mrs. Mills slapping him at O'Hannigan's isn't really enough for me to suspend him, Mandy. He denies all of it. I'm sorry. I just don't have enough to go on."

I let out a pent-up breath. Paget stirred behind me with a groan, followed by a loud yawn.

"I've got to go, Ty. Paget is waking up and I want to talk to her."

"Mandy, wait…I need to—"

"Talk to you later, Ty." I ended the call.

I knew what he was going to say and there was no way I was going to wait for him to get there to question her. I was going to chat with my little sister about her evening's events and I was going to confirm what I already knew: Allyson Harlow was involved in her abduction and I was going to end her torment on my life today.

I looked down at the soft object in my hand. It was a dirtied polka-dot scarf, and I knew just who it belonged to.

* * *

"Mandy?" Paget's voice was small. I looked up and smiled at her, walking to her bedside.

"Hey there, Page. How're you feeling?"

She looked so tiny—so frail. I tried to control my desire to gather her in my arms. I wanted to do that so terribly, but I knew that such an outward display of affection might set her off, and she seemed relaxed at the moment.

She smiled at me and then looked down at her hands. I sat next to her and smiled in what I hoped was a calming way.

"Are you mad at me, Mandy?"

Her words surprised me. A little pain in my chest blossomed like a garden of dandelions.

"I'm never mad at you, honey. Why would I be mad?"

She fiddled with her bed sheet. "'Cause you said that I shouldn't get in a car with strangers. But it was kind of confusing, 'cause it was your car."

I squeezed the back of my neck. Tension knots had formed there. I had to proceed with caution here. If you pushed her in the wrong way, she would clam up, and that would be the end of that.

"Hey, I'll get Ms. Lanier to call Adam and see if he can come by and see you in a little while. Would you like that?" I tried a method of pure bribery. It usually worked on teenagers. Maybe my sister wouldn't be any different.

Her face lit up, and then she started picking at the nail bed of one of her fingertips.

"Page…"

She didn't look up.

"Page, I need you to tell me what you remember about last night."

She picked at her nail again and I almost tried to stop her, but I refrained from the contact.

"Paget, look at me."

She stopped the fingernail assault and looked up at me.

"What do you remember about yesterday? Do you remember who that was in my car that picked you up? My car had a little accident. Do you remember that?"

She closed her eyes and held her breath. I waited.

"She said you sent her to pick me up. She said that I could drive the car. And you know, all the girls my age drive cars. I wanted to drive so badly. But…"

I ran my tongue over my top teeth. I swallowed back the fury that threatened to overtake me.

"But what, Page?" I struggled to keep my voice calm and on an even keel.

Paget opened her eyes and began picking the same nail again. Over and over again. It was a stress-reducing habit she had. She appeared calm to the human eye, but if you were to reach up and stop her, she would go into a fit.

I had to tread carefully here.

"Did you drive Stella? Where did you go?"

"We didn't go very far. I ran into a tree. That driving is harder than I thought. I'm so sorry, Mand." Her words came out in rapid succession and she didn't make eye contact with me.

"Hey, Page. I'm not mad, okay? Are you okay? Did you get hurt?"

Pick. Pick. Pick.

"No, I'm not hurt. But I got scared. I got a little lost. I walked around, but then I wasn't sure if I should come home. I'm supposed to wait for Adam. So I went back to the school. You know, he walks me home from there every day."

"Yes, I know, Paget. I know about Adam."

"He's cute. Isn't he, Mand?"

I looked down and saw a trickle of blood coming from Paget's nail bed. She didn't seem to notice as she stared off into a blank void.

"Yes he is, Page. He's very cute. Can you tell me anything about the woman who was driving my car. The woman who let you drive?"

I pulled a Kleenex from the box on the bedside table and gently wrapped it around her finger. She looked down at her hand then back up at me and blinked once.

"When do you think Adam will come by to see me? I need to brush my hair."

"Yes, Paget. He can come and see you. Don't worry about that right now. I need to know who the woman was that picked you up from school."

Warm tingles coursed up my chest and into my neck. I was trying to hold myself in check but was struggling to maintain patience.

She suddenly seemed sad. "I don't know who she was, Mandy. She looked familiar, but I don't know her. She left that pretty scarf and I brought it for you. Did you get that? I folded it and put it in my pocket."

"Yeah, I got it, Page. Don't worry."

* * *

And just like that, I'd lost my connection with her. It wasn't unusual for her brain to shut down memories when they disturbed her. And right now, her scattered memories were more than disturbing me.

Dr. C. arrived just after I'd settled Paget in with some television and a snack. I left Pickles perched on the foot of her bed.

"Everything okay here?"

"Yep," I lied.

He frowned. "Okay, then." He stood in the living room with me. His eyes knowing but un-accusing.

"Thanks, Dr. C."

"Panda, you know I'd do anything for you girls. Are you sure you can't tell me what is going on? I feel like I'm letting Patty down by not taking better care of you."

I walked to him and put my hand on his shoulder. "She loved you. She would never feel let down by you. And we will be fine soon—you just wait and see. I'm going to get this whole thing settled, and then we'll have you over for dinner."

He grinned, but his eyes remained creased with worry.

"Oh, and Dr. C.—I realized something last night."

"What's that?"

"I won't need you to put Paget on that waiting list after all. I'm the one who needs to take care of her. I'm staying put for now. I won't let anyone hurt her." My voice was surprisingly confident and determined, even to my own ears.

At my words, he reached out to embrace me, and I gave him a brief hug. Then I stepped back toward the door. I had to deal with this.

"You don't mind staying with her a few minutes while I get Ms. Lanier to come over?"

"Of course not, Panda. Are you sure you're all right?" He asked, though I expect he knew the answer.

"Right as rain, Dr. C."

My heart was heavy as I turned and left the house. There was nothing else for me to say here. Everything I had to say was to one high school nemesis, and I knew just where to find her.

But first, I needed some wheels.

CHAPTER TWENTY-EIGHT

———

There's many a ship lost within sight of harbor. –Irish Proverb

"Ms. Lanier, put that thing away!" I wasn't even sure how she was able to hold it up with one hand, but she'd answered the door with gun in hand.

"Oh, sorry, sweetie. With all the car stealing, murder, kidnapping, and other garbage going on in the town, a little old lady has to be prepared to take matters into her own hands. This here's Betty Lou, and I'd like to see someone try to come between me and her."

"Well, put it down for now. Would you mind sitting with Paget for a bit? I need to borrow your Caddy again."

"Aw, heck. I let Adam drive it home last night after he brought Paget home. He's going to bring it by later."

I nodded. It was obvious that Ms. Lanier trusted him. Paget trusted him. And, after last night, his stock had certainly skyrocketed in my estimation. But I really needed a car right now.

"Can you call me a cab, then? Dr. C. is over there with Paget now and I need to get a move on."

Ms. Lanier opened her mouth as if to ask where I was going, but then got distracted. "Did you say Dr. Cavello is there?"

"Yes, he came by to check on Paget again." I stepped inside while she rang Millbrook's only cab company.

"I'll need to freshen up my makeup before I head over, then." Her voice was giddy.

* * *

I took Coosada Concierge Service to The Country Club. Of course, this cab service was really just one eighties-style Oldsmobile Cutlass driven by Scabby Hollon. His brothers owned the wrecker service, but Scabby had decided to go out on his own and start a concierge service—or so he called it. I'm not sure how much business he did—except on homecoming night and prom night. Those nights keep him in business.

He eyed me in the rearview mirror, but he kept silent until we pulled up to the front gate of the club.

"Are you sure you want to go here?"

Sure, I'd been awake all night and hadn't showered before my departure this morning, but geez…I must look bad if a man named Scabby was worried about my appearance.

"Yes, thank you."

"That'll be $19.50, not including tip."

I reached down for my purse and realized that I'd forgotten it.

Oh, crappaccino.

"Um…I don't seem to have my purse on me."

He gave me a look of disbelief as if he'd heard this one a million times. "Well then, we'll just turn around and go back to the house and get it. Then you can pay me double." He shifted the car into reverse.

"Wait…" I shot out my hand in a palm-up motion.

I looked around. What could I do? I just knew that Hussy Harlow would be here at the club this morning. It was brunch time and she'd be here—sucking up to Millbrook's elite and covering her latest crimes. "I'll get you the money, I swear. I just really need to get in there right now."

He shook his head. "Nope. I know how you young kids are these days. Full of promises and you never follow through. That's what's wrong with this whole new generation."

"I'm not a young kid—I'm twenty-eight years old."

He gave me an I-was-born-in-the-morning-but-not-this-morning face.

The beep of a horn drew our attention behind us. There sat a work truck trying to get through the entrance.

"We've gotta move now. I'll run you back to the house."

"Ahhh…" I yelled out, and jumped from the car. There was no way I was going back home right now. Not until I had it out with the hussy.

"You hold it there, missy." Old Scabby jumped out of the driver's seat a lot faster and smoother than I would have ever guessed he could.

"What seems to be the trouble here?"

We both turned to look at the driver of the truck we were blocking. There was the kind face of the groundskeeper for the club. I smiled, and his face lit up with recognition.

"Hi, Rigo."

"It is the cable girl, no?"

I couldn't help but grin at him. He was a sight for sore eyes.

"Yes. I need to pay Mr. Hollon here, but I seem to have forgotten my purse. My sister has been in a little accident and, well, I need to see someone…" It sounded kind of lame to my own ears.

"What can I do to help?" The words were like music to my ears. Finally, someone wanted to help me—no questions asked.

"She owes me $19.50."

Rigo shrugged and reached into his pants pocket, extracting an old, beaten-up wallet. He pulled out a twenty and handed it to Scabby. Scabby grunted in return and got back into the car.

"Thank you, Rigo."

"Hop in the truck, I'll drive you to the main building." I did as he asked and got in, then he backed up—allowing the Oldsmobile to make its departure with a full fifty-cent tip in hand.

We made the ride to the main building and around the back to the service entrance in silence. After he parked, he turned to look at me.

"I don't make it my business to get involved in other people's business, but…I'm not sure if you want to go in there right now."

I couldn't stop myself from blushing. Here was this displaced hurricane survivor, and he actually felt bad for me.

"Rigo. I owe you."

He shrugged. "Twenty dollars is just twenty dollars. You seem to need something much more. What can I do to help you, miss?"

My eyes teared up. Dang these eyes. They kept threatening to cry, and I didn't have time for that.

"Someone is messing with my life. No, no...they've completely wrecked my life—what little life I actually had in the first place. I've lost my job, my life's dream, and they've had me arrested." His eyes softened as he took in my expression. I continued, "And now, some two-bit hussy named Allyson Harlow has made it known to me that she's involved in all of this by hurting my sweet, innocent sister—she kidnapped her from the school and she was lost for most of the night."

His eyes widened. "Have you told all of this to the police?"

I let out a little bark of laughter, but there were tears behind it. I swallowed them down. "The police think I'm crazy. That I've made false reports. And what's worse, some of them may be involved in the whole thing. Of course it's not true—I'm just being used as the scapegoat to protect the mayor for murder."

"Mayor Mills killed someone?"

I shook my head. "I don't know. I thought so, but there are so many suspects and I'm not sure how to iron all this out."

He shrugged. Poor Rigo. I was pouring all this mess out on him, and he was trying his best to make sense of it. That made two of us.

"So, what now? You go in there and confront Ms. Harlow? While she's in there with her boyfriend?"

"Her boyfriend?" My blood ran hot, then cold. Was Ty actually in there with her right now? Or was it Officer Chubby? Who could keep up with all her conquests these days?

"Yes. Uh, the young Mills—I think his name is Matson? Strange name, but no one asked me."

Matson Mills and Allyson Harlow were a couple? My brain tried to connect the dots. The dots. The dots. The polka-dot hussy. Things were starting to become clear. Images popped up in my head one by one like a computer without a good ad blocker.

"Are you sure, Rigo? Mayor Mills' son and Allyson are a couple?"

He nodded vigorously. "Yes, they've been flirting on the tennis courts and in the clubhouse. I don't like it. It is not respectful to the facility. I saw her..." He cleared his throat and looked down at his hands. "She goes topless into the men's steam room this one day, and I saw them together. I thought about telling my boss, but you learn that the less you see the better."

It was *her* perfume. I'd smelled it on Matson when he'd pretended to be the waiter. I just hadn't put her together with him.

Rigo's words were suddenly making me feel better. His calming demeanor made me realize that confronting Allyson was not my best course of action right now. There were more people involved than I thought. Just like Colin said, it was a web of connections and conspiracies. And if there was one thing I'd learned in med school, it was how solve a difficult problem.

We did something call a co-lab. It was all about collaboration—we'd all gather together and bring what we knew to the table and work to solve a complex problem.

Put them all together in the beauty shop and let them hash it out together.

That was what Sundae had suggested, and that was what we needed now. Excitedly, I turned to Rigo and grabbed his arm. He jumped in surprise.

"Rigo, could I bother you for one more favor?"

CHAPTER TWENTY-NINE

———

Reputations last longer than lives. –Irish Proverb

A couple of hours later, Rigo dropped me off at The Back Porch Café. I couldn't help but think that it was kind of like a scene in a movie where everyone stops eating and talking and all eyes are on you. I stood there, frozen in time, and everyone stared back—in silence.

Of course, maybe I was just imagining that. My brain was full of everything that I'd spent planning for the last two hours while Rigo had allowed me to use his office, his phone, and his landscaping dry-erase board. After all, every good co-lab needed a board for brainstorming, and I'd drawn a dozy.

Then my train of thought was derailed as Ms. Maimie Rogers approached me, wearing a pair of gold, glittery pumps and a smile. "Come on, now. Let's seat you over here, sweetie. I have you all set up in this booth."

I watched her feet as I allowed her to lead me to the first booth on the right, and she sat me down with care. Those shiny glitter-embossed gold pumps were something to behold. You could take a girl out of Vegas, but you couldn't take the Vegas out of a showgirl—or a sixty-something-year-old woman, as the case may be.

"What can I get you to eat, shug?"

"Just water, please."

She took a step back and put her right hand over her heart. "Okay, now. I know I'm getting older, but I swear Dr. C. hasn't said a word about my hearing going bad. Did you just say…water?"

I smiled at her—weakly. I was nervous, and my rare lack of appetite became evident when I was at my absolute peak of apprehensiveness. Even then, it was a rare occurrence. "Yes, ma'am, I need to get this behind me, and then I'll feel better."

"Well, all right then." She took a step back and looked as if she wanted to say more, but the bell over the front door jingled and drew her attention that way.

Colin Brooks walked in, and now all eyes were on him. But as soon as he caught my eye, Ms. Maimie made herself scarce and he took the seat across from me.

Colin had asked me to meet him here at noon and here he was—right on time.

"Are you okay?" He reached across the table and took my hands gently in his. I'd be lying if I didn't say that his touch did wonders for both my tired body and my current state of nerves. So much so that a tinge of appetite began surfacing in the form of my stomach emitting a very loud growl.

He smiled, and I bit my lip. Keeping secrets. This had never been my strong point, and I was about to give it all away with the look on my face. This man was no dummy, and he'd figure out my plan before I could count to ten if I didn't keep myself under control. And everything had to go as planned—or this crap storm that I called life would never get back in order.

"Anyway, I was able to question Paget earlier this morning. She didn't know the woman who took her from school, but she did have this, and I haven't shown the police yet." I reached into my pocket and pulled out the polka-dotted scarf. I pushed it across the table, and he examined it.

"And you know who this belongs to?"

"Yes, and I've figured out part of the reason why they did it. You see, when we made our list of suspects last night, we just didn't have enough information to put together all the connections between the suspects. Then today, I found out that two of our suspects were in a relationship, and that was the thing that helped me to start connecting the dots."

"Who was it?"

"Well, we had thought that someone was involved in this who was deliberately trying to involve me. But we couldn't figure out who, or why anyone would want to get me involved specifically. I mean, I only accidentally found the body. I shouldn't have had anything else to do with this. Why me?"

The bell sounded over the door, and I broke my focus on Colin to look up. He didn't turn around, but I saw his jaw clench ever so slightly. It was almost as if he knew who was going to come walking through that door next.

Ty Dempsey strode into the café and made his way to our booth. He slid in next to me, and I was left momentarily speechless by the face-to-face meeting of Colin and Ty. No one spoke.

I caught sight of a waitress as she began her approach to our table, and I opened my mouth to warn her off. But before I could utter a word, Ms. Maimie swooped in and guided her away. I stifled a smile.

"Colin Brooks, I presume?"

Colin sat back in the seat and stretched his legs forward. His jean-clad calf made contact with my leg under the table, and my breath caught in my throat. He tapped his fingers on the surface of the table, but otherwise made no response or comment to Ty's question. But his non-verbal answer spoke volumes.

"I don't know what kind of little games you've been playing, but I know that you won't be leaving my jurisdiction without answering some questions."

I watched Ty. He exuded a confidence I hadn't seen since many years ago. It was the kind of confidence that could make a girl give in to almost, well...to almost anything.

"I'm pretty sure I'll come and go as I please. There are no charges against me and you can't hold me here." Colin's voice jolted me out of a short detour to fantasyland. He used a completely different tone when talking to Ty. I almost didn't recognize it—and it sort of gave me chill bumps.

"Hold on. Hold on. Boys...we have a lot of things to discuss, and let's not get into a mine's-bigger-than-yours scenario quite yet."

They both turned to look at me. Okay, so maybe it was just me who was seeing that scenario play out in my mind.

Ty broke the awkward silence. "What you are doing with Allyson's scarf? You didn't go and do something crazy, did you?"

All three of us looked down at the scarf. I hadn't revealed its owner's identity yet to Colin, but I watched his face as he took in the information. His eyebrows shot up a notch as he watched my face for a reaction.

"No. No dead Allyson. Of course, the day is still young." My voice was wistful even to my own ears. I despised the woman.

Ty cleared his throat. He knew every reason why I had it out for her.

As if on a stage director's cue, Allyson Harlow arrived wearing her signature polka dots, but this time donning a pale pink polka-dotted halter-top, white tennis skirt, and a white sunhat with matching pink scarf tied around it. She sauntered into the café, her Dooney & Bourke bag dangling mid forearm as she removed her sunglasses and surveyed the room.

Out of the corner of my eye, I saw Colin slide the scarf off the table and out of sight.

But all other eyes were on Allyson—as was usually the case.

Her gaze focused in on Ty, and her mouth formed a wide, plump-lipped upward curve. Then she caught sight of me next to him and her expression shifted to a tight-lipped fury. She teetered over and ran her tongue over too-white teeth as she thrust her bosom forward and studied Colin. With no lack of interest, she grinned at him. I got more than a little thrill out of the fact that he didn't seem to return her interest. Score one for Colin.

"I don't believe I've had the pleasure…" she said, addressing Colin, and held out her hand toward him.

Does anyone really say that anymore?

He stared down at her hand, but didn't take the bait. "No, you haven't," was his only reply.

Score two for my secret agent. Internally, I was screaming with delight and cheering on a silent victory. Maybe there was one man in this town who wasn't easily manipulated by Ms. Harlot and her double Ds.

She gave a sultry smirk and seemed to be calculating how to approach the meeting already in progress. So she decided to start with what she did best—attacking me.

"So, when you phoned me, Mandy, you indicated that you had something that belonged to me." She gestured to Ty. "I didn't know you meant *my* boyfriend."

"I'm not—" Ty started to rebut her statement, but she interrupted.

"Well, I don't know if you'd call it a real boyfriend-girlfriend relationship. More like just sex, sex, and more sex."

My face heated up like sun on a vinyl car seat, and I couldn't stop my treacherous head from snapping around accusingly at Ty.

He had the good graces to look embarrassed by her declaration. "It was just that one time, Allyson."

It made me feel a little sick to my stomach, but truth be told...I had no claim to this man and his sex life. I guess I never had.

"Come on, Ty. Tell the truth. It was one night, but not just one time."

Ack. Was there any man in this town that hadn't seen her marshmallows?

"So, you're here with Ty. Is this your way of announcing to the world that you two are back together?" Allyson didn't miss a beat. "I mean, why wouldn't he go for the poor, feeble Mandy Murrin? He always did have a hero complex. And you and your pitiful little sister are just perfect for him. How is your sister, anyway?"

Her voice grated through me, and my skin felt as if it were peeling and cracking. My brain pulsed with long lost words that I wanted to say to this woman. She'd made my life difficult for most of my childhood. And now, she'd personally attacked both me and my sister. It was almost too much for me to fathom.

She tapped her toe on the floor of the café, and for a few moments it was all I could focus on. This confrontation was sinking fast, and I couldn't find my life vest. I was too tired. I just wanted to go home and forget all of it. Then...

"Ms. Harlow, is it?" Colin's voice pulled me back from the darkness.

I hadn't realized that I'd closed my eyes until they sprang open, and I noticed he was watching me. Everyone was watching me. But he was speaking to her.

"Yes. You seem so familiar but…where do I know you from?" Allyson was trying to line up her next victim. It was no secret that she used sex to manipulate men, and she seemed to have her hand in every cookie jar in town. Only, I knew her secret—she'd always loved Ty, and it was clear that he'd never returned the sentiment.

"Oh, you don't know me. But I know you, and I believe you have some explaining to do. Isn't that right, Mandy?"

His leg brushed up against mine again, under the table, and my heart started to beat at a steadier pace. Just that small touch of reassurance directed me back on track. In that moment, I started to refocus, and I reached out my hand to tap it on the table in rhythm to my words.

"Yes, that's right. Care to explain to us why your scarf was in the possession of my sixteen-year-old sister who was abducted from school yesterday in my stolen car?"

As I tapped out the last three words, Colin returned the scarf to the table, and the three of us watched Allyson's smirking face turn sour.

"That's not mine. You can purchase that at any department store," she sputtered.

"Let me see that." All eyes redirected to a deep voice coming from the bar area just behind Allyson.

There sat Captain Owens. He'd spun the bar stool around and was reaching out for the scarf in question.

Yes! He'd been sitting there the entire time—listening in. Just as I'd had Ty ask him to do. I wondered if he'd arranged for the other things I'd asked. Only time would tell. I took a quick peek at the wall clock over the bar.

Ty handed him the scarf and then looked back at me. Question upon question boiled inside his eyes, but I didn't have time for explanations now. My attention was battling itself for focus between Allyson's face and the captain's examination of the scarf.

"I'm not much for fashion. But correct me if I'm wrong, Ms. Harlow—do all department stores monogram their scarves with the initials A. H. down in the corner?"

Boom chica boom, bitch.

"Well, I...I really don't know how it got in the hands of little Paget. I assure you."

The bell over the café door rang again and in walked Mayor Mills. I hadn't seen him in person in, well, years. But he was the same suit-wearing, plump-bellied, fake-smiling politician as always. He took in the gathering of persons of interest in front of him, and he didn't look happy.

"Owens...Dempsey...what is going on here, exactly? And captain, why was I told that there was an emergent issue going on at the café?"

Ty bit back a smile, and Colin made a sound like a laugh-cough, but no one answered the mayor.

Captain Owens stood up and gestured to us. "I believe we have a criminal amongst us, sir."

Mayor Mills looked in my direction, but then his eyes settled on Colin.

"Who is this?"

"I'm Colin Brooks. You might remember my father, Caden Brooks." Colin's voice was as cold as ice.

"Not him. Her." I couldn't stop myself from breaking up the awkward reunion. I nodded toward Allyson.

She shook her head and pressed her well-manicured hand to her chest with indignation. "This is ridiculous. This...this *felon*...who is already out on bail for lying to the police, and Ty Dempsey, who I believe is in a relationship with her, are trying to accuse me of something. I think they believe that I stole Mandy's car and abducted Paget from school and then wrecked her car and left behind my scarf. The whole thing is outrageous. They obviously planted one of my scarves and are just trying to frame me. It is just a ridiculous accusation, and I won't be ridiculed here and made a fool of in public."

"For someone who wasn't involved in yesterday's events, you sure seem to know a lot about it." I interjected.

"Hmmph. Tell her, Ty. I've already been cleared in all that."

"Well, I didn't say you were cleared, exactly." Ty looked back and forth between me and Allyson. "I said that I'd check out your alibi, and it appears to be solid. She was being honored by the Millbrook Service League for outstanding community service at the time of the abduction."

"Community service? Is that what they're calling it these days?" I couldn't resist the jibe.

A beat of silence followed, and then: "Andy, is that what's going on here?" The mayor was addressing Captain Owens.

But it was my voice that answered once again. "Actually, sir, we're here to accuse her of much, much more than that. I believe that she and her accomplice have not only committed this nasty business with my car and my sister, but they've left me a threatening note. I wouldn't doubt it if they were involved in moving Caden Brooks' body to your office and even intentionally poisoning my drink." My voice surprised me. It was as if it had a mind of its own today. Different parts of my body seemed to do that a lot lately. I wondered if that could be a real medical issue.

"Now, let's not get ahead of ourselves," Captain Owens, a voice of reason, jumped in.

Once again, the bell chimed over the door, and silence fell over our mini-mob. Another piece of our puzzle walked in with an attractive older woman in tow. They each wore their own set of country club tennis whites. One of the duo was Matson Mills, and the woman on his arm was Mrs. Mills. She looked at the two men who stood at the end of our booth with a blank expression.

But I watched Matson's eyes, and they were focused on Allyson, although she made a great effort to avoid eye contact with him.

"Douglas, why have you told us to join you here? Are we meeting these people for breakfast?" Her voice sounded a little sluggish, and I wondered if she was on something. Perhaps a little anti-anxiety mixed in with her morning mimosa.

"Hello, dear. I'm not exactly sure myself. Apparently some crime has been committed and Andy Owens here seems to think that I should now be involved in every ongoing case in town. I'm starting to wonder if I need to find someone else to do *his* job."

I watched Captain Owens, and he seemed to be getting a little hot under the collar at the mayor's wrist slap of a comment. He turned to me. "This is your chance, Ms. Murrin. Let's hear your theory. 'Cause one scarf is not going to settle the case here."

I sat up a little straighter and gathered up the little energy I had left. "We're still missing two people, sir. But we'll get started."

Mayor Mills gawked at me. "Do I know you, young lady?"

My mouth dropped open in surprise. Was it possible that this man for whom a cable service call to his house had been the very start of the downfall of my life had no clue as to my identity? Way to hurt a girl's ego.

"Mayor, this is Mandy Murrin. She's the one who reported the discovery of a body in your freezer," Captain Owens said, filling in the blanks.

Mayor Mills looked me up and down. His nose rose and scrunched as if he'd smelled something bad, and I had the sudden urge to sniff my armpits. Geez. I mean, I knew I hadn't had a shower since, well, since yesterday morning. But give a girl a break.

"And we are here to what? Have a community leaders' luncheon with her here in the café?"

Now I knew where Matson Mills got his spoiled brat attitude. I cast a quick glance at Brat Boy, and he stood there with a look of longing directed at Allyson. If he hadn't slipped me drugs, I might almost feel sorry for him.

Almost.

"No, sir, we are here to find out exactly who in your family really killed Caden Brooks," I answered.

CHAPTER THIRTY

———

Patience is a plaster for all sores. –Irish Proverb

In that moment, it felt like the entire café was in a state of suspended animation. So I took the opportunity to bring everyone up to date on the case.

"Ten years ago, I was a senior in high school. I didn't know Caden Brooks, and with the exception of finding his dead body and meeting his son just a few days ago, I doubt I ever would have known anything about the man. But since he and his death have become the focus of my life, I've taken it upon myself to help put this case to rest." I paused to look at Colin. He gave me a small smile of encouragement.

The mayor and the captain both took him in and gave each other a suspicious glance. Mayor Mills pointed at Colin, who was now standing outside the booth, leaning back on a newspaper dispenser as if he were on a midday lunch run. How had he gotten out of the booth without me noticing? I had to get him to teach me his moves some day.

"What are you doing back in town? When you phoned me I told you to crawl back under whatever rock you've been hiding under all these years. No one in my family had anything to do with your father's death."

"Oh, are we telling the truth about things now?" Colin said.

"Are you capable of telling the truth? I didn't know that any of the Brooks clan was familiar with the term." Mayor Mills got in his jibe, but no one seemed to enjoy it but him.

"Are you seriously going to stand here, in front of all these people, and try to convince us that no one in your family had anything to do with my father's death when the body was found in your home and then in your office?"

My heart reached out to him.

"Well, what about you?" the mayor said. "Are we just supposed to believe you because you reappear back in town all of the sudden and the body happens to show up at the same time? Doesn't anyone see how convenient that is?"

He had a good point, but I was feeling protective of Colin right now. "Uh, excuse me…Mr. Mayor. But before you start throwing around accusations at Colin, how about taking a good look at your boy wonder here."

Matson, all but forgotten since his entrance, had started inching his way toward the door. His mother was sitting at the bar, staring off into space.

"Where do you think you're going?" Mayor Mills yelped, and Matson returned to stand beside his mother.

"Dad," he whined, "I want to get out of here. This whole thing is stupid. He did it and she's trying to frame you. Finding that body in the attic and then moving it to your office. They're trying to make a fool of our family. You always said that you can't trust a Brooks. And Allyson said that Mandy was here to destroy our family and that we needed to scare her back out of town. Only she wouldn't take the hint already. Maybe you just need to send her packing. You can do that, right?" He waved his hand at me as if he could sweep me out of the room like a crumb on the floor, and then looked at Allyson for support.

"That's ridiculous, Matty. I said no such thing. I have no idea what you're talking about," Allyson said.

"Yes you did. You told me that when we were in…*bed*." He said the last word in a soft tone, as if he was trying to protect her virtue.

All heads swiveled back and forth between Matson and Allyson—kind of like at a tennis match. It was a good thing they were dressed for the occasion.

"In bed?" The mayor's voice rose an octave.

"Look, am I the only one who can see it? This town belongs to our family, and she's the misfit. Everything was fine until she got here. Right, Dad?"

"He's not your father." Mrs. Mills' voice was barely a whisper, but with an announcement like that—who could have missed it?

Whoa.

* * *

"Myrna, this is not the time and certainly not the place for this…" Mayor Mills' voice was frantic as he stepped back and tried to wrap his arm around his wife.

She shrugged it off and stood up. "Oh, this is exactly the time and place. I can't take it anymore, Douglas. Let's just get all this out in the open and get it over with. You humiliate me at every turn. I've raised this boy while you've pretended to love him, but every time I look at him I see the man I really loved. And every time I turn around I see your slut in my house. Watching me. Waiting for…I don't know, waiting for you to leave me, I guess. And I just can't live with what we've done another day." She burst into tears.

Ty and I exchanged glances. The mayor loosened his tie and stepped back to brace himself on the countertop.

"I'm sorry, Colin." Mrs. Mills turned and looked at him. She reached out a hand, but he didn't take it. "I…your father came by the house that night. He told me how he was going to run for mayor and how Douglas was trying to blackmail him by threatening to reveal the truth about Matson. Caden wanted us to come forward with the truth and beat Douglas to the punch. But I told him that Douglas would never do it. Just to stay calm and keep Matson and I out of it. I knew our family would never survive the scandal."

Gasp.

"So you killed him?" Colin said. His voice was dark.

"Please, Myrna. Don't say anything else. Wait for our attorney, please, honey." The mayor's voice was a little wheezy now, and I took note of his graying pallor.

"You shut up! This is all your fault. The election…the election…that's all you ever think about. What about me? What about my life? I should have just let Caden reveal the truth, but we were all so afraid of scandal. If I had just done what was right that night, none of this would have happened. It would have all been over, and maybe we could have moved on with our lives. But no…I begged him not to tell. Protecting you. Protecting the Mills' name."

"But you loved Caden. You really loved him, and Matson is a really a Brooks? And you hid all this for a decade? Is that why you tried to meet with Colin?" My detective skills were ripening. Things were starting to come together. But if she didn't kill him, who did?

"I'm not finished yet, dear." Mrs. Mills' voice had lost its luster, but she was still trying to spill the beans.

"You're finished, Myrna. Just shut—" The mayor's face had gone white, and a sheen of sweat coated his forehead. He clutched his chest and swayed. I nudged Ty over and scooched out of the booth. I made my way to the mayor and took a hold of his wrist, pressing my index and middle finger to his pulse point. My training kicked in. I didn't care who this old coot was at the moment, but the doctor in me did care if he was about to go into shock or cardiac arrest.

"Are you okay, sir? Take a couple of deep breaths," I told him.

His eyes reached mine, and he saw me—he really saw me for the first time. "Ms. Murrin, I'm sorry. It was my fault you were arrested. Just legal tactics, you see. You come from good stock—you…"

I put my hand on his shoulder and returned his hand to his lap. His pulse was erratic. "Just relax, sir. Right now, I think you need to go to the emergency room and get checked out. This has been a bit of a shock to your system." I motioned to Ty, and he lifted his phone to make a call.

"Find Amika and Trask. They *are* part of our screwed-up family, after all. He's been up to something lately. I tried to find out what, but he lied to me. After all I've done for him—making him a part of this family. He lied to my face and so I smacked his," Mrs. Mills continued her declaration.

Then Myrna Mills pulled on the captain's arm to be certain she gained his attention before she said, "I mean, this is all about family, isn't it? Two families at war, and now we are all mixed up in this together. Mills? Brooks? Does anyone know who belongs to which family anymore?" She started laughing, and then the laughter turned into sobs.

"Wait, Officer Trask is involved in all this?" Captain Owens sounded incredulous.

"Officer Trask is involved in what?" Mr. Jelly Donut strolled in. "What's going on here, cap'n?" His eyes searched the room and landed on Allyson. I caught the look on her face, and I heard the final click in my brain as the combination rolled into place.

"It's you." I held on to the mayor's arm with one hand, but pointed at Officer Chubby with the other. "You're Amika's son, but you're not really a Mills. You've always wanted to be, but you didn't quite make the cut, did you—Traskbauer?"

Trask didn't responded. The café was tomb silent.

"You killed Caden Brooks. Didn't you?"

A few gasps sounded around the café.

"Everything was fine until you stuck your nose into our family's business." Trask's voice was solemn.

I started filling in the blanks. "You were always hanging around the family, trying to become one of the Mills. But you never really made the grade, did you? You and your mother may have changed your name from Traskbauer to Trask, but you both really wanted to change it to Mills. And when you overheard Mrs. Mills and Caden talking about their secret, you saw the perfect opportunity to become the mayor's favorite son. You killed Caden and your mother helped you—a jealous, full-of-rage teenager—cover it up."

I tried to see the look on Colin's face at my theory of what had happened, to see the pain—perhaps the relief. But his face was blank. Absolutely void of all emotion.

"And to think, he still loved that idiot more than me. After all I did for him. I saved the family from scandal. I protected their secret. I killed the enemy. And he still loves this feeble-minded brat more than me." Trask pointed at Matson, and all heads turned that way.

Mrs. Mills was sobbing full force now, and the mayor was starting to wheeze.

"Let's handle the rest of this at the station. Dempsey?" Captain Owens interjected. Perhaps he was afraid this was about to get heated.

But I wasn't finished. There was still the matter of how my life had gotten wrapped up in this tortilla filled with terror.

"And when I found Caden Brooks' body, Amika decided that she had to protect you at all cost. She followed me that day, trying to make sure I reported it. Maybe she'd had enough of the waiting. Waiting for the mayor to leave his wife for her. Waiting to become his real family just like you wanted. So she decided to point the finger at Mayor Mills. Let the police come and find the body. Make sure that her son would be safe. But what she didn't know was that I'd already told the police, and you were the first one to hear about it. Before Ty could get a warrant, you must've moved the body." I paused, one piece still not quite fitting in this puzzle. "But why *did* you move the body?"

All eyes were on Trask, but he looked pleadingly at Allyson. Unfortunately for him, help was not forthcoming. She continued to stare down at the tiled floor, studying the pattern as if her life depended on it.

"She told me how much she hated you," Trask said. "How she wanted you to leave town. And…I thought if I made you look crazy or something that you'd go away. I wanted to impress her. But you didn't take the hint."

Captain Owens spoke up: "You moved the body and destroyed evidence to impress a girl?"

Trask hung his head. Mrs. Mills' sobbing reached a louder level, and I checked on my patient, who was fading fast.

"Ty, where's that ambulance?"

"On the way. It should be here any second."

Our exchange seemed oddly out of place amongst all the confessions, but I wanted to be sure I got in one more.

"And you've been harassing me ever since. Leaving threatening notes for me, stealing my car, and hurting my sister. I overheard Allyson on the phone reassuring you that you wouldn't get caught. She's in on this. I know it."

"Is that true, Ms. Harlow?" Captain Owens asked.

"Look, my personal life isn't a part of this. If *he* did any of these things—moving corpses, harassing people—I wasn't involved in any of it. And obviously, if he was trying to impress me, I don't go for that type of thing. I'm a community leader, not a common criminal." She stuck her chin up in the air as if all that was beneath her.

"What about my car? What about my sister? And how did your crummy scarf get in her possession?"

"I'm sure I don't know." She looked down at her nails and began to examine them as if determining the date of her next manicure.

"Allyson, baby (cough), you said we'd be together forever (cough), you said that she made you unhappy and that a girl doesn't like to be unhappy. You said that I should do whatever it took to make you happy (cough)."

"You told me the same thing," Matson chimed in. His voice sounded full of withheld tears. I felt a little sorrier for him now. Finding out that your real father was dead was something I didn't wish on anyone—even if that someone had poisoned your drink.

"Did you tell Matson to slip a drug in my drink at O'Hannigan's to make you happy?" I had to know.

"You shut up!" she barked at me. "These men are big babies. I show them a little affection and they go off the deep end. I didn't tell them to do anything. What they chose to do to prove their loyalty is all on them. And you…" She focused on Officer Chubby. "How stupid are you? Who did you give my scarf to? 'Cause I definitely wasn't involved in any car stealing and child abducting."

"I keep it with me all the time (cough, hack). I love you (cough, choke). She said she just needed to borrow it."

Uh-oh. Officer Chubby was about to evolve into a full-blown asthma attack and we'd have two down in here.

"I think I've heard enough," Captain Owens said, trying to rein in the confessions.

Things were getting solved left and right around here. This was better than I could have ever dreamed. My mind was absolutely full of a-ha moments right now. And I had an idea of just who took my car and my sister.

The mayor's body began to sink down to the ground, and Colin stepped forward to help me lower him the rest of the way down.

"Where are those medics?" I asked no one in particular.

"Is he gonna be okay?" Matson stepped forward. His face full of hurt and confusion.

The sound of ambulance sirens sounded in the distance, and a temporary hush fell over the café. Then the bell above the door rang, and pandemonium ensued.

Because there stood the last invited member of my impromptu beauty shop blowout.

It was Amika, of course. But she came holding a gun.

CHAPTER THIRTY-ONE

———

The longest road out is the shortest road home. –Irish Proverb

Amika waved the gun around, her hand shaking. She didn't know who to point it at first.

Her eyes seethed anger at Allyson. She glanced down at the mayor's limp body and sniffed—no love lost there.

"Amika, I'm going to have to ask you to put your gun down and put your hands up." Captain Owens' voice was a beacon of calm as he reached down to his right hip holster.

"No. I'm here to get my son. You back off. I take him. We go."

Then her eyes found Trask. He was standing by our now-empty booth, and he was…crying.

Her face softened. "Come on, baby. We go now. I heard everything."

"How did you hear everything?" my big mouth, of which I seemed to have no control today, asked.

She pointed the gun in my direction. "You don't think I'm smart? You call up and ask to meet with me and you don't think I'm suspicious? I come in through the back door. I listen from the kitchen. My son—he is a slave to his emotions. But we are done with this family and this town. But I not mean to hurt your sister, ma'am. I know he's been playing tricks on you to impress her." She shifted the gun to Allyson, who emitted a little squeak. "I want to show my liebe—my Heiner—that this woman he thinks he loves is not worthy of him. I see her scarf at his apartment and I come up with a plan."

"Who's Heiner?" I follow her gaze toward Trask, who was now sobbing louder than Mrs. Mills.

Heiner Traskbauer? No wonder he wanted to change his name to Mills.

"I'm sorry, but I can't let you do that. Put that gun down, Amika," said Ty.

That's Detective *Ty Dempsey.*

"No. No. We go now. Come on, my liebe."

"It wasn't a question. You have until the count of three. One. Two. Thr—" The captain had his gun drawn, and it was pointed at her chest.

"Don't hurt her," Trask yelled, and dove between Captain Owens and Amika right as her gun went off.

Mrs. Mills screamed and crumbled to the floor as sobs tore out of her throat.

Ty tackled Amika to the ground, pulling her arms behind her back and securing the gun. Matson attempted to take advantage of the chaos and grabbed Allyson's hand and tried to pull her out the door. But she stomped her heel into the toe of his shoe, and he yelped in pain.

"Where do you think you're going, Matson? Your butt is about to be in a sling, son. Attempted murder, for one," Captain Owens directed.

Matson did as he was told and then sank down into a booth, holding his foot, and now he was crying.

This was quickly becoming a Lifetime Movie moment.

As the paramedics entered the scene, I turned my attention to them as one headed for Trask, also known as Heiner, and the other for Mayor Mills.

When I took a moment to look up from the two traumas before me, I noticed one thing—Colin had vanished.

* * *

"So do I get any credit at all for giving you the scoop of a lifetime?" I asked Penny Dempsey as she stood by me and Ms. Maimie while the cops finished clearing the scene.

She didn't answer, but she gave a little head tilt at my question. With Penny, that was a good sign.

"Guess I get the rest of the day off, then. With blood on the floor, I doubt we can serve up any food," Ms. Maimie said matter-of-factly, and turned to give me a kiss on the cheek. "This was some setup, girl. How'd you figure all this out?"

I shrugged. "I didn't, really. I just know how no one can keep a secret in a beauty shop, and I figured that getting all these people into a beauty shop together would have been a lot more hassle than getting them into the café together. And these were a lot of secrets that were busting a gut to get told. I just figured if we got all the culprits in the same place at the same time, maybe we could bust it wide open."

"You did that and more," Penny said.

"You sure did." Ty interrupted our girl talk. The three of us looked up at him, and a sudden happiness welled inside me.

"Do you need a ride home?" Ty said. He never forgot about me. I'd give him credit for that.

I smiled—a little warm and fuzzy was still there as well. I couldn't deny that.

"I'll get her home safely," Penny responded. "You've got enough to deal with here."

"Well, all right then. Ladies…" Ty offered us a fake tip-of-the-hat move and then turned around to leave.

"Oh, and don't forget the assault charges against Stella! I want those brought up as well," I yelled out just as the captain headed back into the café for something and Ty held the door for him.

The captain stopped short—blocking the entrance and causing Ty to almost collide with him. He looked at me and then at Ty. "Dare I ask? Who is it now? Stella?"

Ty grinned. "I'll explain it to you later, sir."

"I can hardly wait." The captain eyed me.

* * *

On the way back to the house, Penny remained quiet, but somehow I knew the tension between us had lessened considerably. I wouldn't say that we were back where we should be, but maybe my little tip-off about the big confrontation was a start at showing her that she was still important to me.

"Wow, so will you be putting out a special evening edition on this one?"

Penny let out a low whistle. "I think I'll have to. There were quite a few witnesses at the café, and if I want to nail this story I need to get the fingers to the keyboard pretty quickly."

"Understood. Hey, thanks for giving me a lift home."

We stayed silent for a few beats.

"What's the deal with you and that hottie Colin Brooks?" Penny looked at me out of the corner of her eye, but her face remained expressionless.

Her question caught me totally by surprise. "Why, do you know something about him?"

"Maybe."

"Penny, spill the beans."

Now she smiled. A wicked one if I'd ever seen one. "Maybe some mysteries are better left unsolved."

"Oh, gee, thanks."

"What are friends for?"

I opened my mouth to ask if that meant that we were still friends but changed my mind. Some things were better left unsaid.

I wondered when or if I'd see Colin again. He'd ghosted out of the café during all the ruckus. But I hoped he'd be back—bearing food.

We pulled up to the house, and something occurred to me. "Hey, hold on a second, will you?"

She nodded. "But hurry up…I have a story to run."

I exited the car and entered the house. I ran to my bedroom. *My* bedroom? The thought crashed against my skull as I stepped across the bedroom threshold. I'd been calling it Aunt Patty's bedroom for as long as I'd been alive. Was it truly *my* bedroom now? Sad, but necessary. At least for the time being.

Seeing the source of my mission on the nearby table, I grabbed it and ran back out the front door. Penny was drumming the dashboard and singing along to Tom Petty on the stereo.

I handed her a photograph of us from the night of our senior graduation party, her smile reached her eyes, and her face lit up. Now, *that* was Penny.

"Oh my Lord, where did you find this thing?"

"It was in my old stuff. I did a major clean the other night and came across it. Look how happy we were at that moment."

"Yeah, the night went sort of downhill from that point on…"

"You could say that." We didn't need to discuss it further. It was old news and better left in the past. On that, we could agree.

She started to hand it back to me. I shook my head at her. "No…that's for you."

She squinted at the photo. "Okay, Mandy. Okay."

"Hey, Penny, thanks again for the ride. See you around."

"Yep. Yep. Yep." She backed out of the driveway and was gone.

* * *

After a quick shower and a change of clothes, I prepared to hotfoot it over to Ms. Lanier's. She'd left me a message that she'd have lunch waiting for me, and that she had Paget and Pickles as well. I needed a big, big hug from both of them.

As I passed through the kitchen, the phone was ringing. I snatched it off the receiver. I seriously need to cancel this house phone thing.

"Hello?"

"Mandy Murrin?"

"Yes." I didn't recognize the scruffy voice, although it sounded vaguely familiar.

"This is Hollon Brothers' Towing. We have an estimate on yer car repairs, and it is a doozy."

"Oh, gee, great, but I doubt I'll have the money for that anytime soon. I don't suppose you'll let me work out some sort of payment plan?" How could I agree on a payment plan when I was jobless? I hadn't spoken to Barry at Flicks Vision yet, but his lack of calls spoke volumes. I knew that ship had long since sailed.

"Well…see here, we don't usually do that." He paused while he hacked up a lung.

"Okay, I understand."

More hacking followed by a gurgle. "Well now, we don't do payment plans, but…"

Guess I wouldn't be getting Stella back anytime soon.

Silence on the other end. I wondered, briefly, if the man had passed out from lack of breathable oxygen.

"Sir?"

"Yeah, listen here. We have a need for an office girl here. Maybe do an odd pick-up or two with the rig. You need a job, we might can work something out."

I let out a pent-up breath that I hadn't realized I'd been holding. "How did you know I was looking for a job?"

Suddenly, the voice seemed very familiar. "Well, I figured that if you had to borrow cab fare from that there yard man over at The Country Club that you were in some kind of sitch-e-ay-shun. And a fifty-cent tip? What year do you think this is? 1950?"

Scabby Hollon to the rescue.

"Okay then, Mr. Hollon. When can I start?"

"We'll see you in a couple days. I'll send my boys over to pick you up. Seein' as how you don't have your car and all."

I grinned. "All right. I'll see you soon."

"Oh, girlie?"

"Yes, Mr. Hollon."

"What size coveralls do you wear? I've gotta get the boys to check the storage and see if we have your size."

More coveralls. Oh, goodie.

* * *

After my phone call, I joined Ms. Lanier and my family for some baked ham, black-eyed peas, and sliced bell pepper. She fussed over having missed the big scene at the café. Pickles kept moving his head back and forth between my lap and Paget's. Between bites of his food, of course. He seemed worried about his girls. Of course, on second thought, he could have just been hoping for twice the scraps.

"Dessert will be another half-hour. I'm baking up one of those Hummingbird cakes. And then we'll have to wait for it to cool before we can frost it."

Did she say Hummingbird cake?

I was definitely sticking around for that. "Sounds good. We'll hang out for a bit."

"Okay, hon. Listen…while we are waiting for dessert…and if you feel like it…"

Oh, boy.

"Could you take a look at my ear?"

"What seems to be the trouble with it?" I asked, with no lack of reluctance.

"Aw…nothing to worry over too much. I think it's just what you'd call an extreme build-up of wax. It won't take long to wash it out. I bought a kit and everything."

Oh, for the love of all that is…Millbrook.

ABOUT THE AUTHOR

Kerri Nelson survived a fifteen year career in the legal field and then took her passion for crime solving to the page. But her journey to become a mystery author took a decade long detour into the world of romance where she penned twenty two novels and novellas in various sub-genres.

Born and raised a true southern belle, Kerri holds many useful secrets: how to bake a killer peach cobbler; how to charm suspects with proper batting of the eyelashes; and how to turn your parasol into a handy weapon.

Kerri is an active member of Sisters in Crime and Romance Writers of America which includes various volunteer positions such as Board Member at Large and Daphne Published Contest Category Coordinator of Kiss of Death RWA (Chapter for Romantic Suspense Authors).

To learn more about Kerri Nelson, visit her online at
www.kerrinelson.com

Enjoyed this book? Check out these other fun reads available in print now from
Gemma Halliday Publishing:

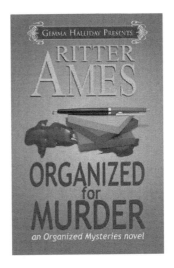

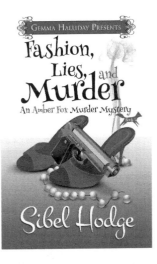

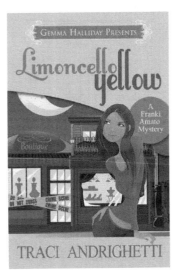

www.GemmaHalliday.com/Halliday_Publishing

Made in the USA
San Bernardino, CA
19 May 2014